By Tracy Sh

The Grace of Crows
Floating Underwater

Table of Contents

The Grace of Crows
A Novel

Tracy Shawn

Turbulent Muse Publishing
California, United States

ISBN: 978-1-7366649-4-0 (Paperback)

ISBN: 978-1-7366649-5-7 (Ebook)

Library of Congress Control Number: 2024904334

This book is a work of fiction. The names, characters and events in this book are the products of the author's imagination or are used fictitiously. Any similarity to real persons living or dead is coincidental and not intended by the author.

The Grace of Crows

Second Edition

Cover Design by Lynn Andreozzi

Author Website: www.tracyshawn.com[1]

---

1.   http://www.tracyshawn.com

Author's Disclaimer

Please note that Dune Beach is a fictionalized town inspired by several communities along the Central Coast of California. Likewise, there is no Breakers Point at the northern end of Malibu. Breakers Cove Pier is inspired by Paradise Cove Pier in Malibu, but again is fictionalized. The present Paradise Cove Pier would not provide enough space for someone to live under. Also, the secluded Breakers Cove Beach of this author's imagination provides a different emotional setting than the real Paradise Cove Beach, with its smoothly paved entrance road, popular restaurant, and fancy cabana rentals.

CHAPTER ONE

Saylor walked in rhythm to the words she had scribbled across her journal before leaving the house: *I'm in control. I will stay calm. I know I can.* She quickened her pace and repeated the commands, silent marching orders to keep moving forward under autumn's brisk dusk.

When she was just one block from the bookstore, a man pushed by and then stopped to glare at someone behind her. On edge, Saylor turned to look. Against the red-orange horizon, a silhouette of a slump-shouldered teen trailed up the sidewalk.

"Jesus Christ, can you go any slower?" the man called.

The girl stopped in her tracks. "Go on ahead of me, then." Even though her tone was hesitant, anger still tinged the edge of her words.

"No," he bellowed, "you need to get a move on." He stood in the middle of the sidewalk, blocking Saylor's path.

What an awful father, Saylor thought. She tried not to look at him, worrying that her most irrational fears might come true. But she couldn't help herself. When she glanced over, he stared back with what she was sure was contempt. Finally, the girl caught up to him, and they walked toward the bookstore.

Mouth clamped shut, Saylor reminded herself how great she was at magnifying the meaningless into the irrational, and continued down the sidewalk. Most of the locally owned businesses had already closed for the night, their windows etched with seaside-themed names that still made her smile: Ocean Mist Flowers, Dude's Surf Shop, Mermaid's Menu Café. But not tonight. Tonight, her mind was too preoccupied with what-ifs.

Telling herself to calm down, that the man's glare was just because he was an all-around jerk, she gritted her teeth. She couldn't have blurted out her thoughts without knowing it—could she? No, she didn't—this was just fear and only fear, nothing more. She inhaled the scent of California Sagebrush from the café's border garden and focused on the entrance of the bookstore.

Inside the small, but well-stocked shop, she headed for the art section, paused before the row of possibilities, and then grabbed the thickest book on the shelf. Transfixed by its emotional colors, Saylor slowly turned pages until landing on a self-portrait by Vincent van Gogh. She traced her fingers over the image, sorry for his long-ago torment and at the same time admiring his determination; even when he had been overwhelmed by severe mental illness, he painted. If only she could be so tenacious. Every time she thought about painting, anxiety drained any desire and all she had left was getting through the day, pushing down the fear.

She straightened her back. She had to stop feeling sorry for herself, and thought about how her best friend, Lucy, would remind her to "Quit debilitating yourself with such asinine quibble."

Saylor breathed in the art book's glossy-paged newness and focused on the safe anonymity of Dune Beach's sole remaining bookstore. A slight, freckled woman surveyed the cookbook section. An old man wearing a canary-yellow sweater thumbed a paperback from the bargain table, and a young guy with a wolf tattoo howling up the side of his neck sat cross-legged on the carpeted floor by the magazine section, a thick literary-looking publication open on his lap while he texted on his phone.

But when she caught sight of the man from the sidewalk, her stomach lurched. Under the fluorescent light, Saylor eyed his profile. He looked to be in his early fifties, just a few years older than herself, but a hell of a lot thinner. He sported a black workout shirt and running shorts, his legs showing the taut leanness of an over-disciplined marathon runner, his face, the gaunt-cheeked look of self-deprivation.

Arms crossed, he faced his daughter and spoke to her in a loud whisper. "I'm telling you—you need to lose weight *now*."

The girl's doe-like eyes and old-fashioned Dutch boy haircut made Saylor feel even more protective. Although the girl was bigger-boned and taller than Saylor's fifteen-year-old daughter, Brooke, she looked a couple of years younger.

With the normal, yet self-conscious pudginess of a budding teen, the girl tugged her T-shirt down to cover the doughy skin between her stomach and jeans. Frowning, the girl tried to shrug off the hawk-like clasp of her father's hand on her shoulder.

"Leave me alone." The girl looked at her father with a red-faced, twisted-mouthed expression of hurt and defiance.

His grip still on the girl, the father pushed his face too close to hers. "If you don't care what you look like, don't be surprised if no one else does either."

The girl's eyes watered, and her fists clenched over her stomach in a protective fighter-like stance. Finally, the father released his hand from her shoulder, but continued to stare her down, unblinking as if he were trying to hypnotize her. Eyes averted, Saylor worried again that her irrational fear would come true—that in her agitation, she would blurt out invading thoughts without any filter of control. Her heart thudded so hard that all sounds became muffled. Panicked, she wanted to bolt, but didn't want to abandon the girl.

With his face cemented with judgment, the father leaned toward his daughter. "You don't want to get as grotesqué as your mother, do you?" He paused. Then a slithery grin. "No, I bet you don't."

That did it. Unable to resist, Saylor snapped the book shut and looked straight into the man's eyes. A shout flew through her brain: *You goddamn bastard*. She held her breath, telling herself that she couldn't have possibly said it out loud.

But the man glared at her. "What," he bellowed, a venomous growl in his voice that sounded as if he were about to attack. The whole bookstore felt as if it were suspended in time.

Like a stupefied rabbit, Saylor froze, her heart thudding so hard against her chest that she wondered if she might be having a heart attack. Looking down at her hands, she swallowed. Finally, she found her voice. "Nothing," she managed to say, straining to sound innocent. This could not be happening.

"Bitch." He narrowed his eyes, then turned to his daughter as if Saylor had disappeared. "I'm going to check out some running magazines. If you don't pick out a diet book by the time I'm done, your cell is gone for a week." For a moment more, he stood with the challenging stance of an overbearing coach while his daughter determinedly looked past him. Finally, he walked away, and the girl exhaled. She flashed Saylor a quick, sly smile, then left.

Saylor wanted to follow the girl and tell her that she was perfectly fine. It was her father who had the problem, yet her legs had grown nightmare-paralyzed, and beneath her shoes, the puke-brown carpet stuck like the muck of unhappy memories. She told herself the man must have just been pissed off with her for slamming her book shut and challenging him with her narrowed-eyed look of disdain, but he did say bitch, didn't he? That was surely too vehement for what she had done, even if he was such an asshole. And the girl's smile was conspiratorial, as if she thought it funny that Saylor had called her father a bastard. Yes, the possibility was more than strong that she had blurted it out. Now instead of just grappling with the what-if anxiety, she had to seriously consider that her fears might be true.

She needed to get a grip. Not knowing what else to do, Saylor turned her attention back to the book. Maybe the renowned artist had some kind of answer. She flipped through the pages, and randomly pointed a shaky finger at a sentence, landing on the last words Van Gogh had supposedly uttered to his brother, Theo: "The sadness will last forever."

Saylor shoved the book back on the shelf, reminding herself how Van Gogh had been struggling with more than just anxiety. Near the front door, she knocked her hip against a table stacked with the latest slick-covered self-help books. She heard the man chortle and could feel him watching her.

Instinct told her not to look back. Still, her head jerked over her shoulder. Immobile in the spotlight of his scrutiny, she felt the roll of her stomach over the too-snug waist of her increasingly tight jeans and wished that she'd worn her looser sweatshirt instead of the unforgiving thermal that exposed every bulge. He held up a rolled-up magazine and winked, seemingly enjoying his power over her, a smirk spreading on his thin lips.

Before her trapped feeling of nausea grew, she made herself break loose from his gaze, turned her focus on the door, banged it open and fled outside. Now her fears had really got her.

CHAPTER TWO

Saylor closed the front door behind her just as her dog, Neptune, got up from his dog bed to greet her. She wrapped her arms around his neck and breathed in the dried-grass smell of his fur. Trudging upstairs, he followed on her heels. She entered her bedroom without uttering a sound. It'd be ridiculous to cry about what happened in the bookstore. Simply ridiculous. But there she was with an ever-expanding lump in her throat and an all-too familiar ache in her chest.

"You're home early." Brian glanced up from his book, a mystery novel, its cover embossed with gunshot holes splattered across a Miami beach, with neon-blue ocean and bone-white sand. Still in his carpenter pants and work shirt, Brian's sturdy body was sprawled on their bed's frayed quilt, his shoulders propped up against all four pillows.

At the foot of the bed, Saylor fidgeted, envious of his peace. "Brian..." Not sure if she wanted to tell him what had happened in the bookstore, she still closed their bedroom door as she always did whenever she spoke of her fears. She never wanted Brooke and Devin to know about her irrational thoughts, never wanted them to know that their mother was continually hanging on by the thinnest of threads. She bent down to pet Neptune, who was still by her side, her ever-loyal sentinel who seemed to sense whenever her anxiety was on high.

"What's stressing you out now?" Brian reached for his bottle of beer and swigged down the last sip.

She paused. If she didn't talk about it, maybe she'd be able to diffuse the fear on her own. But when Brian started reading again, her throat constricted. She needed to air it out, needed to try and make some sense of it. "This guy in the bookstore..." She swallowed, telling herself to keep her voice low. And level. To not act hysterical. "This guy acted as if I had blurted out what I was thinking."

"I'm sure it was just a coincidence," he muttered, flipping a page.

"But he yelled 'what' right after I had thought the words 'You goddamned bastard.'"

With his reluctant I-really-don't-want-to-hear-this-again expression, Brian shook his head. But she hurtled on, smelling her own sweat, a metallic stink that always grew more pungent with fear.

"He was an awful man, Brian. He was badgering his poor daughter to lose weight. And when he told her that he didn't want her to get as *grotesque* as her mother, I couldn't help it. I slammed my book shut and looked right at him. He then called me a bitch—but I don't think what I did should warrant that kind of reaction. And after he walked away, the girl smiled at me as if we were in on the same joke. I must have said it out loud."

"What if you did say it? It sounds like he deserved to be called a bastard."

"So, you're agreeing that I must have said it out loud?" Saylor bit her lip, angry with herself for telling him. Now the fear was worse than before. "I can't walk around thinking that I'm going to unknowingly blurt out anything at any time."

"You shouldn't be so afraid of this." Brian exhaled. "We all mumble what we're thinking sometimes."

"But you know that the more stressed out I get, the more crazy things I think—things that aren't even true sometimes—"

"Look, you didn't hear yourself say it, right?"

"No, but you don't understand." She tried to keep her voice from rising. "I've told you before, when I'm in my anxious mode, my heart beats so hard, I'm afraid I can't hear anything."

"A pounding heart would not make you deaf to your own words." He gave her his smile with eyebrows-raised expression, the one that was supposed to make her realize how irrational she was being. "And you'd hear yourself even more if you were so afraid of saying things out loud."

Brian was only trying to help, and what he said did make sense. Still, she couldn't let go of the possibility. "I'm sorry—."

"Your anxiety comes in waves. It'll be better tomorrow." He yawned.

"You're right." The angry rash at the base of her neck stung as if she'd run into a patch of nettles. Her fingernails dug in despite herself.

"Quit doing that and put on some of the ointment your dermatologist gave you."

"It stopped working a long time ago."

"You're going to give yourself a scar scratching like that."

"I think I already have." She pressed her palm against the inflammation and headed to the bathroom with Neptune in tow. With quiet force, she shut and locked the door, a barrier against any well-intentioned intrusion.

Against the wall, she sank down onto the cool linoleum, her eyes wide open to the dark. Neptune sat beside her. She leaned into his reassuring warmth as she reassessed the evening. The man in the bookstore had acted too much like her own long-dead father. Maybe that was why she had become so anxious. But did that only increase the possibility that one of the most upsetting of her irrational fears had come true? She tried to steady her breath and focused on the two facts that sometimes calmed her: Everyone dies in the end, and in billions of years, the sun will explode and melt the earth. Even if her fears were valid, she was just another passing speck on a doomed planet.

With a sigh, she pictured her friend Lucy exclaiming, "This just shows how screwed up your anxiety has gotten. You have to laugh at yourself when you realize you're actually comforted by such morbid thoughts." Lucy was right. She had to lighten up.

With her palms braced against the floor, she unhinged her knees. Like a blind woman, she ran her hand across the wall until she felt the plastic rise of the light switch. Under the halogen's crisp shine, she stared at her reflection in the mirror. She shook her head. This was not the person she was supposed to be.

Aware that Brian was probably wondering what was taking so long, she reached for her toothbrush and thought about going back into therapy. Her last psychiatrist, Gail, a woman with perpetually watery eyes and a pressed-together mouth, had talked her into going on several anti-anxiety meds. When she had tried to explain to Gail how the second round of meds had been even worse than the first, Gail's face had soured, and after a long silence, she tucked her ghost-white calves under the chair. Saylor felt her impatience, but didn't blame her—she figured that reasoning with the fear-ridden was no easy job.

After spitting out the froth of toothpaste into the drain, Saylor stuck her toothbrush with its bristles facing opposite from Brian's in the chipped ceramic holder and grimaced for the mirror. A thin, bright line of blood grew between her gums and teeth.

"You okay in there?" Brian rapped on the door.

"I'm fine...I'll be right out." She wasn't fine, but she sure as hell didn't want to spend any more of their dwindling savings on seeing another psychiatrist. And the thought of gambling on yet another kind of medication felt as worthwhile as jumping over an open fire pit. No. She'd find a way to battle this herself.

The morning sun appeared as spiritless as Saylor felt. She forced herself out of bed and trundled downstairs for the required cup of coffee, last night's anxiety continuing to fray her mind. The kitchen's black and white tiled floor cold against her feet, she surveyed the adjoining living room's scattered-looking décor. Although her 1950s home was cheerful enough with its big windows and cozy bedrooms, Saylor had felt the need to reduce its tract home vibe. They had bought it when she was pregnant with Devin. It was the upstairs room, which the previous owner had added on, and the real estate agent had billed as a "parents' haven," that had been the deciding factor. Before her due date loomed too close, Saylor worked to make it her own. She painted each wall a different color and collected mismatched thrift-store furniture, coating wooden chairs and tables with thick layers of blue, yellow, or red paint. She draped her couches with old Hawaiian prints and hung antique pictures of exotic birds and flowers throughout the living room, hallway, and bathroom. Visitors often exclaimed how wonderfully eclectic her home was, and Saylor always took it as a compliment. But with her increasing fears, it just looked more and more out-of-control.

She squeezed honey into her coffee from a smiling plastic bear and tried to concentrate on the moment, but instead stopped to listen to seventeen-year-old Devin wash his hands while he counted out loud in the downstairs bathroom. He had never done this before. She pictured her Uncle Silvio's haunted face, but shook her head. Devin would never get that bad. Saylor sipped her coffee, wishing she had the answers to banish his distress. Just as she felt her eyes sting, Brooke plodded into the kitchen in faded black pajamas and skull and crossbones slippers.

Saylor pasted on a smile and faced her daughter's groggy-faced irritability. "Can I fix you some breakfast?"

Brooke rolled her eyes and went to pour herself a cup of coffee.

"If I were you, I'd have at least a piece of toast with that," Saylor said in the most casual tone she could muster. How could Brooke concentrate in school with nothing but black coffee for nourishment? And how, at fifteen, had she developed a taste for something so bitter?

"You're not me—so back off, Mom." Brooke scowled, sliding her chipped purple nails through dyed-black hair with its glaring blond roots.

"Just looking after your health."

"You never listen when I tell you that I'm too stressed out every morning to be able to deal with anything in my stomach," Brooke said. "I wish you knew what it felt like—"

"But you're starting to look too thin, honey—"

"Stop body shaming me."

"But I'm..." Saylor was going to finish with the word concerned, but thought better of it. This was probably just a phase.

Red-faced, Brooke stomped out of the kitchen and banged Devin on the arm. Saylor couldn't tell if it was on purpose or accidental. Devin grunted and went back to the bathroom. Saylor listened intently, hoping that he wasn't washing his hands again.

Guilt constricting her chest, she pictured Devin's solemn face on another autumn morning when he was almost three. They had started to play catch in the backyard, the sun bouncing off his caramel-colored hair and dried oak leaves crunching beneath their tennis shoes. Saylor had finally made time to have fun with him after getting Brooke down for a nap. Then she'd heard the phone ring in the kitchen and raced to get it, leaving Devin holding the red rubber ball, the happiness in his brown eyes dimming. On edge, she was convinced that Brian would get in a fatal car accident simply because they had a spat right before he had left for work. By the time she got off the phone with whoever had called, Brooke woke up, crying with the urgency of baby hunger. While Saylor was feeding her, Devin came in, lay his head on her shoulder and whispered, "Mommy, why are you so nervous all the time?"

Saylor opened the kitchen window, trying to shrug off the pressing weight of regret.

Once Devin and Brooke left for school and Brian raced off to his first jobsite, Saylor went into the office Brian had built at the back of their garage. Although it was cramped with office furniture, Brian's enormous drafting table, and piles of paperwork, Saylor liked how the outside spilled in. Right above the desk, a window looked out on an old oak tree and branch-patterned sky, and just outside the glass door, stepping stones led to Brian's neatly rowed vegetable garden.

She turned on the computer and breathed in the quiet. Beneath her computer desk, Neptune exhaled onto her toes. Ever since she'd rescued the mixed breed, wolf-gray Neptune from the shelter, he had stayed close, especially when she was alone. Saylor smiled. "We'll take a walk later."

Even though inputting job accounts and billing for Brian's general contracting business was not her idea of a dream job, Saylor liked the fact that she could go at her own pace and didn't have to deal with people like her former boss at the frame job, a tense-shouldered woman who'd been constantly annoyed at Saylor's "haziness." And when Saylor had overheard her mutter that Saylor's brain seemed to have developed a layer of perpetual fog, she was so embarrassed with the knowledge that her boss was right, she pretended she hadn't heard and then quit within a week.

Grateful for the morning's peace, Saylor input numbers, her mind starting to float in the wonderful pool of the mundane. But the cruel eyes of the man from the bookstore intruded. Why, why did she have to cross paths with him? Saylor tried to banish the image of his pinched, hostile face while she leaned over the keyboard, but her vision started to blur and she caught herself inverting numbers. Each invoice became a strain instead of the usual comfort of her mindless routine. She had to shuffle back to each previous invoice, double-checking her figures.

Hand pressed against the stack of invoices, she looked out the window and stared at the placid sky. Then her phone chirped, making Saylor start as if an alarm had jolted her awake.

"You okay?" Lucy asked without Saylor saying nothing more than hello.

"I'm slogging along. How about you?"

Lucy inhaled, a craggy sounding breath that always put Saylor on edge. She wished Lucy wouldn't smoke her "organic" cigarettes," but had given up badgering her; besides Lucy's rich voice was a welcome distraction today, and she didn't want to say anything that might cut the conversation short.

"Okay, Saylor, what's wrong?"

Lucy could read her better than anyone. They'd met on the first day of kindergarten when Saylor stood at the door, her mother's sweaty hand gripping hers so tightly that she imagined her mother wanted to break it off and take it home with her. Saylor had gone rigid, not wanting to see the hurt cut into her mother's eyes if she dared squirm away. Luckily, Lucy came over and took her by the wrist, leading her miles away to a corner of the room where she proceeded to instruct Saylor on the art of wooden block building. Saylor fell in love with Lucy's fire-engine red tights, blond pigtails tied up high with lime green yarn, and huge smile; and now she was still the friend who guided her back to reality whenever Saylor became frozen.

Saylor relayed the encounter at the bookstore, trying to keep the agitation out of her voice. Even though Lucy had always been in her corner, had always been that one friend she could count on—she still got annoyed whenever Saylor acted *too* anxious.

"Maybe you should think about meds again," Lucy said in her matter-of-fact voice after Saylor had finished agonizing over the what-ifs.

"I knew you'd say that, but you don't understand. I want to get over this without them. And I want something permanent. Anyway, don't you remember? Taking them actually increased my anxiety."

"There are better ones available now, I know a lot of people they've helped—"

"But when I read about all those side effects, I get even more anxious."

Lucy laughed. "Now I remember. You were afraid that you might become some kind of nocturnal zombie doing God knows what because the side effects included somnambulism."

Saylor realized she was picking her neck again and tucked her hand under her thigh. "It's not just a joke. I had read in the paper how a man said he must have been sleepwalking due to the bizarre side-effects of his antidepressants when he strangled his wife."

"Come on, Saylor, don't you think that the guy was just concocting an alibi?"

"Stranger things have happened. Anyway, the second meds I took made me feel like I was about as alive as a leftover potato." She knew Lucy would only become more frustrated with her if she tried to explain how it felt as if her emotions had seemed to be wrapped in cotton stuffing with the anxious thoughts just as strong, an ongoing riptide beneath the calm.

"I don't think you gave them enough time to work, and I'm telling you, there's a good chance that there's a better one for you. Also, if there're any side effects, I've heard that they go away after a week or two, plus they aren't as monstrous as you imagine—if they're going to happen at all, which is almost never."

Saylor wasn't in the mood to battle against Lucy's upbeat practicality. "I know how bored you must be with all of this."

"What about just seeing a therapist who specializes in anxiety, but doesn't prescribe medication?"

"Lucy, I've been through five health care professionals in the last ten years, and none of them helped." Saylor paused, realizing her own negativity. "I know therapy helps lots of people—but it just doesn't work for me."

"If you won't take meds or see a therapist again, then after all these years you really should learn to laugh at your fears. Like I've always tried to tell you: What's the worst that'll happen?"

"I'll lose everyone."

"No, you won't," Lucy snapped.

Saylor shook her head, even though Lucy couldn't see her. "You can't know that—"

"I know that you're spinning, Saylor—and when you spin, even the most outrageous of scenarios seem plausible."

"But," Saylor said, "if the worst of my fears came true, there'd be a chance." The sound of Lucy tapping away on her laptop keys echoed in Saylor's ears, and as always, she marveled how Lucy was able to carry on a conversation and concentrate on work at the same time. She pictured her in front of her monitor with Bluetooth in ear, keen brown eyes unblinking behind her retro-chic Oliver Peoples glasses, her cigarette traveling from clasped fingers to vintage kidney-shaped ashtray.

"Just because you're afraid that you'll do or say something, doesn't mean you will. That's just a lot of superstitious psycho-babble you've convinced yourself of."

Saylor noticed the change of light coming through the window and saw that the pale blue sky was half shrouded in late morning fog.

"Saylor, did you hear me?"

"Lucy, how am I ever going to get over this?"

"I know that you've been through your share of therapists, but really, don't you think there's someone you can learn to trust and let in? That's sometimes the bravest thing you can do—"

"I'm not sure what you mean." Saylor's voice rose with irritation. Did Lucy think she hadn't tried hard enough?

"You need to be stronger and knock down that brick-wall thinking that makes you believe nothing can change."

Saylor bit her lip. Lucy was right. Of course, Lucy was right. But knowing and doing were two different things.

"Look at it this way," Lucy said, "at least you're not afraid that you'll un-knowingly run over a pedestrian and then have to drive up and down the street to make sure there isn't a dead body on the road."

Grateful that Lucy had fallen back on her dark sense of humor, Saylor laughed, remembering the self-help book that Lucy had given her last year. The author shared the ways he had overcome his debilitating obsession that he had ran over people without knowing it—a fear that had developed after several years working as a taxi driver in New York City, where he'd mistakenly hit a pedestrian. Although his deep breathing exercises and thought replacement techniques had helped a bit, Saylor's fears still continued to rage.

"You have to admit I'm a lot better off than some people." Saylor didn't dare add that at least she hadn't become agoraphobic. If she said it out loud, then maybe it would cement it into her future, create a reality that couldn't be avoided.

"Whatever," Lucy said. "But you do need to get out of your own head—so we're going to have a girls-only weekend—and you're not allowed to say no."

"What do you have in mind?"

"You're coming down to visit me. And I'm going to take you to a new nightclub in Malibu where we can run into some old friends, dance, and drink something wickedly good." Lucy paused, taking in a hungry sounding inhale. "And you, my dear, are going to forget about everything else."

"I don't know, Lucy. Let me think about it and check in with Brian—"

"Does he ever check in with you about all his surfing trips with the guys?"

"It's not just that. I'm not sure I'm up for that kind of weekend."

"Come on, Say, when was the last time you had any fun? You're allowed a life outside of the house and that little hovel you call an office. How long has it been since you've come down and visited?" Lucy's tone had grown accusatory. "How long has it been since you've done anything for yourself?"

"You're right." Saylor didn't want to argue, knowing that no matter how strong and sure Lucy acted, she was still raw and lonely since her divorce two years ago. And Lucy did have a point: How long had it been since they had a complete weekend to themselves?

"Damn right I'm right," Lucy said.

"Aren't you always?" Saylor smiled into the phone.

"Only about everyone else's life..."

"What are you talking about?" Saylor said. "You're a successful accountant, funny, smart, and to top it all off— gorgeous, too."

"And that is why you are my best friend. You always tell it like it is." Their connection cut out.

"Lucy, you there?"

After several seconds, Lucy said, "Can you hear me?"

"Yeah—"

"I have to go and check in with a client now. I'll call you later." Lucy clicked off before Saylor could say goodbye.

The chill of outside air filtered through the window. Saylor gently nudged her foot against Neptune's paw. "Let's go for that walk now."

Under a sky that was now completely blanketed in fog, Saylor pulled her red Hyundai out of the driveway. She could have taken Neptune for a short walk through her beach bluff neighborhood, heading down the concrete, graffiti-strewn steps, which landed on the rocky beach below. Yet the open, clean sands of Diablo Dunes sounded more appealing on this lead-gray morning, so she decided that the ten-minute drive was worth Neptune's overenthusiastic-car slobber.

Neptune pulled her along the wooden boardwalk between the rise of sand dunes. The damp leaf smell from the eucalyptus grove behind her and the scent of saltwater-soaked driftwood ahead gave her an unexpected rush of energy.

When they reached the end of the walkway, she kicked off her shoes, unleashed Neptune and followed him down to the shore. Grateful that no one else could be seen on the wide expanse of beach, Saylor exhaled. The air was standstill calm, the calm that Californians describe as earthquake weather. She watched Neptune chase a squawking gull and wondered why she didn't dwell on more normal fears like natural disasters, crime rate, or even money. These were the kind of concerns you could talk about in public without people thinking you were crazy.

She shook her head, angry at her own weakness. When the white froth of incoming tide lapped her toes, she backed away and then paused to watch her brown-skinned feet sink into the damp sand. And for no reason at all, she began to cry. But just as quickly, she straightened up, making herself stop. She looked ahead at Neptune tromping into the surf after a gull that had just landed beyond the breakers. Sometimes her old dog forgot that he was ten years old. Every time he got closer, the gull lifted off and landed again, bobbing just out of reach. Saylor had heard that over-exuberant dogs had been known to drown playing this exhausting game. As loud as possible, she yelled his name. He ignored her at first, but after several hoarse calls, he finally trotted to her side.

With her energy zapped from sleep deprivation and her brain's constant playback of the man's unsettling reaction in the bookstore, she hadn't planned on taking a run. Yet adrenaline had kicked in now, and jogging seemed the only thing that could stop her from spinning into an even worse state. She aimed for the far-off Diablo Creek, which no matter what time of year it was, flowed straight into the ocean, creating a muddy mixture of earth and sea. If she could make it there and back, it would be a good thirty-minute run. Her hand reached for Neptune's wet fur. "Stay with me, boy."

Determined, she began to jog, but her body would not go as fast as she wanted. Her lower back ached and her lungs already burned as if she were scaling a mountain. The saggy sweatpants and thick sweatshirt didn't help. But she kept on, trying to ignore it all. After some time, the strain in her back subsided and she could breathe in without her lungs feeling as if they'd explode. With the sand's give beneath her bare feet, and the mist coalescing into drops on her hair and face, Saylor inhaled deeply, knowing she would make it. She checked to make sure Neptune was still with her and pressed on.

And as she sprinted for a pace, her mind transformed the fear of what had happened in the bookstore into a satisfying kind of anger. She pictured slapping the man in the face, rendering him speechless with shock. She grinned, seeing herself purposely confronting him and then telling the daughter how damaged he was. *Don't take in any of his bullshit*, she'd say. Saylor ran faster than she had in a long time.

CHAPTER THREE

Lucy gunned her yellow Mini Cooper through Malibu and turned off Pacific Coast Highway onto a small side street Saylor had never noticed before. Across the way, a neon sign featured an indigo-blue bird with outstretched wings. Illuminated below the bird, in a 1940s round script, the words *The Wild Sky* glowed in the same brilliant blue.

Saylor watched Lucy apply her lipstick, admiring Lucy's rowdy curls, clever brown eyes, and expansive grin. With a tinge of envy, Saylor thought how the chronic anxiety and sleepless nights had dried her up, making her appear older than her friend, although they were both forty-seven.

Lucy turned to eye Saylor, head cocked and eyebrows raised as if she sensed Saylor's thoughts. "You know, Saylor, I wish you could learn to own your own beauty."

Saylor flipped down the passenger side mirror, but could only see a weary-looking woman with dark shadows under uneasy eyes. Still, she mustered a smile for Lucy. "Thanks. I was just thinking how beautiful you are," she said. "But even more than that, you look happy."

"Looks are deceiving, my dear."

"I know the divorce has been hard on you," Saylor said. "But somehow, you still seem so open and unafraid."

Lucy laughed, rolling down her window. She lit a skinny brown cigarette and made sure after her first inhale to dangle it out the window. In the bluish light of the car, Saylor studied her friend's face. She could still see the young Lucy, and wondered if they viewed each other in a better light than the casual onlooker, who could not overlap them with memories of their smooth twenty-year-old faces and open-hearted hope.

"The way I look at it," Lucy said, "it's like this—at any moment, for any one of us, the world can pull the rug right out from under our feet. There's always some disaster—earthquakes, tsunamis, cancer, car crashes, pandemics—and there you go. In order to stay sane in this world, you have to plow along as if nothing bad is going to happen—otherwise you stall. Fretting about it all doesn't change anything. When something happens, it happens." She flicked her ashes on the road and grinned. "Look at my mom. She smoked until she died at age seventy-nine, not from lung cancer but from a drunk driver ramming into her when she was heading to a matinee in her beloved Eldorado. You might as well be obliviously happy while you can."

"You're right. If only I could train my brain not to worry so much—"

"Remember what I think about your obsessive thoughts?"

"I know, I know. You think I've locked up my creativity and it's coming out any way it can."

"Yes—besides the fact that your parents screwed with your psyche—the creative part of your brain goes over to the dark side when you don't give it the outlet it needs." Lucy scrunched her eyes the way she always did before she was going to say something confrontational. "And I'm sorry, Saylor, no matter how safe you feel working for Brian at home, you're not reaching your full potential. I remember your art. You were damned good. For your own sanity, you have to get back into it."

"I don't have the time right now. Maybe after Brooke and Devin both graduate."

Lucy shook her head, then glanced over at a pair of men walking toward the Wild Sky's entrance. "We'd better get going before the line gets any longer." Abruptly, Lucy stepped out of the car, her leggings and slinky top accentuating her strong, capable body.

They crossed the street and Saylor noticed a model-thin girl standing in line. She wore a licorice-red dress and her skintight boots rode up to perfectly shaped knees. Her turquoise-painted nails fluttered in the air while she laughed at something a young, and very handsome man, in leather pants said into her ear.

Saylor glanced down at the outfit she had picked to best de-emphasize her expanding muffin top and middle-aged hips, a long black blouse over dark jeans. "Are you sure I won't feel too old for this place?"

"You shouldn't be so self-conscious." Lucy exhaled as if she were still smoking. "Anyway, I told you it draws a diverse crowd. You'll see people of all ages and walks of life." Lucy quickened her pace, impatience emanating from her sharp shoulder blades. "The last time I was here, I met a biker guy, a software designer, and one of those vice presidents of industry types who can never really tell you what they actually do—and none of those men seemed to be worried about their age, so why in the hell should we?"

"I don't know...maybe we could just go out for a movie instead?"

Lucy rolled her eyes. "Just stop thinking and let me buy you a drink."

After they joined the line, Saylor spotted a couple that looked to be about her age. The woman wore the same dark jeans and below-the-butt blouse motif as Saylor. She exhaled, guessing that the woman had probably picked out her outfit for the same reasons.

When they finally made it to the door, a bald-headed bouncer, who had just checked a young man's ID, nodded at them. "You two should try our newest drink," he said, peering past them at a group of young twenty-something women. "It's called Sapphire Sky."

Lucy licked her lips suggestively. "Thanks for the tip," she answered in a husky voice, winking at the guy with innuendo.

Saylor's body heated with embarrassment for her friend. After they were out of earshot, she whispered in Lucy's ear, "Are you going to be flirting like that all night?"

"And what if I do?"

Saylor shrugged, realizing how uptight she had sounded. "You're right...let's have some fun."

They entered a sedate-looking room painted the color of cream with blond wood tables and chairs. Only a few people sat in small clusters, drinking wine and eating hors d'oeuvres.

Saylor looked at Lucy. "This is The Wild Sky?"

"This is just the upstairs bar," Lucy said. "We're going downstairs."

"Oh, downstairs." A blast of fear hit Saylor in the chest. Yet vibrating up through the floor, Marvin Gaye's soulful voice beckoned her on.

Lucy took her by the hand. "Let's go."

They descended the narrow staircase and Saylor squeezed Lucy's palm. "Don't leave me alone down there."

Lucy grinned as if she couldn't hear her and kept leading her down the steps with bossy confidence. Her pulse racing, Saylor hemmed in her unwarranted panic by focusing on the surroundings—a technique she had learned from the numerous self-help podcasts she subscribed to—and noticed the contrast from the brightly lit room upstairs.

This crowded downstairs bar felt subterranean in its compact darkness with midnight blue walls and dimly lit tables. The air cool yet dense, like the charged pressure before a downpour. Saylor watched a cocktail waitress in a vintage dress and maroon lipstick hand a drink order to the bartender. He read it with bunched-eyebrowed concentration.

Across the red laminate floor, Lucy led them to a back table, the farthest from the small dance floor. Saylor made sure to slide into the cushiony booth first so she could be closer to the wall. No one was dancing yet, but a young couple kissed near the dance floor's corner, the white-blond man's razor-cut hair and the black-haired woman's slick bob reminding Saylor of yin and yang.

"Look up." Lucy pointed above their heads. "Isn't that cool?"

Saylor tilted her head back and saw that the ceiling had been painted with Van Gogh-like swirling blues and golden-yellow star bursts. The memory of what had happened in the bookstore invaded her mind, but it dissolved quickly, seeming much less scary, almost dreamlike in this place far from home. A sudden gratitude overtook her. Here she sat with her best friend—someone she knew would never abandon her—in a strangely beautiful place where someone cared enough to think about art on the ceiling of a bar. Her gaze still upward, she said, "It's wonderful, Lucy."

"It's good to get out of your usual routine, isn't it?"

"You're right." Saylor sighed. "I should listen to you more often."

Lucy flashed her a knowing grin and then nodded in recognition at the cocktail waitress making her way to their table. The waitress smiled and Lucy grinned back, gesturing toward Saylor. "I planned to buy my friend here a whiskey on the rocks, but the door guy recommended the Sapphire Sky. What's in it?"

The waitress leaned in. Saylor smelled her green apple body spray—the same kind that Brooke sometimes doused on before going to a party—and marveled at how very young the world of waitpersons, cops, and teachers seemed to be getting. With the efficient recall of youth, the girl fired off the ingredients: "It has blue Curacao, pineapple, guava and lime juice mixed with Bombay Sapphire gin and premium tequila."

Lucy and Saylor exchanged glances. They both knew that tequila gave Saylor a buzz way beyond any other alcohol. Saylor remembered nights on the town with Lucy, both of them still single, when she'd down tequila sunrises. Cool, loose freedom would crack open her ordinary world and Saylor would find herself dancing and flirting without the filter of her usual shield. Lucy always managed to get them home before Saylor got too wild.

"Great. Make sure to tell the bartender to be generous with the tequila," Lucy said.

"No way, Lucy, I can't handle that much alcohol—besides, don't you remember that I swore off tequila a long time ago?"

"Just think of this as your medicine with only a passing hangover as a possible side-effect." Lucy winked at Saylor and then beamed her smile at the waitress.

The waitress smiled too as if she was in on the joke, and turned to go without giving Saylor a chance to change the order.

The drinks came in oversized glasses, and Saylor closed her eyes, taking her first sip. It tasted sweet and sparked an immediate thirst for more.

"Lucy, don't let me drink too much of this."

Lucy shook her head, a mischievous grin on her face.

They sat back and proceeded to down their drinks as they people-watched, Lucy occasionally leaning over the table in order to share her wry observations. Aware that she was laughing too loudly, Saylor felt the freedom of not caring. By the time she had reached the bottom of her glass, the world wasn't such a dangerous place after all. Lucy ordered her another round, and Saylor, this time, found no reason to protest. She started on the second drink as soon as it arrived, and smiled, watching a trio of girls practicing their dance moves.

"I better be careful. It tastes too good." Then a flash of sober thought made her set the drink down before she could take another sip. She didn't want to get too out of control. "Lucy, do I seem drunk?"

Saylor turned toward Lucy to see why she hadn't responded. A lanky red-haired man wearing serious-looking glasses was offering his hand to Lucy with an exaggerated bow of old-fashioned chivalry. His raised eyebrows and crooked smile made him look as if he hoped that Lucy understood he was making fun of himself while still hoping she'd dance with him. Lucy laughed and stood, then motioned for Saylor to join them. With what Saylor hoped was a convincing smile, she shook her head no. She felt too self-conscious to dance without a big enough crowd to camouflage her. Besides, she felt safe sitting in the dim corner with the buffer of music padding the air. She leaned back, allowing herself tiny sips from her cocktail, trying not to drink too fast or too much more. But when she watched Lucy dance to a Rolling Stones song, a carefree rebellion bubbled up and she tipped her glass to her lips. So what if she got drunk?

Saylor felt the drink muffling her thoughts; she also sensed someone eyeing her. Perched on a barstool, a woman about the same age as her mother stared at her. Even in the dim lighting, Saylor noticed the overstretched effect of repeated plastic surgeries. Still, the smiling woman was pretty. Saylor smiled back, even though a wary kind of familiarity made her rash sting.

She held her hand against her neck and watched the woman walk toward her. The woman, who kept her gaze locked on Saylor, wore a long crochet skirt, a silky white top with flowing, diaphanous sleeves, and Victorian lace-up boots, a Stevie Nicks getup that reminded Saylor of parties her parents used to throw. Though the woman had to be in her mid-seventies, she still managed to pull off the hippie-chic style that not only took a fair amount of fashion sense, but also a good amount of cash.

Without a word, she slid into the booth next to Saylor, setting down her glass of red wine. "Saylor?" The woman tilted her head. "Saylor Leoni?"

"I'm Saylor Crawmore now." Saylor hadn't heard her maiden name in so long that it seemed as if she would be a liar in not correcting her. "How do I know you?"

"So little Saylor is now a grownup," the woman said.

Saylor finally knew who she was. The breathy voice hadn't changed much through three decades. Now she could match the light green eyes and striking cheekbones with the past. It was Billy Underwood's mother. The Billy who haunted her thoughts and made her feel—even after all this time—as if she'd lost something important. "You're Faith Underwood." Saylor blinked, trying to remember exactly why Faith had disappeared so many years ago. "I can't believe you recognized me. I was only fifteen the last time I saw you." It'd been at her father's funeral, and Saylor remembered thinking how weird it was that her mother's peripheral friend, Faith Underwood, was crying harder than she was.

"I knew right away who you were," Faith said. "You're the exact image of your teenage self—but thirty-five years older!" She laughed, clasping a thin hand on Saylor's forearm. All at once, Saylor felt like the dumpy, frizzy-haired girl who everyone always exclaimed was the spitting image of her short Italian father—and who looked nothing at all like her tall and elegant Swedish mother.

Faith leaned closer. "Some things never change, do they?"

Saylor inhaled Faith's expensive smelling, powdery-linen perfume and sour wine-breath, remembering how Faith and her mother had been friends for a time, Faith and her husband, Cliff, sometimes-guests at her parents' house. And when all of them were busy in the living room drinking sangria and smoking pot, Saylor and the Underwoods' son Billy sat in her room listening to records and consuming the Fritos and 7Up that Billy had smuggled in his backpack.

Saylor eyed Faith. "How is Billy?"

"Billy?"

"Yes, your son Billy." Saylor pictured him singing along with her to Jackson Browne's "Doctor My Eyes." Her patient Billy, with his pitch-perfect tone, never once made fun of her when he accompanied her out-of-tune enthusiasm. Then Saylor saw Faith press her wineglass against her lips and suddenly remembered why Faith had disappeared. Soon after the funeral of Saylor's father, Faith had supposedly gone to some meditation retreat in Bali, leaving fifteen-year-old Billy in care of the often-absent Cliff. The Breakers Point gossip was that Faith had really ended up living with some wealthy Frenchman. Regardless, she was supposed to return from Bali after a month, but never came back at all.

"Billy always had a soft spot in his heart for you," Faith said, glancing down at her myriad of chunky-chic tiger's eye, amber, and agate rings.

"When was the last time you saw him?" Saylor could tell her questions were making Faith uncomfortable, but the tequila made her act bolder than her usual self.

"It's been a while." Faith stopped and Saylor wondered if it could have possibly been since Billy was just fifteen.

"How long?" The need to know what had happened to him grabbed Saylor so hard that she didn't have time to worry about how Faith would take her incessant questioning.

Faith drained the last of her wine. "I don't have to explain myself to you," she said. "I don't have to explain myself to anyone. I waited till Billy was a teenager before I left, and he did have his father."

Saylor nodded in embarrassment. Who was she to judge Faith Underwood? No matter how closed-off the woman acted, maybe she'd been going through her own emotional turmoil. "I'm sorry, Faith. I didn't mean to—"

"You should know that he's not the same boy you remember." Faith's voice faltered. "When I got back into the country, I looked up Cliff, and he told me that Billy ran away before his eighteenth birthday." With a challenging stare, Faith continued, "Cliff said he had lost touch with reality."

"Lost touch with reality?"

"Yes, that happens sometimes," Faith said. "And unless you have a loved one who has gone through something like this, you'll never understand." She glanced at her thin Bvlgari watch and slid out of the booth. "I have friends I need to meet upstairs."

"Wait," Saylor said, trying to break through Faith's guarded smile "Do you have any idea where he could be now?"

"Cliff mentioned..." Faith looked up at the ceiling as if searching for an answer. "Cliff told me that he was living under Breakers Cove Pier."

Saylor's throat went dry, but maybe she had misunderstood. "Living under the pier?" At her last high school reunion, Saylor had asked what had happened to him, but no one had a clue. Most people didn't even remember who he was.

"It's exactly how it sounds, Saylor." Faith shook her head. "And, no, he refuses to get any kind of help."

"Do you think he's still there?"

"From what I understand, he's not exactly someone you want to visit."

Faith's mouth twitched. Although Saylor felt sorry for her, she needed to know. "I don't care what kind of state he's in, I want to see him."

But Faith only gave her a cool nod goodbye, acting as if she couldn't hear. Saylor watched her glide away, wanting to chase her down to try to get a real answer, but knowing that Faith didn't want to provide it.

Faith disappeared up the stairs, and Saylor pushed the rest of her drink aside.

"I told you we'd see some old Malibu faces there." Lucy opened Saylor's car door for her. "Can you believe how much plastic surgery Faith Underwood has put herself through?"

"She's an interesting one—"

"Has she moved back to Breakers Point after all these years?"

"I don't know," Saylor said, hearing the weariness in her own voice. "We didn't get that far. She never even asked about my mom."

Lucy grabbed a cigarette out of the glove box. "Yeah, those two always seemed to bristle at each other like pissed-off cats guarding their territory."

"Do you remember her son, Billy?" Saylor turned to face Lucy.

"The super-cute, but totally shy boy who went to school with us?"

"According to Faith, Cliff had told her that he ran away before he was eighteen—and that he had lost touch with reality. But I would have never thought that about him, would you?"

Lucy inhaled her cigarette and then exhaled the smoke out her window. "No, but maybe he had gotten into heavy drugs, or he could be schizophrenic. My cousin Daniel was fine until he hit his early twenties. They didn't diagnose him until he had unraveled so badly that he believed he had become victim of a government experiment in which they planted a tiny electrode inside his brain to see how sick they could make him."

"I don't remember you ever telling me about that." Saylor knew Lucy's older cousin had been mentally ill, but Lucy had never told her that he was schizophrenic, let alone shared any of these details before.

"I don't like to talk about stuff that freaks me out," Lucy said. "He was a normal kid—no one would have predicted it."

"I'm so sorry."

"It wasn't anyone's fault; people are just born with that gene—and then boom—for some reason, the symptoms wait to invade a young person's life just as they're about to start living it." Lucy sighed. "Anyway, I hope Billy is okay."

"Me too," Saylor said, knowing she had to find him—but not sure why.

CHAPTER FOUR

"I don't understand why you're leaving so early. It's only ten in the morning." Lucy reached for her coffee, the citrus scent of her just-washed curls reminding Saylor of summer. A beam of sunshine slanted across Lucy's red Formica table, illuminating her tan arm. "I was hoping we'd go shopping and have lunch out. It's such a nice day for the end of October."

"I'm sorry, Lucy." Not wanting to tell her the real reason, Saylor grasped for a likely excuse. "You know it's a long drive—and I want to get going before the Sunday traffic gets too fierce."

"Then leave later tonight."

"I hate driving long distances in the dark." Without thinking, Saylor scratched her neck. "Maybe I could visit you again next month."

"Your rash is getting worse." Lucy tightened her mouth in disapproval. "Aren't you doing anything about it?"

"The prescription cream stopped working."

"With all that scratching, you're going to scar yourself. You'd better see the doctor again."

"Listen, Lucy, I..." Saylor looked down at her last dregs of coffee. "Do you remember anyone saying anything about Billy running away?"

"You're obsessing." Lucy stared at her. "Stop."

"I want to find him. I want to know what happened to him. Faith had said that he was living under Breakers Cove Pier, but she didn't seem to know if he's still there."

"Why's it so important? Didn't you guys only hang out when his mom and dad came to your parents' house for some dinner parties?"

"I can't explain it, Lucy...I just need to know." She had never shared with Lucy how often she thought about him because she knew that Lucy would only chide her for it, telling her that she was hanging onto the past and fixating on someone who didn't matter.

After a quick eye roll, Lucy stood. "I'll check online and see if any info pops up." She picked up their mugs and strode through the double doors to her kitchen.

Saylor waited, appreciating the view of impossibly tall palm trees.

Lucy abruptly materialized by Saylor's side with their refilled mugs. "I wonder if he still goes by Billy—or if he's even still alive. So many people we went to school with have died from overdoses." She set down their cups and turned toward her credenza. On top of the polished walnut sat her glasses and laptop alongside a stack of Vanity Fair magazines. She whipped on her glasses and grabbed her laptop, placing it on the table next to Saylor. Behind her tortoiseshell frames, Lucy's unblinking eyes stared at the screen.

I'm getting a lot of Billy Underwoods, but I don't think any of these are a match." Lucy's fingers tapped away between sips of coffee. "And also, lots of William Underwoods—but again—not your Underwood."

"Besides saying that he'd lost touch with reality, Faith also mentioned something about him not being someone you'd want to visit—you don't think that means he's dangerous, do you?"

Focused on her laptop, Lucy clicked away. "Your mom still lives in Breakers Point. Maybe she's heard something. By the way, how is your mom doing?"

"I haven't talked to her in a while," Saylor said. "I didn't even tell her I was visiting you because I didn't want her to guilt trip me about not making the time to see her."

Lucy winked. "I get it. You wanted to keep this weekend fun. Besides, your mom always seems to forget that the coastal route makes it a way longer drive for you."

"That's part of the reason I'm leaving early; I've decided to go there to try and find Billy."

"I don't understand. How are you going to find him that way?"

Saylor paused, annoyed that Lucy had only been half-listening to her. "I'm going to see if he still might be living under the pier." She knew that Lucy would only think she was obsessing again, but didn't care. "It's worth a try."

Lucy shook her head. "Promise to call me when you get home."

"I will." Saylor nodded.

"And promise me that you won't let yourself fixate about him if you don't find out anything," Lucy said. "Sometimes certain things aren't meant to be."

"And sometimes you have to make things happen too," Saylor said, reaching for her coffee.

Saylor rolled down her window. She had forgotten how congested Pacific Coast Highway could get on a Sunday and wondered how many people on the road were tourists and how many were just fleeing their cramped city lives to try and find a spot on the ever-narrowing string of beaches. When she glanced at the dashboard clock, she saw that almost an hour had already passed since she left Lucy's Ocean Park bungalow. The drive, so far, should have been only fifteen minutes. Still, she knew she had to do this. She pushed down the button to open the passenger window and leaned forward to let the crosswind cool the sweat beading down her back. The weather was what her mother called Indian Summer; autumn having been overtaken by the out-of-season heat of a dry summer's day.

Amid the honking horns, Saylor gave in to the stop and start traffic, memories of Billy floating in her mind. He had been a beautiful boy, with curly brown hair and eyes the color of a clear, green sea, yet he always walked with a hunched-over back, his shoulders in a perpetual wince—as if he were always waiting for something to fall.

The first time he had shown up at her house his head was bowed as his parents laughed at how even though he was thirteen years old, they didn't want to leave him at home since Saylor was the same age—and "wouldn't it be nice for him to hang out with someone from school?" Because Billy was in a different class than hers, and because he was so shy, melting into the edges of school grounds and cafeteria, she had never taken note of him. Within hours, though, Saylor had felt like he understood her—maybe even more than Lucy did. With her bedroom door closed to their parents' ridiculous laughter and the skunky smell of pot smoke, quiet Billy looked straight at her as if he were reading her thoughts. Hoping his parents would stay longer than the other guests, she turned off her light, lit one of her homemade sand candles, and stacked her well-worn Jackson Browne, James Taylor, and Loggins and Messina records on the turntable. With the burning candle set on a stack of books between them, they sat cross-legged on her carpet.

Billy's shoulders relaxed. "I know this is a weird thing to say, but I trust you."

She didn't know how to reply, wondering how he could think that when it'd been the first time they ever really talked. And why say it out loud, anyway? Yes, Billy was what Lucy would call *different*, that was for sure.

Thankfully Billy seemed to sense her discomfort and studied the words on the back of a nearby album jacket, acting as if he hadn't said anything. Then he quickly changed the subject. "Let's sneak out with some rafts and take the bus down to Breaker's Cove. It's a red tide, so we'll be right in the glow when the waves break."

She readily agreed, knowing from science class how the ruddy daytime ocean color caused by invading phytoplankton would create bursts of bioluminescence at night. Clamping their hands over their mouths, they refrained from giggling out loud as they tiptoed out the front door. Saylor grabbed two rafts from the garage and signaled Billy to follow. They ran up the street, rafts under arms, and waited for the bus under a flickering streetlight.

Once the bus deposited them on the side of the highway by Breaker's Cove, they trekked down the windy road to the beach. When they made it to the sand, they stood watching the glow of breaking waves.

"Let's be part of that," Billy said.

Surprised that he stripped down to his boxers without hesitation, Saylor watched him race into the tide, the splashing water shimmering electric-blue around him. Clad in her suit, which she had put on under her clothes before leaving, Saylor followed, smiling in the dark at his joy. He definitely was different from the other kids she knew, the kind of different that made her feel as if he was aware of something bigger than himself, something that no one else understood, let alone sensed. But what that *something* was, she could not guess.

With the water on the side of their rafts flashing by like a liquid star system, they paddled over a wave. "Let's take this one," Billy said, his face illuminated by the water's phosphorescence.

She couldn't get over how happy he sounded and turned her raft around. They caught the wave and when it broke, they were immersed in an otherworldly brilliance.

The rest of her memory now vanished, Saylor wiped her brow, realizing that she'd better pay closer attention to the road. Traffic had finally subsided, and cars were now whizzing past. She passed the famous Malibu Colony and put her car into fifth. In a daze, she continued to drive through the rest of Malibu, leaving behind the sprawling homes of movie stars, directors, and producers, heading toward Breakers Point. The small cluster of houses past the outskirts of Malibu drew more of the avant-garde, drop-out-of-society crowd. Cut in two by Pacific Coast Highway, Breakers Point's cliff-side homes clung onto the mountainside's unstable earth, and on the ocean side, beachfront properties balanced on stilt-like pilings, the incoming tides roaring beneath. Saylor's mother still lived in the northernmost beach house, a 1960s box-like design, gray and faded, exhausted-looking with its crumbly stucco exterior and cloudy plate-glass windows.

Saylor knew better than to visit her mother, Erika, unannounced, never knowing if Philip would be there or not. It had been over thirty-five years since her mother started seeing the still-unavailable and increasingly goblin-faced Philip A. Kentsmoth. About a year after her father had died, her mother had taken up with the prominent movie director. Erika had always insisted that they were very dear friends—and nothing more. But Saylor had known better, having heard her mother's theatrical moans verging on screams whenever the couple was behind Erika's bedroom door. As a young teen, Saylor had turned up the radio, trying to drown out the sound, as she wondered how her mother could stand his touch.

After all these years, Saylor couldn't figure out why her mother continued with Philip. Not only was he arrogant and rude—he was a married man. A married man who had told Erika from the very beginning that he'd never leave his wife due to 'monetary concerns.' Insisting that it was of utmost importance, he insisted that Erika had to take special care in hiding their ongoing affair. As far as Saylor knew, he never took her mother out, never even for a clandestine weekend away. The two main reasons Saylor guessed why Erika had stayed with him was that her mother got off being with a man of power—as well as being the desired one, the *other* woman who still had a hold on him.

Not long after Simon Leoni's death, Faith Underwood had made sure to tell Erika—in front of Saylor—that she had found out that Simon had slept with Philip's wife numerous times while Philip was on location. Soon after that, Erika had flirted with the bulbous-eyed Philip when they happened to run into him, insisting that he write down her number 'just in case.'

No, Saylor didn't think she'd ever stop by her mother's house unannounced. Even if Philip wasn't there, Erika would act as if Saylor had interrupted her, even if there was nothing to interrupt. Instead, she would call her mother a day or two after she got home—not to tell her that she had been in Breakers Point, but to ask about Billy.

Before the highway curved into Breakers Point, Saylor anticipated the turnoff for Breaker's Cove, remembering the long crescent of sand with its 600-foot-long pier. When she spotted the entrance sign, Saylor flipped her left turn signal and waited in the middle divider for the southbound cars to clear. She turned down the road and smelled the faint scent of ocean. Even if she wasn't going to find out anything, she still had to look.

She made it down to the lot and parked facing the water. After she unfolded herself out of the car, she held her hand over her brow and surveyed the pier. It didn't match the mental picture from the past. Her memories were of seemingly brighter days when she and Lucy bought Popsicles at the Snack and Bait Shack, a tiny shop located on the middle of the pier, painted with surfers on orange boards riding turquoise-blue waves. Even at sixteen, she and Lucy had still skipped over the cracks that showed the flashing ocean below, had still raced to the end as if they were little kids to grin at the seals barking on buoys.

Now the Snack and Bait Shack had been torn down and the pier itself was much shorter, having been damaged years ago, as Erika had informed her, from an El Niño storm. But Saylor hadn't pictured it having this severe of an effect. A single blotchy-skinned seal lay motionless on a faded buoy that bobbed much farther away from the pier's end than it had in the past. The beach itself had narrowed, rocky and wet where even in the highest of tides it used to be smooth and dry.

Male voices caught her attention. Three men hunkered by the edge of the lot, their weathered faces and beaten-down postures reminding her of the homeless guys that hovered around Dune Beach's main shopping center. Two of the men leaned back and laughed at something the third, a wiry man in a wheelchair, had just said. They all wore faded plaid shirts just like the surfers used to wear when Saylor was in high school. For a moment, she stood studying their animated conversation, wondering if any of them could be Billy.

She clutched her keys and walked toward them. The closer she got, the more certain she was that none of them were Billy. Still, she hoped that one of them might know something about him. When she came within a couple of feet, the man in the wheelchair stopped talking and stared. With pulse racing, she stepped forward.

"Excuse me, but I'm trying to find an old friend of mine. His name is Billy Underwood." Embarrassed by how shaky her voice sounded, she tried to cover it up with a plastered-on smile. "You guys don't happen to know him, do you?"

The two young men looked at the older man in the wheelchair as if he were their spokesperson. The man widened his eyes for a split second. But then he tightened his lips, not saying a word. He reminded her of poor Uncle Silvio with his bleak stare, only this man appeared angry instead of fearful. His irate eyes and bitter mouth made Saylor feel defensive, as if he was just waiting to point out how stupid she was.

But what if this man was her only clue? She hesitantly touched his shoulder, amazed at her own courage. "Please tell me if you know him." His neck muscles tightened as he glanced down at a faded bubblegum wrapper. Then he shot one defiant glare at her and rolled away. Saylor stood mute, watching the sharp-edged retreat of his back muscles underneath his thin shirt.

The other two men stood in awkward silence. The closest one avoided eye contact, nervously scratching his patchy beard. The other took off his frayed baseball cap, pushing his hair back from a sweaty forehead. "I'm sorry about Wex. He's what you would call the suspicious type," he whispered. He first looked at the direction Wex had gone and then looked toward the pier, raising his eyebrows. "But I'm thinking," he said, "that who you're looking for is close."

Saylor nodded and the two men turned in unison, bolting like spooked horses to catch up with their friend. The one who had last spoken, glanced back. He wore an incongruous expression of naïve sweetness and street-worn formidability. A raw burning in her throat, she inhaled the salty air, trying to keep down unexpected grief.

As she made her way toward the pier, her eyes watered in the heated glare. At the point where the lot met the sand, she sat on a rock and took off her shoes before she stood. She stared at the pier's underside and continued on. Once she was close enough, she could smell the odor of dank seaweed and the tarry scent of creosote oozing from the pilings. Her fingers tightened around her keys and she ventured into the shadows. Except for the intermittent lull of a lethargic tide, there remained a stagnant kind of stillness that reminded Saylor of the underworld air of a cave.

The mixture of apprehension and quiet made her shiver. Yet she didn't feel as fearful as she knew she should. She didn't feel as fearful as she had in the bookstore, or when irrational thoughts kept her from sleep while cocooned in the safety of her bed. What the hell was wrong with her? She should leave right now, get home, and make an appointment with a therapist.

Yet her feet remained fixed in the sand; it didn't feel right to give up now. She half-turned, trying to decide if it was braver to continue or go back. But something caught her eye. Did she see part of an elbow? It appeared for a split second behind the piling just a couple of paces ahead. Mesmerized by a rivulet of cigarette smoke drifting from the same location, she froze. For a moment she forgot why she was there. She shook her head, telling herself that this was crazy, but continued toward whoever was there. Her heart pounded so loudly she could hear it inside her head.

He sat against the piling, staring straight ahead. He looked like Billy, but then he didn't. His skin was dark, dark as earth. His matted hair reminded her of an abandoned dog. Stony-faced, he didn't even register that she was there. In the shaded quiet, Saylor paused, thinking how much coarser his features were than she ever might have imagined on her grown-up Billy.

When she took a step forward, he flinched, finally noticing her. Then recognition flashed in his eyes. Not saying a word, he stubbed his cigarette in the sand.

Saylor swallowed. *Maybe I'm just imagining he could be him.*

But his eyes were the same shade of sea-glass green. "Billy?"

He hesitated for so long, she wasn't sure he had heard her, but then a hoarse whisper came out. "Yes. You know me."

"Are you...Billy Underwood?"

"I know who you are," he said. "You're my old friend, Saylor."

Now her heart felt like it had stopped beating. "It is you."

He motioned for her to sit. She kneeled on the sand next to him, but the stench of urine and mildew made her turn her head. She averted her face, catching a quick intake of air that didn't reek of devastation. Not sure what to say, she turned her attention back on Billy. With unfocused eyes, he rocked back and forth, seemingly forgetting that she was there. She knew she should be careful, but somehow the old childhood trust pushed away any trepidation. Finally, his body calmed down, and he clasped his hands around his knees, turning his gaze toward the ocean.

"Billy, I've missed you." It was the first thing she could think of to try and break into wherever his mind had gone.

He turned to face her in an unnaturally slow mechanical way, his eyes glassy, creating an improbable green in his coffee-brown face. "I missed you too. I missed so much." His voice sounded unused and rusty.

"Have you..." Saylor scratched her neck. "Have you been on your own for a long time?"

"Time is not what you think it is." Back and forth he shook his head, a scowl on his face.

"Oh," Saylor said, not knowing how she should respond. Billy was definitely suffering from severe mental illness. Yet she wasn't afraid. She thought about the warmth of the day saturating the planks of pier over their heads and turned to him. "Let's walk out in the sun."

"Out there?" Billy said, a bewildered look in his eyes.

"Yes," Saylor answered. "Out there." She got up and held out her hand.

"I like it better at night," he said. But then, his fingers, the texture of stone and sand, tentatively grasped her palm.

They crossed into the sunlight, and he ducked his head, keeping it bowed while they walked in silence. They continued on. Saylor thought about the strangeness of time and how all those years ago, she would never have envisioned that she and Billy would be these middle-aged tragedies: an unbalanced homeless man and an anxious woman too afraid to trust in happiness.

Billy stopped. "The Snack and Bait Shack has ceased to exist." He withdrew his hand from her grasp.

"I noticed they tore it down."

"You used to like their root beer Popsicles," he said, staring ahead.

"You're right." Saylor wondered how he could have remembered that, or have even known. He had never been on the pier with her, and she couldn't recall him hanging out with any of the other kids either.

"I was always invisible," Billy said, uncannily echoing her thoughts.

"Billy, do you remember being at my house? Do you remember how we used to talk?" Squinting against the glare of sunlight off water, Saylor held back tears.

"It must have been hard for you—your father being so cruel to you the night before he died," he said.

Saylor's chest constricted—a sudden tightness that made it hard to breathe. "What are you talking about?"

"My dad had brought rocky road ice cream for dessert." Billy nodded as if in agreement with his own memory.

Billy's father had loved sweets—especially ice cream—and had been disappointed when her parents didn't offer desserts at their dinner parties. Saylor's father had banned all things with sugar as 'poison to the masses.' She pictured Simon's haughty-faced disgust, and without warning, an inconceivably insane sentence invaded Saylor's mind: *You're rotten and I wish you would die.* Panicked, she stole a look at Billy, but his eyes still had the same far-off daze. Why in the hell would her irrational fear pop up now?

"He was mean to you," Billy said. "Ugly mean."

"I know that he was too strict about what I ate, but I don't remember him being especially mean that night."

Billy did not respond. With his hands in pockets, he clenched his mouth into a tight line. The ocean surged forward, stretching within inches of their feet, and they continued on.

As they walked side-by-side, Saylor gently touched his arm. "Why did you say that my dad had been cruel to me the night before he died?" She wondered if Billy had mixed facts and delusions. His own mother had said that he'd lost touch with reality. She did know, though, that he and his parents had been over the night before her father's death, and her father had gotten mad at her for sneaking some ice cream with Billy. But all he did was spout out his same speech about how evil sugar was and how he was going to dump the rest down the sink.

Billy flinched the same way he did when he first noticed her. "I remember what he said because *I* wasn't the one who had to bury his words."

He wasn't the one who had to bury his words? Fearful that she was falling down a rabbit hole of Billy's misguided memories, she still had to ask: "What exactly do you remember?"

"He said..." Billy shook his head. "Your dad said that you were a disgusting pig."

She didn't recall any of these things, but her stomach roiled at the words as if her father himself had just said them. "Do you recall," she said, "what happened next?"

"After he caught you eating the ice cream, he went into a rage," Billy said, his voice just above a whisper. "He took the rest of it out of the freezer and dug his hand in it and threw it all over you. You cried, but he wouldn't stop."

She didn't know what to say, the scenario Billy was painting sounded too out there. But then the memory of her father's face, red and distorted with rage, pushed into her mind.

"Don't you remember how the ice cream hit you? How it got all sticky?" Now, Billy tapped her arm. "Don't be afraid."

Saylor wrapped her arms around herself to stop from shaking. Billy stood next to her without saying a word. She squeezed her eyes shut, seeing her fifteen-year-old self. She was cowering by the kitchen sink. Billy, standing in front of her trying to protect her. There was her father shoving him aside. She had tried to pretend it wasn't happening, but still held her hands up to deflect the ice cream as if it had the impact of fists. So much crazy anger had been fired at her, she grew paralyzed—a girl trapped in a bizarre dream that made no sense. Ice cream slid down her neck. Stickiness like blood.

After her father stormed out the kitchen, Billy led her to her room and brought a towel, its end warm and damp from where he had let it run under the bathroom faucet. He attempted to clean her neck, tried to console her. "Don't listen to him. He's sick, you know."

"This could have been a semi-funny story about my father throwing ice cream at me" she had said, "but he acted too much like a monster."

"I know," Billy said. "His head is full of demons."

Now, the tide crashed at their feet, and Saylor shook her head. It was un-settling to have a memory redefined, as if a skeleton resting inches under the sand had just been exposed.

Then, out of the corner of her eye, she saw a teenage couple walking to-ward them. The boy bent down to give the girl a shell. On her open palm, the girl held it with reverence as if it were a perched butterfly ready to take wing. The boy grazed her arms with his fingertips. They didn't seem to notice Say-lor or Billy.

"You know..." Billy cleared his throat. "Two things happened that night."

"What?" Saylor tilted her head, hoping to catch every word.

"One is that your father took all his fear and threw it even harder on you—so hard that it stuck. Two is that you came to believe that your words were actual weapons."

"You think so?" What an enigma Billy was: unstable and alone—and, yet, so perceptive and connected. But maybe some of the wisest of sages in-habited the outskirts of so-called civilization.

Billy continued, "Even though he was a bad father, he didn't *want* to throw his fear on you—but he was too sick to stop. Too sick to control him-self."

"What do you mean by my words being actual weapons?"

"You had said that night that you wished he would die—and you know the next day he did—and by his own hand too," Billy answered.

"You mean he died in the catamaran accident." She didn't remember say-ing that she had wished her father would die, but didn't doubt that Billy was telling the truth because she had so often thought it. "He drowned after an incoming wave crashed into the boat. He fell off and hit his head against the hull," Saylor said, trying to remind him.

"It was an accident that he wanted to happen," Billy said. "I believe so."

CHAPTER FIVE

Saylor could tell that Billy had gone someplace inside himself again, his body rigid as a mannequin while his unblinking gaze fixated on the surf. She stayed next to him, a strange sense of calm coming over her, the kind of calm that arrives with sudden clarity. Billy's poetic words perfectly described what had happened and probably why her fears had developed. Her father had thrown his fear on her and she had taken it in. And, before her father had died, she did live with the constant worry that he was going to take his own life.

Although Simon had never said anything about wanting to do himself in and had never attempted to kill himself—at least as far as she knew—she still sensed, even at an early age, that he had been suicidal. It was especially scary during what he had called his 'dark blue' phases—periods that lasted for days at a time when he was unable to go to work, hardly ate, and wouldn't speak. She would check to make sure he hadn't killed himself like Uncle Silvio had. She would creep up to the locked bathroom door, pressing her head sideways on the wood floor, trying to see what she could under the crack. He would be in there for hours, the ongoing silence making her want to scream. Though she never saw anything but her father's veined feet planted against the pink tiled floor, she would walk away relieved, telling herself that he was okay since she couldn't see any blood.

She had always wondered, as well—though no one else had ever spoken of it—why her father had decided to take the catamaran out by himself that day. Her mother had begged him not to because of the high-surf warnings that blared all morning from the kitchen radio. Still, he insisted, saying that it was a Sunday and it was the only thing he could think of to take his mind off things. The very last memory Saylor had of her father was the vacant look in his eyes that made him appear as if his soul had already been sucked out of him. Before he turned to walk out the front door, he briefly faced her. His hollow gaze sliced right through her body to someplace she could not see.

With a sideways glance at Billy, she wondered how he could have known so much, amazed at how much insight his frayed soul had been able to give. Years ago, she had read an article that dived into a theory about how some people dealing with mental health conditions are highly intuitive because their brains do not filter out the multitude of stimuli that most people don't even register. If that were true for Billy, she could only imagine how scary and confusing his world would be. She tried to swallow down the ache in her throat.

The incoming tide splashed past their ankles. Saylor leaned down to roll up the ends of her wet jeans. She noticed that Billy didn't seem to mind, or perhaps even notice, as he didn't make any attempts to push up his soaked pant legs. He just kept staring straight ahead. "I need to go back," he whispered.

"Billy, wait." Saylor touched his shoulder, wanting to make contact. "Thank you."

His eyes shone. "You're strong, Saylor."

"I'm far from strong, Billy." Saylor answered, feeling a sudden unease.

In hunched-over silence, Billy turned toward the pier.

Not sure what to say or do next, she did her best to keep up with his furious pace. She debated whether she should mention seeing his mother, Faith. When she looked over at his unhappy profile, she decided not to. Her fingers scrunched into fists, angry that her sweet Billy had fallen through the cracks. Had he really been struggling with his mental illness before he ran away, or did this perilous existence, which he had been possibly surviving through all the way since he was just a teen, create his mental condition?

Even with her unrelenting anxiety, she felt ashamed at how easy her life had been compared to his. Now her fears seemed frivolous. She scratched her rash, wondering how she could help. "Are there any shelters around here?" she said, trying to keep her voice from shaking.

Billy frowned, freezing in mid-step. "Shelters?"

"You know, a place where you can sleep inside, get some warm food."

"No," Billy said. "I don't ever go anywhere inside. It's too dangerous."

"Too dangerous?"

"Don't try to talk me into it." His voice had grown loud with both anger and fear.

"Okay," she said, not wanting to provoke him. "I don't want to talk you into doing anything you don't want to do..."

"You have family, yes?" Billy nodded, his tone now gentle, his eyes kind.

"Yes," she answered, relieved that he sounded like her old Billy again. "I have a husband named Brian, and two teenagers—a boy and a girl."

"Good." His face softened. "Make your way back home. Open your eyes. Unshackle yourself by letting others in. Then you can help them."

"But I want you to let me in, too." She was about to ask him if he wanted to know about his dad, but he was loping ahead again, his attention turned inward.

"Wait," she said, trying to keep up. "Maybe you might want to come home with me?" It was a long-shot, but she had to try.

Billy tucked his head as if he were fighting a headwind. She wasn't sure if he just chose not to answer, or if whatever was happening in his turbulent brain had drowned out her words. He headed under the pier, muttering things under his breath that Saylor couldn't make out. She followed on his heels, sensing his trepidation. "Please think about it," she said.

With downcast eyes, he turned around. "Be on your way now," he muttered. "Be on your way."

"But I—"

He held up his hand. "No," he said and then turned in the direction of the piling where she had first seen him.

"I'll come back then," she called. "I'll come back to see you again." For several long minutes, she waited, hoping that he'd change his mind, but the only sound she heard was the insistent caw of a far-off crow.

Saylor sat in the comfort of her car and eyed the pier, wondering how she would ever be able to reach him. There had to be something she could do, but the longer she sat there trying to figure out what, the sadder and more useless she felt. She turned on the ignition, realizing how free she was in just being able to drive a car. The heat of guilt trickled down her back. Outside the car window, she saw Wex and the two other men watching her. Without warning, Wex yelled, "That's right, lady, go back to your own world." His dead-gray teeth formed into an angry grin. "Billy is fine just the way he is."

She didn't answer, sensing that this Wex character felt he was protecting Billy. After she drove out of the lot, she briefly held a palm against her rash, queasy from the sickening memory of melting ice cream against her skin.

CHAPTER SIX

When Saylor was just a couple of minutes away from her mother's house, she debated if she should stop on the side of the road and call her from her cell. Maybe Erika wouldn't mind the impromptu visit if she gave her some kind of warning, even if she were only minutes away. It did seem strange to be all the way out here and not see her. It was her mother, after all. But when Saylor's stomach twisted at the thought, she stepped on the gas.

After some miles had passed, the knot in her belly softened. Then nearing the first tight bend in the road, she slowed down. This was the windy part of PCH with ocean pounding against rocks by the edge of the southbound side while cliffs bordered too close beside the northbound lane. Saylor knew there was always a chance that the next rainy season could bring landslides, obliterating the highway and taking out drivers like insects. Even now a loose boulder could come out of nowhere, crash down on the car, killing her in an instant.

Saylor reminded herself not to catastrophize. She let out a breath, picturing how Billy's eyes seemed to glow when he had said that she should unshackle herself and then help her own family.

She tried to concentrate on the road ahead, knowing that Billy was right, as the sunlight's reflection off the ocean flashed in her peripheral vision. As a young child, she used to shield her eyes from the sun glinting off sand and the glare of light bouncing off water. Those days were sometimes so raw with sunshine that she used to have nightmares of going blind under blazing, white-yellow skies.

Now that she was older, the brightness was no longer overbearing. Rather, it was something she craved. She drove on until she saw an outlet on the ocean side, turned left across PCH, and parked so that her car wasn't too close to the drop-off. After she walked to the bluff's edge, she stared down at the crashing surf. A light spray misted her face, and she breathed in the contradictory smells of highway asphalt and ocean brine, not sure why she had stopped.

She sensed someone looking at her and scanned the water's surface, spotting the dog-like face of an inquisitive seal. Its unblinking eyes stared straight

into hers. She smiled. When Brooke had been about five, one of her favorite
stories had been about a selkie. Saylor must have read it to her at least once
a week for nearly a whole year. The myth told of how a selkie was a seal that
could assume human form when she shed her sealskin. When a handsome
fisherman spied this transformation from shore one day, he stole her skin so
she wouldn't be able to return to sea and was made to become his wife. She
learned to love her husband and had children with him. She was a good and
kindly wife and mother, yet she desperately yearned for her earlier life in the
sea. In the end, one of her children found her sealskin and gave it back to her.
The selkie then returned to the sea, free from the restraints of land.

Saylor kept her gaze on the seal. How similar an average woman's life
was to the selkie's tale. Mother's journeys, she mused, evolve from freedom
to caretaking, and then back again to freedom after their children are grown,
and how with time, women often become less emotionally dependent on
their spouses. The seal now popped her head under the water. Saylor held her
hand over her brow, searching left and right to see where the seal would reap-
pear. Finally, the shiny head resurfaced. Instead of traveling up or down the
coast, the seal went farther out, but still seemed hesitant to leave the green
coastal water for the expanse of deeper blue. They kept a distant, fixed gaze
on each other until Saylor's vision blurred. She closed her eyes and rubbed
her lids as if she were a young child trying to wake from a long sleep. When
she opened them, the seal was gone.

She raced to the car, remembering Brooke had left an old spiral notepad
in the trunk. Sure enough, under canvas shopping bags, she spied the
turquoise cover. After searching the glove box, she found her second treasure:
a soft-leaded pencil left by Devin.

It had been years. Years since she took the time to contemplate the layout
of the land and imprint its character to paper. On the edge of the cliff, Saylor sat cross-legged, the sun-drenched earth warming the back of her thighs
through her jeans' worn denim. She studied the horizon, the folds of unbroken waves, the ocean cliffs jutting from the north. As if it were a wand,
her fingers directed the pencil. Barely glancing at the paper, she sketched the
delineation between sea and sky, the curves of water, the exposed, eroding
bluffs. Finally, she looked down. Even over the lines of college-ruled paper,
she liked what she had created, surprised by the looseness of her work. With

a deep breath of accomplishment, Saylor realized that she had finally been brave enough to dip her artist's hand into the stream of actual doing. She couldn't wait to report this to Lucy. Somewhere over the ocean waves, she heard the far-off bark of a seal, and guessing it was her seal, she closed the notebook with satisfaction.

After some time back on the road, the sky's brilliance diminished into a cool, blue evening. The car window still open, she held her hand out, letting her fingers trail through the rush of air. She imagined how it would be to continue her art, fantasizing about her work progressing to the point where she could show at art shows, maybe even selling some of her better stuff. Then, while stopped at a light, she flipped open the notebook and glanced at her sketch. It looked like scribble, the pathetic attempt by a too-hopeful amateur. Who was she kidding?

Her father had tried to be an artist, too. Had he been any good? She couldn't recall. She did remember, though, that he suffered from debilitating regret and self-doubt. When she was young, he had told her that when he graduated from high school, he had wanted to go to an art institute, but his mother only scoffed at him, telling him that she would never pay for such an indulgence and how it would be a waste of time and money since Simon lacked any natural talent. Instead, Simon had been coaxed into getting a business degree and then working for his father's industrial supply company, where he stayed year after miserable year.

After her Grandfather Frank had retired, Simon took over the business even though he hated everything about it: the trapped hours sitting as a 'soulless suit' behind his desk, the endless business lunches at 'mediocre restaurants' with clients 'who couldn't give a crap' about the real him (and whom he didn't give a 'crap about either, for that matter'), and the 'asinine employees' who were both soft in the head and belly.

All of this, Simon had shared with Saylor. And as he reminded her about a year before he had died, since he had a wife and daughter to support, he had no choice but to stay in the only career he ever knew. He also confided to her that if he hadn't married her mother (the woman his own mother had introduced him to after she became enamored with 'the class-act sales girl' who sold her a mink coat), then maybe he would have had a chance in life.

One foggy Saturday, Simon did set up an easel in their living room. He stood tense-backed before it, wearing a white T-shirt and his weekend khaki pants, which he had to belt in order to keep them up, his body bone-lean from years of low-fat, no-sugar, no-white-flour diet, and predawn calisthenics. He stared out the window at the muted colors of a winter's ocean, a nervous energy bristling from his olive skin and the ends of his black, defiant hair. With a severe swipe of hand, he wiped his forehead even though the day was cool. After drawing in a deep breath that sounded as if he were about to dive under the ocean, he muttered under his breath, "I have more talent than anyone realizes." He squeezed the blues, greens, and whites of his acrylic paint tubes onto his palette and furiously stabbed the canvas with his brush. Saylor had been about five at the time and wondered if she should pick up her crayons and coloring book from the coffee table and run back to her room. Yet she remained on the couch. Maybe he wouldn't give up like he did last time when she had left the room. Maybe if she smiled and hummed as sweet as she could, he'd stay calm. They could both be artists together. And, then, maybe he would be happy.

She didn't dare say a word and colored the best she could within the lines, listening to her father's breathing. But when the room became too still, Saylor looked up from her yellow and purple giraffe to see her father gripping the brush in his hand, his eyes too big and scary to look at. She held her breath, pretended she was invisible, and tiptoed out of the room. She pulled her door shut, but Simon's bellow still intruded into her room.

"Fuck everybody." He yelled so loudly that she crouched against the door with hands over her ears, hoping he'd stop before her throat squeezed too tight, so tight that she wouldn't be able to breathe.

Saylor shook her head at the memory and narrowed her eyes at the approaching headlights. After exiting onto her shortcut, a rural stretch of road between farmland, she turned on her high beams and rolled up her window against the manure stink that infiltrated the fields she was passing by. She stared straight ahead, thinking how Lucy was wrong; she didn't need to "let out" her creativity in order to conquer the anxiety. It was easy enough for Lucy. She had no idea how futile it all felt. There could never be enough room in this world for all the artists to ever make any kind of living or gain any kind of recognition. Why be yet another one of the frustrated? Why put all that time and energy into something that could never amount to anything?

She pressed her foot on the gas. Suddenly, an animal the size of a small dog darted straight in front of her car's path. Saylor had to brake so hard that her calf spasmed. Luckily, she missed whatever it was. She exhaled, seeing now that it was a coyote. He stood for a moment, appearing just as surprised as she was. Then he regained himself and trotted off to the other side of the road. Before he edged out of view from the headlight's beam, he turned one last time and stared at her with a penetrating look of disapproval. Saylor remained stock still, waiting for something that she couldn't name to happen. But this was ridiculous. She was in the middle of the road and had to get going. Her calf, though, remained knotted with pain, so she pulled onto the dirt and leaned over, hoping to knead it out. The ache eased a bit and she sat back, an overwhelming loneliness descending over her in the blank quiet of the car. She thought about Billy and what he had said about her father throwing his fear on her.

She shook her head. She would never allow herself to become the self-defeating, self-hating wretch that her father had been. Her art wasn't about proving herself, and it wasn't about recognition. It wasn't about anything except doing something that made her forget about everything else.

After the pain eased into a dull throb, she turned the car back onto the road. The rest of the way home, she fantasized what it would be like to see Billy again, how she would help him start a new life.

CHAPTER SEVEN

A young Billy Underwood, with eyes the luminescent green of an unbroken wave, lay on the beach, his gaze wide open to the sky. The summer afternoon offered only a cloudless sense of listlessness. Her young self was there too, her body lying on the sand next to him. He looked at her and said something, but the surf pounded too loudly. She asked him what he said. Suddenly, he disappeared—and she somehow knew that he had been swept out to sea. She stood, desperate to save him. But her legs would not work. Fear pounded in her throat.

Saylor woke herself up yelling Billy's name.

Brian patted her arm. "Did you have another one of your nightmares—or is there something I should know?"

She could hear the smile in his voice. "There's nothing you need to know," she answered, her heart still galloping. "It was just a nightmare."

"But who is Billy?"

By the time she had made it home that night, she didn't have the energy to tell Brian about finding Billy—and the memories he had dug up for her. But now she wanted to explain.

"I knew Billy way back in grade school. His parents were friends with my parents. But he's homeless now."

"Homeless?"

"I found him living under the pier."

Brian yawned. "Living under the pier? How does someone live under a pier?"

"I don't know, Brian—but you're missing the point." Saylor's rash itched so much that it burned. She scratched with a vengeance until she felt blood pooling under her nails. Balling her hands into fists, she told herself to stop. Told herself that the more she scratched, the more it would ultimately itch.

"I'm sorry," he finally murmured back. "That must have been weird for you to run into someone from your childhood who's become homeless, but at least you had Lucy there—"

"I was by myself." Saylor inhaled as deeply as she could, trying to keep the agitation at bay. "And I purposely went looking for him."

"You did?" Brian's voice had become slurred with the half-aware drone that told Saylor he was about to nod off.

Regardless, she still wanted to talk. "I had run into his mother the night before, and she had told me that he had become mentally ill and had run away when he had been just a teen." She paused, hearing the slow, steady breath of slumber. How Brian could wake up and then fall back to sleep so quickly was a mystery to her. Once she was awake, her mind behaved like a neurotic hamster stuck in a cage, relentlessly racing within the confines of a mental exercise wheel. She breathed as deep and slow as she could and ran her fingers through a patch of moonlight, a perfect square between her and Brian. She considered moving closer and resting her head on his shoulder, but thought better of it. His calm body would only make her feel more un-nerved.

Determined to find rest again, she closed her eyes, counting to three with each inhale and again with each exhale, trying to keep her mind blank. Yet she couldn't help but ponder why thoughts of Billy had seemed to catch her over the years. She'd been unloading laundry from the dryer, and the way the afternoon sun fell on the blue tiled floor brought on a memory of him squint-ing in his serious, tense way. Or she'd be washing dishes on a winter's day and the rain dripping down the eaves would somehow make her cry for him. It was as though she was mourning him, even though he had only been part of her life for a few short years. With a sigh, she remembered that sometime during high school he had faded even further into the background, until she no longer had seen him at all.

Saylor often went for a walk with Neptune and showered before she called her mother, a routine that made her feel more cheerful and sharp-witted, an emotional shield to deflect Erika's brittle tone and even sharper words.

Ever since she could remember, Saylor sensed her mother's unhappiness, saw her joy continue to dissipate over the years. Once she was old enough to hear Erika's sad background, she attributed her mother's temperament to a forlorn childhood, where her two older brothers received the lion's share of attention and love while she was considered the leftover girl no one wanted.

And it sure didn't help that Erika had married an emotional monster—the man who ended up being Saylor's father. Still, as a child stuck between her parent's tangled emotions, Saylor often wondered if she were the main reason behind her mother's misery. She just wasn't good enough.

When she was younger, she thought that if she could dance as well as the other girls in the ballet classes her mother forced her to take, then maybe—just maybe—her mother would be able to smile at her. Unhindered by the "pound cake thighs" (just one of the many derogatory nicknames Saylor's father, Simon, had bestowed upon her body), these girls moved with smug entitlement, turning up their noses whenever Saylor got too close. Dressed in whisper-pink leotards, the girls pranced around the room in a way that reminded Saylor of the proud little ponies that she'd seen on Saturday morning cartoons, their mother's faces warm as sunbeams nodding and smiling at their daughter's delicate embraces of air. Saylor's mother, though, only looked angry and embarrassed. With a sour-looking mouth weighing down her face, Erika's eyes darted around the room, never once landing on her own daughter. Saylor tried to keep up in the thick black leotards her mother had insisted suited her better than pink, had tried to tilt her head just so, had tried to raise her arms as if they were as light as fairy wings. The harder she tried, though, the angrier her mother grew. Then one day, Erika yanked her out of class without explanation. Regardless, the anger and disappointment continued.

And later, when Saylor became a teen, if only she could be as smart and sophisticated as her mother had been at her age. If only she could be as disciplined as Erika had been—a "determined young lady" who had not only dieted herself down to a fashionable weight, but had also learned three languages by the age of fifteen. If only Saylor could establish that certain *je ne sais quoi* that her mother claimed to have developed before she even hit adolescence. But, no, Saylor remained what Erika had once blurted out as 'mediocre,' a girl who made average grades, a girl who made average effort. And while Erika surrounded herself with dinner parties and lunch dates, Saylor had Lucy—the loud and crass girl whom Erika bitterly disapproved of.

Saylor flattened her hand against her rash. She envisioned scraping layers of itchy skin off with the ragged ends of her fingernails, but knew it would only make things worse. Instead, she unloaded the dishwasher and waited for her mother to pick up her home line—the one Erika insisted she use because she liked to keep her cell free—no matter how many times Saylor tried to explain how she would still be able to pick up a call-through from Philip on her cell. On the fourth ring, Erika answered with a curt hello, the Swedish accent still distinct after more than five decades in the United States.

"Hi Mom, I hope I caught you at a good time," Saylor began.

"It is nice to hear from you, but I am in the middle of bills."

"I could call back later..."

"No. I haven't heard from you in weeks, and I'm desperate to know how my grandchildren are doing."

Her mother's cell chimed in the background. "Hold on," Erika said, her voice suddenly breathless. "I have to get this."

Saylor let out an unintended sight. "Is it Philip?"

"Please hold, Saylor."

The rude clunk of the phone being set down echoed in Saylor's ear. She debated if she should hang up and make Erika call her back, but thought better of it. Her mother would only call her oversensitive. Saylor sighed and continued to unload plates. About five minutes later, her mother finally picked the phone back up.

She didn't apologize for taking so long like a normal person would, but continued where she had left off. "So how are my grandchildren doing?"

"They're fine, Mom. Listen, I want to talk to you about Billy Underwood."

"Billy Underwood?"

"You must remember Faith and Cliff's son, Billy—"

"Why are you asking about him?"

Saylor clenched her jaw, hoping beyond hope that Erika would show some compassion. "Did you know he's homeless?"

"Yes," her mother said. "I've known for years."

"Mom, how could you not have told me?" Saylor stopped unloading the dishwasher and leaned against her kitchen counter, waiting.

"He became a drug addict and ran away when he was a teenager and never came back. I didn't think you needed to know."

"You didn't think I needed to know?"

The other end of the line was silent.

"For all these years, Billy's been on his own?" A familiar tightness squeezed Saylor's heart. "He's been surviving on the outskirts of Malibu—and no one has been able to help him?"

"I do know that Cliff put him in a half-way house at some point," Erika said. Saylor pictured her mother sitting straight-backed as she spoke, her cool gray eyes appearing just as indifferent as the tone of her voice. "But he ran away from there too."

"There's got to be something someone can do." Saylor wondered if something bad had happened at the half-way house. Something that had triggered Billy's fear of being inside. Something that would make even Erika want to reach out.

"Honestly, Saylor, you must not obsess about this." Erika sighed. Loudly. A frustrated outtake of air that let Saylor know she was getting under her mother's skin. But she wasn't going to stop.

"I don't think that wanting to help Billy means I'm obsessing." Saylor exhaled. She hardly ever contested anything her mother said because it wasn't worth the ensuing fight—or worse, the probable belittlement.

"But you didn't even really know him."

"That's not the point, Mom." Once, just once Saylor wished her mother wouldn't contest her every word, wouldn't assume she was *obsessing* just because she cared about something—or someone.

"Don't you have enough on your plate without worrying about this? There are needy people everywhere; you can't help them all, least of all someone you barely even knew."

Saylor swallowed; she certainly wasn't going to share with her mother about finding Billy now. "I'm sorry I brought it up." She went back to the dishwasher and reached for a still-damp glass. Just as she was about to place it in the cupboard, the glass slipped. It crashed at her feet, scattering slivers of glass across the kitchen floor.

"Shit!" She grabbed a paper towel to pick up the pieces.

"What just happened—did I hear something break? And why do you have to be so vulgar about it?"

Saylor made sure to put on a calm voice. "Mom, I just broke a glass—I need to get going."

"There's no need to get so hysterical just because you broke something."

"I'm not..." Saylor gritted her teeth, "being hysterical."

"I know you better than you think. I can hear it in your voice."

Saylor placed her cell on the floor and then wet the paper towel. She bent down to clean up the larger shards of glass. The clear splinters, which were nearly impossible to see, would take a second, third, and probably fourth going over. "I'm sorry, but I have to get off the phone and clean this up."

"I want to make plans first. I haven't seen *my* grandchildren in quite some time. I don't appreciate when too much time has gone by like this...and, besides, I miss you, too."

Saylor pinched her lips together; the way her mother emphasized *my grandchildren* made it sound as if she were claiming some kind of ownership over Devin and Brooke. Yet Erika did say she missed her and it had been nearly six months since they last visited—and she knew the longer she put it off, the more grief she'd get. "I'll check with Devin and Brooke and call you as soon as I can."

Then came the standard line that Saylor knew was coming: "Time slips by too fast—"

"Yes, Mom, I know how time marches on. I'll try my best to make it happen."

"Thank you," her mother answered in her clipped way that made her thank you sound not at all grateful, but rather like a command that had better be carried out.

Dinner that night started out unusually peaceful. Brian made it home at a decent time. Brooke seemed to be enjoying her food. And Devin was able to sit at the table without his usual leg jitters. Saylor bit into a piece of honey-glazed chicken, remembering her mother's request.

"I talked to my mom today and she wants us to visit." Saylor looked at Brian, knowing that he was going to try and squirm out of it, but he kept on eating as if he hadn't heard a thing.

"I can't this weekend—I have plans with Penelope," Brooke shot out before anyone else had a chance to respond.

"And I'm going to be busy studying," Devin said. Saylor felt a slight vibration on the kitchen table from his leg hitting against the side.

She didn't say anything at first, trying to figure out the timing. In just a few weeks, it would be Thanksgiving, and since Brian had already told his parents that they'd be coming, they were cornered on time. Although they had also invited Erika, Saylor could count on her mother not showing. Even though Brian's family tried, Erika acted stand-offish at their functions, because, in her own words, his family was *too provincial*. But even more distasteful to Erika, Saylor knew, was that they didn't give her the deferential treatment she had come to expect of others.

The combination of her mother's refined beauty, Swedish accent, and cultivated air made most people react as if Erika were royalty. And even if her mother wasn't as stunning as she used to be, strangers and old friends alike still commented on her beauty, still acted as if they better please her above anyone else in the room. As time marched on, Erika seemed to crave the attention all the more.

Saylor exhaled. Her mother would hold it against her if they didn't see her before they spent Thanksgiving with Brian's family.

"What's wrong?" Brooke asked. Her dark eyebrows were downturned in such a way that it made her look both angry and concerned at the same time.

"We have to visit my mom, and we have to do it before Thanksgiving. I think we better go this weekend."

Brian smiled. "Do I have to go, too?"

Saylor glared at him. Sometimes it felt as if she had three teenagers instead of two. "Yes. You know my mom; she'll be mad if you don't make it and then blame it on me."

"Well, I'm not going," announced Brooke. Saylor watched her daughter splat a half teaspoon of sour cream over her baked potato.

"Please explain to Penelope," Saylor said, hoping to sound like the confident mother figure, "that you'll have to make plans for the next weekend."

"But she's the only friend that—" Brooke cut herself off by taking a gulp of water.

"If Penelope's any kind of friend, she'll under—"

"Understand?" Brooke stared at her, anger flashing in her eyes.

"Brooke, honey, it'll be okay." Saylor studied her daughter's narrow face. Had the girl lost even more weight? "Just try to enjoy your dinner."

"I've lost my appetite." Brooke stormed out of the kitchen and slammed her bedroom door so hard that Saylor felt her back jolt. She looked over at Brian who still chewed on his chicken leg as if nothing had happened.

Devin tapped his fingers against the table. "I told you I have too much studying to do."

"I'm sorry, Devin. You can study there." Saylor knew that he usually overestimated how much schoolwork he had anyway.

"Whatever," Devin mumbled, his leg thudding loudly against the table.

Saylor's stomach churned, yet she continued to stuff down the starchy white of her potato, wishing she could go back in time. It didn't seem that long ago that the four of them would eat dinner without a hitch, the younger Devin and Brooke appreciating whatever simple meal she had made, the munching and slurping interrupted only by their chatter and outbursts of laughter. And even those times when her mind had been racing, she still relished those nights when they used to settle on the couch together and watch a corny, laugh-out-loud movie. Those simple, sweet times that had evaporated before she could even catch her breath.

Finally, after all the dishes were done and laundry was folded, Saylor flopped onto the bed and flipped through one of the fashion magazines Lucy had given her.

Turning a page in his latest crime fiction novel, Brian glanced over. "Why are you lying on top of the covers?"

"I'm having a hot flash." Saylor set the magazine down and swept her hand over the tattered queen-sized quilt that her grandmother Rosa had made for her mother and father as a wedding present. Since Erika had bestowed it to her when she and Brian got married, it was one of those things that she never quite summoned enough nerve to get rid of or even tuck away in storage.

"Aren't you too young to get hot flashes?"

She'd been telling him for months now that she was starting to go through *the change*, but he didn't want to hear it. "Listen, Brian, I haven't had a chance to tell you about Billy."

"You did." Brian spoke through his teeth with forced restraint. "You said that you found him living under the pier."

"But I didn't get to tell you everything else."

"Like what?"

Saylor paused, hoping he would understand why this was so important to her—why *Billy* was so important to her. "I had started to tell you last night why I went to look for him, but you fell back asleep—"

"I don't understand...how'd you know where to find him, anyway?"

He was missing the point—as usual, but Saylor decided to plow on. "I had run into his mom, Faith, at a nightclub in Malibu the night before and—"

"So, Lucy took you out—did you guys close the place down or what?" Smiling, he raised his eyebrows as if he was expecting her to regale him with a juicy Lucy anecdote.

"Just," she said, "listen to me."

"I'm trying." Brian shook his head as if he had no idea that he'd interrupted her.

"I need to tell you what Billy said."

He snapped his book shut. "I'm all ears."

"Wait—I need to close the door," she whispered, suddenly feeling out of control. What if she yelled something insane in her own room?

"For God's sake, Saylor, we're upstairs—the kids can't hear you—I can barely make out what you're saying and I'm right next to you."

"Just forget it." She turned her back to him. "It's no big deal." She knew by the kick in her gut that if she said anything more, her anxiety would only get worse.

"Fine." Brian went back to his reading.

She couldn't take it anymore. Her need to connect. His desire to withdraw. She got up and started to walk out the room.

When she was almost to the door, Brian finally looked up. "What're you doing?"

"I'm sleeping on the couch tonight."

"Don't be so sensitive." He patted her side of the bed as if he were beckoning a dog.

His overbearing tone set her teeth on edge. "I can't sleep up here." What she really wanted to say was "with you," but refrained.

"Don't..." he said, "be like this."

"I'm not being like anything, Brian. I just need some time to myself."

"Okay, I give up—what did Billy say?"

She wanted to tell him—and she longed to fall back into bed as well—but it was too late. "It doesn't matter."

She trudged downstairs but paused on the landing, wishing she could peel away the layers of hostility, the ever-expanding stain of contempt. She imagined running back upstairs and kissing him. Holding him so tight that both past and future dissolved. Yet, she continued on, her throat constricting as if a thousand sorrows were trying to escape. She grabbed a blanket from the hall closet and settled onto the couch, doubting the possibility of change but still wishing for it anyway.

CHAPTER EIGHT

Her mother wore a crisp white blouse and straight black pants with red flats. Her hair, which she had never allowed any gray to invade, was dyed ash blond and cut in a stylish bob, slightly longer in the front and efficiently shorter in the back, so no bothersome hair could touch the nape of her neck. She greeted them by saying, "You must excuse the mess."

Why did her mother say that when it was never true? "Mom, you always keep your house clean." Saylor smiled, determined to get along.

Erika waved them in. The familiar scent of her signature Chanel No. 5 perfume, which she had dabbed on her wrists and collarbones for as long as Saylor could remember, wafted from the doorway. When the four of them made it inside, she immediately beamed her attention on Brooke and Devin. "Hello my Brooke and greetings to my Devin. How is my pretty girl?" She gave Brooke a hug and then turned to give Devin one too. "And how is my smart boy?"

Brooke and Devin mumbled their hellos. Erika gave them her up and down inspection. "Brooke, you've managed to stay nice and trim," she said.

Out of the corner of Saylor's eye, she saw Devin flinch.

Erika continued, "It makes you look a lot more sophisticated than other girls your age."

Brooke grinned. "Thank you, Grandma!"

"Sometimes people gain weight in their teens, but that won't happen to you; you have more will-power than that, don't you?"

Brooke nodded. "My mom thinks I'm too thin."

"You're perfect just the way you are." Erika winked at Brooke.

Saylor bit back her anger. Why couldn't her mother see how this was making Devin feel? Why couldn't she see that Brooke was beyond thin—looked close to emaciated, in fact? And...why did it always seem as if Erika was trying to win Brooke and Devin over and against her?

Before Saylor could think of what to say, Erika took Devin by the shoulders. "And you, my young man, I have missed you so much!"

"I've missed you too." Devin gripped the straps of his overstuffed back-pack, shifting from side to side as if he were having a hard time maintaining his balance.

Erika peered at Saylor; her gray eyes sparkling. She nodded with a satis-fied smile, looking as if she had just won some kind of game against her own daughter.

Brian, who had been silent the whole time, stepped forward. "Good to see you, Erika."

"It's wonderful to finally have you all here." Erika linked arms with him and put on her exaggerated, damsel-in-distress pout. "May I count on my son-in-law to fix a few things this weekend?"

Brian stood straighter and nodded, succumbing to the good son-in-law role. "Of course. And if you don't have the right tools, I'll go to the hardware store."

"That's quite a drive, Brian." Saylor shook her head. "I'm sure my mother will understand if you don't have time to get everything done." She directed her attention onto her mother. "And, Mom, I'm sure you can always hire someone if Brian can't find the tools."

On top of wanting to be the nice guy, Saylor knew that Brian was looking for any excuse to get out of there—even if that meant that he'd end up with a far longer to-do list than he was expecting. He always seemed to forget, too, how Erika would often gripe about how he didn't do what she had asked him—how she had to end up hiring someone else who had to charge more because he only made things worse.

Saylor looked at him, hoping he'd get it. "Besides, you've been working all week, maybe you want to go to the beach—you could even surf. Remem-ber there's an old longboard in the garage."

"Honestly, Saylor, it's just a few simple things," Erika shook her head. "The bathroom faucet is leaking, my kitchen window is stuck, and my show-er drain is clogged." She smiled at Brian. "I'm sure you enjoy this kind of work—especially when you can do it for your own mother-in-law."

Saylor bit her lip. Erika's requests were reasonable, and it was Brian's busi-ness if he helped her or not. And, so what if her mother complained about his work later? It wouldn't be her fault.

"I'm sure I can handle it." Brian grinned as if he really was looking forward to the work—loved, in fact, doing favors for his bossy mother-in-law.

"Thank you." Erika unhinged her arm from his. "Let's everyone come into the living room for some iced tea." Before she turned to walk down the hallway, she glanced at Saylor. "That shirt looks very nice on you. Is that the one I sent?"

"It is." Saylor looked down at the blue silk blouse her mother had sent as a "just-because" present. Not only was it Saylor's favorite color, but also the cut was more flattering than Saylor's usual baggy T-shirts. It was obvious that her mother had taken both the color and style into account when she had picked it out for her. The silk, though, was definitely more Erika's taste than Saylor's. She gave Erika a smile; her mother was trying "I really like it, Mom. Thank you again."

Erika led them into the living room. After all these years, the ocean and sky view shining through the old plate glass window was still breathtaking. Saylor paused, taking it in while listening to the waves roll beneath the house. Then she looked down and saw that the once plush carpet was even more threadbare than when she had last visited, the tweed couches even more faded. The white marble coffee table—the one that had been there since she could remember—still sat in the middle of the room completely unadorned by any knick-knacks, magazines, or books.

The kids sat on the opposite-facing couches, and Brian went to stand in front of the window. Saylor turned to her mother. "Can I help you with the iced tea?"

"That would be nice. But you don't need to bother."

"I want to." Saylor's stomach growled, reminding her that she hadn't eaten since breakfast. "I'm hungry, does anyone else want some snacks?"

"Let's wait for dinner," Erika said. "I want all of us to go out tonight. It will be fun." Her cell rang and she excused herself. She whisked out of the room, greeting Philip in her excited whisper that, even after all these years, still sounded as if she got off on being the other woman.

Erika insisted on driving because she said that it was good for her car to take it out every day or so. Saylor kept her mouth shut; the reality was that Erika really wanted everyone to see that she was still a proficient driver. Saylor resigned herself to her mother's slower-than-traffic pace, gazing out the window from the front passenger seat of the old sky-blue Volvo. She had to admit that she was impressed with Erika for keeping the same car running for over four decades.

Saylor glanced over the seat at Brian, Devin, and Brooke scrunched in the back. Both Devin and Brooke had their earbuds plugged into their skulls, oblivious to any conversation, and Brian was texting on his cell. She watched the red-orange color of sunset deepen the sky and thought about Billy.

"Mom, do you ever go down to the pier?"

"No, why do you ask?"

"Have you..." Saylor's throat caught. "Have you ever seen Billy?"

"Have I ever seen Billy?" Erika's tone was even more sharp than usual. "Saylor, I told you not to obsess about this."

"Well, have you? After all these years, I'd think you'd have seen him somewhere—in front of a restaurant, walking down PCH, maybe hanging out in front of the market?" Saylor still hadn't shared with her that she had found him herself, but she wanted to know any little piece about Billy her mother could provide.

"I have not seen him," Erika shot back a tad too quickly. So quickly that it made Saylor wonder if she was lying. "And even if I did, I doubt I would recognize him."

"But what about when he was just a teen? Didn't you see him around after he had run away—when he was still a young man?"

Erika cleared her throat. "This is my family time, Saylor. I want to enjoy my grandchildren without you badgering me. Let's just have a nice dinner."

"I'm sorry," Saylor muttered. She slumped against the ugly sienna-brown leather, feeling like the depressed teenager she had been when she was sitting in this same seat so many years ago, and her mother had called her a *Goddamned Rottweiler who tried to tug out information that did not concern her*. It happened about a year or so before her father's death. Until then, she had held the information inside herself. For weeks, as she was riding the bus from school, she had spotted her father's car in the driveway of her mother's friend,

Marie's house. Day after day, Saylor spied his Porsche perched like a spider, the glare of Marie's afternoon-lit front window reflecting off its black body.

When her mother was driving her to a doctor's appointment later that month, they saw Marie meandering down the street with a familiar rose-patterned scarf fluttering around her neck. A scarf that was the exact match to the one Simon had given Erika just weeks before. Saylor couldn't help mentioning the similarity, which her mother rolled her eyes at, telling Saylor that she was *too observant*—whatever that meant. It was then that Saylor dropped the bomb, finally informing her mother that Simon's car had been parked outside of Marie's house every day for at least two weeks. She didn't want to hurt her mother; she just wanted to wake Erika up from playing the fool. But Erika only acted more loving with Simon after that—and even more annoyed with Saylor. Because of this, Saylor never bothered to mention that about a month later—while her mother was visiting family in Sweden—her father had the gall to inform her how understanding Marie was, how soft, and giving as well. Saylor knew. He was comparing her mother to Erika. But why in the hell did he share it with her, his fourteen-year-old daughter, who of all people, wouldn't want to know? Saylor changed the subject at the time, trying to act as if she didn't really hear.

Erika cleared her throat, pulling Saylor out of her memories. "I hardly get to see my grandchildren," she said. "Please try and be pleasant for the rest of the evening."

Saylor's stomach hardened. Was there anything she could do or say that would be right? "I think I'm being pleasant enough, Mom."

"Then why do you have to look so downtrodden, for goodness' sakes?"

Saylor looked at Erika's own bitter-looking face, but knew not to challenge her, so she answered in the most benign way she could think of. "Just thinking..."

Brian leaned forward. "I think we passed the turn-off for the restaurant that you wanted to go to, Erika."

"So, I did." Erika chuckled as if she'd done it on purpose. "I'll just have to drive a couple of miles up the coast and back track at the next light."

Saylor held a hand against her neck. A couple of miles really meant ten to get to the signal—and then ten to drive back. "Can we please just eat at that Mexican place coming up? I know the kids like their food, and it'll be so much easier—it's a right-hand turn."

Erika gave her a sour look. "Is that what you want, Brian?"

"I don't care." He flashed his best nice-guy smile. "Wherever we eat is fine with me."

"I had really wanted to take you all to this new restaurant, but if you really want to go to the old Mexican one…" Erika sounded as if she were choking out the words. "I guess we can do it *your* way, Saylor."

Anxiety hit, unintended words screaming in Saylor's head: *I can't take you anymore.* Panicked, Saylor caught her mother's hard stare. Was it shock or merely Erika's usual harsh expression? "What are you looking at, Mom?"

"Are you feeling alright?"

"I'm fine." She smelled the stink of her own sweat as it pooled under her arms and trickled down the back of her silk blouse. Saylor turned, hoping she could catch eyes with Brian, but he was checking messages. Devin and Brooke still had their earbuds in. Could she have said it out loud, and only her mother had heard, but didn't know how to respond? The Volvo's engine was loud and Brian was distracted, the kids tuned into their own worlds.

"Why did you ask if I was feeling okay?" Saylor tried to sound as if she really was okay.

Erika shrugged. "Nothing, Saylor. We'll go to the Mexican restaurant, then."

"Okay." Saylor didn't know what else to say. For one brief moment, she imagined opening the car door and hurling her body onto the highway. She wiped her palms on her jeans, her mind racing. What if intrusive thoughts were self-hypnotic and could make someone do something that they didn't want to do? What if constant fear created a self-fulfilling prophecy? She clenched her fists on her lap, reminding herself what she had learned from the latest podcast she subscribed to: Lots of other people suffering from anxiety have irrational thoughts—thoughts that they never act upon. Irrational, Saylor told herself, was something not governed by reason. She exhaled, focusing her thoughts on what it would be like to find Billy again. Her breathing slowed.

With a sigh, Erika pulled into the parking lot and found a space right in front of the restaurant. The kids reluctantly unplugged themselves after Saylor gave them her let's-be-respectful-of-grandma look.

"I had wanted to take you all to a fancy restaurant up the coast, but your mother was too impatient," Erika said. "Maybe you two could come with me another time."

"That's okay," said Brooke. "I like this restaurant."

"It's gone downhill." Erika turned away from Brooke, looked at Devin and smiled. "Devin, be a good grandson and escort me up the stairs."

They walked ahead with Brian beside them and Saylor and Brooke trailing behind. Brooke leaned into Saylor and whispered, "What does she mean by downhill?"

"Maybe the service hasn't been as good as it was in the past," Saylor whispered. "But you know Grandma."

"Yeah, she's beyond critical," Brooke said.

Erika whipped around. Her gaze focused on Saylor. "What did you just say about me?"

"Nothing, Mom." Saylor bit her lip and flapped the bottom of her blouse, knowing that the light blue silk had become stained with perspiration's dark underarm circles and down-the-back streaks.

"Then why would my own granddaughter say something about me being critical as if she were agreeing with you?"

"We weren't even talking about you, Grandma," Brooke piped in. "We were talking about my friend's mom."

"All right then," Erika said, turning back around.

Saylor looked at Brooke and mouthed a thank you.

Once they entered the restaurant, Erika put her hands on her hips and tapped her foot. The hostess, who'd been taking a call-in order, got off the phone and apologized. "Do you have a reservation?"

"Of course not," snapped Erika. "Why would we need a reservation?"

Saylor touched her mother's arm, hoping to shut her up. The place was busy—in fact there were only two tables open. She looked at the hostess. "I'm sorry—do you happen to have a table available for five?"

The hostess nodded and motioned for them to follow her. As they neared the back of the restaurant, Erika tapped her on the shoulder. "I don't want to sit back here. It's too dim. Please put us closer to the front."

The young woman turned around and put on a shiny-hostess smile. "The lighting is all the same. I thought you'd like to be away from the door, but I'll put you up front if you'd like."

"I'd like to make sure you get that front table cleaned again, though," Erika said, "it doesn't look as if they did a good enough job."

It wasn't so much what her mother said; it was the haughty tone she said it in that made Saylor's face heat up.

"Of course," the hostess said. She pressed her lips together, looking as if she'd like to say something entirely different. When Erika turned her back to them to survey the rest of the room, Saylor smiled and shrugged apologetically. She hoped the hostess wouldn't equate her mother's behavior with the rest of the family. The girl grinned back with an understanding nod. So much, Saylor thought, for her mother's "je ne sais quoi."

They were seated at a window table, which was already spotless. Erika motioned for Brooke to sit next to her and instructed Devin to sit on the chair at the head of the table so that he could be kitty-corner from her; Saylor and Brian sat on the other side facing Erika and Brooke. Uneasy silence descended until the waitress handed them their menus, and then placed a basket of warm tortilla chips on the table, their grease staining the white paper lining. Before the waitress scooted away, Brian made sure to order a beer, saying that he couldn't eat Mexican food without a Tecate in hand. Everyone but Erika began munching on the chips and scanning the menus.

Saylor crunched two at a time, thinking how if she made it to seventy-five, she'd let herself be round and happy instead of the increasingly sharp-boned, unhappy creature her mother had become.

"Mom, you really should try these. They're delicious." Saylor looked up to see that her mother was eyeing the door with a pained expression.

"Oh God, it's her," Erika said, and then eyed Saylor. "I told you I didn't want to come here—it's one of *her* hangouts."

Saylor turned around. Faith Underwood, wearing a tie-dyed shirt and designer jeans tucked into the same Victorian lace-up boots she had on at the Wild Sky, strode toward them. Her arm was linked around a much younger-looking man's waist. As she made her way to their table, Saylor swore that she heard her mother whisper "bitch."

"Why, Erika, you have your whole family with you, how nice." Faith laughed too loudly as if what she had just said was funny. "And Saylor, I can't believe we're seeing each other so soon again."

Erika scrutinized Saylor and then Faith, her brows scrunched in disapproval. "When did you two last see each other?"

"We ran into each other at the Wild Sky," Faith said. "By the way, this is Warren." Her slender fingers visibly tightened around his side.

"Nice to meet you all," Warren said. He flashed a huge grin, a shocking white against his salon-tanned face. Saylor recognized him as a bit actor who always played clueless jock roles.

Erika sniffed the air as if in disgust.

Faith laughed. "Careful, Erika, your s-h-i-t is showing." She spelled out the offending word as if only she and Erika could understand its meaning.

Erika's cheeks turned the sour-red shade of unripe cherries. "Don't you dare," she said, "talk to me that way."

"Lighten up," Faith said. "It was just a joke: instead of slip, I said s-h-i-t—because you looked like you had just taken one." She tilted her head up as if challenging Erika to raise the bar, while Warren, looking as if he was having a more than a difficult time not chuckling, studied his leather Vans. He rubbed a manicured hand against his lips and then scratched the days-old stubble of his unshaven face, a current trend, Saylor thought, among hungry young actors.

Saylor pursed her lips. It was all too absurd, and Brooke's eyes popping wide in disbelief made her want to laugh and cry at the same time.

Still flushed with anger, Erika stared at Faith. "The only reason I was ever friends with you..." she straightened her back, "...was because I felt sorry for you." She grimaced as if lemon juice had been squirted into her gums. "And look where that got me."

"Just like everything else you've lied to yourself about, you're dead wrong, Erika," Faith retorted. "The only emotion you ever felt for me was jealousy."

Erika's mouth opened, but no words came out.

"Come on, Warren, let's get out of here." Faith grabbed Warren's hand, pulling him away. Before they were completely out of earshot, he said something that made her burst out in laughter.

Saylor gaped at her mother, who had already masked her face with icy composure. "What was that all about?" She hoped Erika would answer honestly.

"That is what happens when a woman can't face her age." Erika said. "She ends up acting like a fool."

Brooke smirked. "I don't know, Grandma, she looked like she was having a hell of a time to me."

Saylor watched the veins on her mother's temples pulsate. Brooke, as forthright as she was, had never challenged her grandmother.

Erika shot an irate look at her. "No, Brooke, you're too young to understand. She didn't look like she was having a hell of a time—she just was being ridiculous—and you shouldn't talk like that at your age. It makes you sound precocious."

"I was only kidding." Brooke twisted her hair.

Like an impatient old man, Devin cleared his throat. "Can we please order? I need to get back and study."

"You're such a nerd, Devin. It's the weekend." Brooke kept her menu shut and began texting.

"You're going to let her use her cell at the dinner table?" Erika said, looking only at Saylor.

"I was just going to remind her—"

Brooke's nostrils flared. "I have to go to the bathroom anyways."

"What if the waitress comes?" Saylor said. "What do you want me to order for you?" Hungry and tense, she couldn't wait to get this night over with.

"I don't know," Brooke said. "I can't handle too much food right now."

Erika nodded in approval. "I see they have ceviche. That's nice and light—and it's also low in calories."

Saylor wanted to kick her mother's skinny shin. What was wrong with her? Did she want to enable Brook's excessive dieting? She tapped Brooke on the arm. "Why don't I order you a chicken tostada?"

Brooke's face became a stone. "I already said I'm not hungry."

"Let the poor girl alone," Erika said, her tone now over-indulgent sweet. "There's nothing wrong with her trying to stay nice and slim. Is there, Brooke?"

"I'm not trying to stay anything, Grandma," Brooke said. "My stomach just hurts when I get stressed out."

"I doubt, at your age, that you experience any real stress—you just think you do." Erika smiled as if her dismissive words were full of sympathy.

Saylor shook her head. "Mom, that's not true—"

But Brooke cut Saylor off before she could defend her. "Excuse me, I really do need to go to the bathroom." Brooke stood, but Erika wouldn't budge.

Not knowing how to diffuse Erika's anger, Saylor sat mute while Brian kept his head in the menu and Devin tore away at the loose skin near his cuticle. Saylor cringed, thinking how much it must have hurt.

Brooke finally broke the silence. "Please move over, Grandma. I need to get out."

Slowly, Erika stood to let Brooke by. With hands gripping the edge of the table, Erika watched her granddaughter walk away with what Saylor thought looked like a rare moment of unguarded frailty. When Erika sat back down, she turned her gaze to the window and studied her reflection in the glass. She patted her hair, her fingers trembling in the fragile way that made it look like her connection between mind and body had become unsure. Saylor had never seen her mother's hands shake before. All at once, she saw her mother as weak and old, and it brought on an uncomfortable empathy. It had been way easier, just moments before, when all she felt was anger.

CHAPTER NINE

Saylor sat up in the twin bed and inhaled the scent of her childhood. Even though the damp beach-home odor of seawater and mildew wasn't the sweetest in the world, it did make her nostalgic—and it reminded her of something else from her youth, something good, but what was it? She turned on her stomach and remembered her raft. How the musty-storage smell of its saltwater encrusted canvas always made her anticipate summer. Nothing made her happier than riding belly-flat on that striped red and blue raft, descending a wave's downward curl and crash, and then the tide pushing her all the way to shore, her body staying afloat through it all. She wished she still had it, but guessed that it had been tossed long ago. She sighed, wishing that her own kids enjoyed the ocean as much as she did when she'd been their age.

Even though she and Brian had often taken Devin and Brooke to the beach when they were little, Devin didn't completely trust the water, never venturing farther out than waist-deep, and although Brooke thought that the ocean was pretty, she complained that it was too cold and *seaweedy* to stay in for any length of time. Saylor had always wondered if their trepidation had been caused by the knowledge that her father—the man who would have been their grandfather—had died in the surf. By the time Devin and Brooke were in their early teens, Brian had given up on the idea of teaching them how to ride waves, and Saylor resigned herself to the fact that she had to enjoy braving the swells without them. She stretched between the worn pink-striped sheets, wondering if she would be able to find a similar raft online. If she did, would she be too old to use it? Would Devin and Brooke still be too wary of the ocean to give it a try?

The loud snort of Brian's intermittent snoring interrupted her thoughts. He slept face-up and opened mouthed on the twin bed across from her, the rise and fall of his stomach visible under the matching chenille bedspread. When she was a young girl, would she ever have imagined that she'd have married this man? She turned her back to him, thinking how fast her youth had vanished. It seemed such a short time ago that her mother had bought that other bed. Soon after her father died, Erika had insisted, even though Saylor had told her that she didn't want it. "Nonsense," Erika had said, "now

71

you can have friends over to spend the night without having to roll out sleeping bags."

After the bed had been set up, her mother stood by its side, grazing her fingertips on the shiny-blue mattress with what looked like longing. Her eyes watered. In a hushed voice, she apologized to Saylor about not giving her a sibling, explaining that after Saylor had been born, Simon had been adamant that he didn't want any more children since they already had a daughter—that he couldn't chance it a second time and possibly have a son. When Saylor had asked why, her mother said how she thought it had to do with him having to grow up with his brother Silvio's "mental condition." But when Saylor prodded her further, Erika turned around, mumbling that it was too exhausting to explain.

Sunlight shot through the lower height of the shutters, and Saylor forced herself out of bed. She sighed; most likely, Erika was already making breakfast. Since Devin and Brooke were bunking on the living room couches, she hoped her mother's typical morning cupboard slamming hadn't woken them up yet.

Her stomach hollow, Saylor ventured into the drab kitchen. Erika had never bothered to replace the ugly yellow and orange daisy-patterned wallpaper or cracked beige tiled floor, yet she managed to keep everything clean and organized. Hardly anything seemed to get lost or broken. She still had all the same stoneware plates, pink and white-flowered mixing bowls, and dented utensils, including the aluminum measuring spoons that Saylor remembered from childhood. At the square oak table, Erika sat with one hand clenched around her coffee cup while she hovered her spoon over a bowl of muesli and yogurt.

Saylor said good morning and wiped her nose with the wad of tissue she had stowed in the pocket of the polyester robe her mother had bought for her visits. For some reason, every time she stepped into Erika's house, an immediate congestion set in. Maybe it was from the disinfectant assault of Pine Sol her mother religiously swiped the counters and sinks with, or the simple fact that no matter how much her mother cleaned, she'd never be able to keep the ongoing mildew at bay.

With a thick coat of make-up painted on her face, Erika eyed Saylor. "There's coffee; I made enough for everyone." She pursed her lips, her pink frosted lipstick making her mouth appear even more crinkled with age.

From the dark brown cupboard, Saylor found a mug, then poured herself a cup of coffee from the old 1960s Corning Ware percolator, its white exterior imprinted with the blue cornflower logo, still remarkably clean and free of nicks. "I can't believe this thing is still going strong."

"Yes, not everything breaks down in just a couple of years," Erika said, her Swedish accent making her sound as if her world was so much more efficient than Saylor's.

"Mom, I want to ask you something."

"Have some breakfast, Saylor."

"I will." Saylor sat on the chair next to her, the uncomfortable wicker seat prickly, even through her robe. "Why's there so much animosity between you and Faith?"

"She's just a drunkard." Erika spit out her words, her tone both snarky and bitter.

"Is that really true?" Saylor shook her head, guessing it wasn't.

Her mother tsk-tsked her. "Of course, it is!" She shot Saylor a cut-glass look. "And she's not just your typical lush. She's also the worst kind of slut."

"Mom!" Erika did, indeed, hold a huge amount of resentment toward Faith. But why? "What makes you say this?"

"She deserves it, Saylor." Between prim lips, Erika sipped her coffee.

"But I remember you and Dad used to have her and Cliff over. You guys used to be friends—you used to laugh and drink wine and—" Dare she say it? But why *not* let her mother know what she had observed as a child. "You used to *even* smoke pot with her."

Erika's head jerked back in surprise, but she quickly regained control, jutting her jaw forward as if she were commanding the troops. "You just assumed I smoked pot because everyone else did. I have always limited myself to two glasses of wine—and that is all I've ever done."

Saylor had a very clear memory of seeing her mother inhale a joint as she sat cross-legged on the living room's frosted gold carpet next to Faith. She remembered thinking how odd it was to see her mother giggle. But it wasn't worth confronting her about this. For all she knew, her mother only did it once or twice, and feeling embarrassed, had pushed it out of her mind. What had happened between Erika and Faith, though?

Saylor inhaled, steadying herself against Erika's prickly cover of defense. "How many times have you seen Faith since she's been back?"

Erika took a small bite of yogurt and cereal, her elegant fingers poised around the spoon. "Much more than I'd like." Then she shoved her spoon into her breakfast as if stabbing it. "The woman not only moved back to Breakers Point, but also decided to buy a house right down the road from me."

"Mom, I can't believe you never mentioned she was back in town, let alone is one of your neighbors now."

"What's there to mention? I do not like the woman and would rather not think about her."

"I'm sorry, Mom. It's just weird to me that you had never told me about her—or Billy."

Abruptly, Erika stood. She marched to the cupboard, clanging down another brown-rimmed cereal bowl. "Saylor, I know how you obsess. It is not healthy. You need to stop. Faith is a lush, and Billy, poor soul that he is, was just a boy who became deranged from drugs and never came back."

"You've said that before, but how do you know for sure it was from drugs?"

"Cliff told me years ago."

"Whatever happened to Cliff?" Maybe Billy's own father could help—or, at least, could provide more insight on Billy than either Faith or Erika had.

Erika puckered her lips as if the past had left a bitter taste in her mouth. "Cliff's acting roles dried up some years ago, and he moved to L.A., hoping the proximity would get him more work." She poured Saylor a bowl of muesli, and then topped it off with a dollop of plain yogurt. "I haven't seen him in anything for a long time. I doubt he was ever able to make much of a living at it again." She handed the bowl to Saylor and sat back down.

Saylor thanked her and swallowed a spoonful of the sour-tasting yogurt. "I feel sorry for that whole family," she ventured, "Even Faith."

"You need to stop. I'm sure Cliff is fine—and you can see that the self-involved Faith hasn't changed." Her mother cleared her throat like she always did before abruptly changing subjects. "By the way, how does Brian feel about you going off and gallivanting about in night clubs without him?"

"It was just a girls' night out." She nudged Erika's elbow, hoping to make a joke out of it. "Don't be so old fashioned." So old fashioned, Saylor thought, that it was okay for her to be having a four-decades-long affair with a married man.

Erika sniffed the air. A sharp, angry sniff that told Saylor she'd better not say a word more.

Brian's footsteps thudded toward them, interrupting the tense silence. Sleepy-faced, he slogged into the kitchen in jeans and an oatmeal-colored sweater. With swollen eyelids and bloated face, he didn't appear his usual handsome self. Saylor stared at him. Was she noticing this because she sensed Erika's judgment? He scratched his hair, one side sticking up like the fur of an alarmed cat, the other section, crushed flat.

"You look absolutely lopsided, Brian." Erika pointed to his head.

He felt the top of his hair and laughed. "I bet your coffee will straighten me out. Is there any left?"

"Of course, there is," Erika said, "I am quite sure you need it after last night."

"What makes you say that?" Saylor looked at her mother. But why ask? She knew very well where Erika was going.

"He downed quite a few beers. Didn't you, Brian?"

Yep, thought Saylor, *exactly what I knew she'd say.*

Brian shrugged, smiling at Erika as if she were a child. "I had a few—nothing more."

Saylor wrapped her arms around herself. What was worse? Her mother's constant judgment...or her husband's arrogant, I'm-just-being-a-guy demeanor.

He sauntered to the cupboard and reached for a mug, his thick muscular body looking like it could withstand almost anything, especially Erika's accusations of alcoholism. Even though Saylor found it hypercritical that her mother had lived in denial about Simon's having a multitude of affairs—but now rejoiced in putting down Brian for having a few beers, a thick unease settled in the pit of her stomach. Although he never came home falling-down drunk, his drinking did seem to make him act even more removed from what was happening around him, more cut-off from his own family and marriage. What right did she have to complain, though, when he had put up with her ongoing anxiety?

Erika went to pour Brian a bowl of muesli. "After you have breakfast—and get yourself straightened up, I'd very much appreciate it if you could start working on unclogging my shower drain. It's even worse since yesterday."

"I'll get to it." Brian slurped his coffee. "Sometime today..."

Erika gave Saylor her sidelong glance of disapproval. Saylor pretended not to notice and spooned a bite of cereal while averting her gaze from her mother's unblinking eyes. Yet, her mother's critical stare still bore into her, still seemed to penetrate all layers of defense. And, soon enough, a bolt of anxiety shot through Saylor's body, making her heart race and limbs tingle. Rubbing the back of her neck, she silently repeated to herself: *I am safe. I am strong. I am safe. I am strong.* Over and over again. But no matter how many times it looped inside her skull, she continued to feel *unsafe.* Continued to feel *weak.* Continued to wonder at her own sanity. Luckily, Erika and Brian went back to discussing the day, oblivious to her silent turmoil.

Drenched with sweat, she felt as if she were suffocating within the four walls of the kitchen, the ancient tiled floor and peeling wallpaper, more depressing than usual. "Do you mind if I open a window?"

"If you must." Erika sighed as if it were a huge imposition.

With shaky knees, Saylor got up from her half-eaten bowl of cereal and leaned over the sink, a sudden queasiness hitting her gut. She told herself not to succumb to it and pushed up the window's sticky wooden ledge. Her body leaning against the counter, she breathed in the cool scent of ocean. "I think," she said to no one in particular, "I'll go down to the pier today."

Neither Brian nor Erika responded. Instead, they continued on about the house repairs as if she had already left the room. Still facing the window, Saylor mouthed *I will find Billy* three times in a row, and then after pouring some more coffee, excused herself.

Mug in hand, Saylor went into the living room and crept by Devin and Brooke, who were still cocooned in their sleeping bags. She stood in front of the window and watched the ocean's cool, blue surface ripple in the morning breeze. Relieved her heart had settled down and anxiety's heat had already passed, she imagined what it would feel like to jump in and swim as far out as she could.

"Hi Mom." Brooke came up to her side and leaned her head on her shoulder.

Saylor smiled. It was such a wonderful surprise whenever her daughter slipped back into being the girl she was before teenage-hood had abducted her—even if it was for the briefest of moments. "I didn't wake you, did I?" she whispered, looking back at Devin, who was still asleep on the couch, his body huddled inside the green sleeping bag with only a mass of brown, curly hair sticking out.

Brooke yawned. "No...I never sleep very well here."

Saylor put her arm around her daughter's narrow shoulder. "Sorry about that. It must be all the light. But isn't the ocean beautiful?"

"Not when you feel like crap," Brooke said, lifting her head off Saylor's shoulder.

Saylor withdrew her arm, wrapping both hands around her cup's warmth. "Watch the language. You are in Grandma Erika Territory, you know."

Brooke rolled her eyes. "I wish our house looked right over the water. You were so lucky to grow up here."

"I've always loved the ocean," Saylor whispered. "I'd feel trapped if I couldn't live near it."

"That's funny because when I was a little girl, I used to pretend that you were a mermaid."

"You did?" Saylor turned her head to look at her daughter's profile. How very young she looked for her age. "I bet it was because you loved that story about the selkie so much."

"No, it was because when I was really little, I had never seen you look so happy as this one time when you were out swimming in the ocean. I was building a sandcastle with Dad and Devin, and then I looked out at the wa-ter." Brooke sighed as if she were just waking up from a dream. "And there you were, gliding between the waves, not even looking like my mom."

"That's a nice memory." Saylor tried not to frown. How sad it was that her daughter had remembered her as looking the happiest—not when she was with her—but when she was out swimming in the ocean a good distance away.

"Mom?" Brooke stretched her skinny arms overhead. "Are you okay?"

"I'm fine, sweetie." Saylor put on a smile, gazing at her daughter. "Why do you ask?"

Brooke shrugged. "No reason."

They stood next to each other in silence, mother and daughter each absorbed in the endless expanse of rolling ocean. Suddenly, Brooke broke the silence. "I know you told me before, but how did you get your name again?"

Surprised that Brooke hadn't remembered, Saylor turned to look at her. "What makes you ask?"

"I'm just wondering if it's because the way your name matches the sound of the word sailor, like a sailor of the sea."

"That's pretty close—are you sure you don't remember?"

"You told me when I was just a kid—it's kind of fuzzy now. But didn't you end up naming yourself?"

Saylor pressed her index finger against her lips. "Remember to keep it low; your brother's still sleeping."

"Well?" Brooke eyed her.

"My real name was Seraphina."

Brooke snorted. "I can see why you wanted to change it."

"Seraphina isn't that bad. In fact, now that I'm older, I think it sounds pretty."

"But tell me again how you got the name Saylor."

"I will...but feel free to stop me if you get bored—"

"Mom, out with it already. I swear you make such a big deal out of the simplest things."

"Okay, okay," Saylor answered, trying to remember how she had edited it before. "When I was about four, I was in my room one afternoon, having what my mom called 'hush-time.' I was supposed to be resting, even though I was too old to nap anymore." She didn't tell Brooke how she had clamped her hands over her ears, her parents fighting raging through the bedroom door, the sound of the front door slamming shut, and her mother's crying, loud and jagged, as if she were a little girl herself. That upset her more than any of the razor-edged words thrown by her father before he had left. After her mother's sobs finally subsided, Saylor ventured out from under her bed to find her crayon box.

"I think I remember you did something naughty, didn't you?" Brooke grinned.

"I was naughty," Saylor smiled back at her daughter. "I drew huge pictures of sailboats on my wall with my lightest blue crayon because I thought no one would be able to see them but me. I hadn't wanted to draw on paper because I didn't want them ever to be thrown out or lost. Then your Grandma Erika opened the door."

"So, you got in trouble, right?"

"Surprisingly, I didn't." Saylor remembered how her mother alternately laughed and cried as she tried to scrub off Saylor's design. Saylor had found a rag under the kitchen sink and joined in, wanting to help her shaky-handed mother. Even at the age of four, she knew that she wasn't the only one making her mother's life so sad—but, still, maybe it was her fault that her father had left. Maybe she was just one more thing in his life that made him run away.

"What happened next?"

"After Grandma Erika let me know that it wasn't okay for me to draw on the wall, I told her that my name was no longer Seraphina; it was Saylor. I even spelled out the first part myself because I already knew how to spell the word 'say.'"

"No wonder the spelling is so weird," Brooke said. "But why did you change your name that day?"

"I changed it because I loved sailboats."

"I knew it had to do with the ocean." Brooke eyed her as if she were trying to solve a puzzle. "Still, I loved lollipops as a kid—but I didn't change my name to Lolli."

"But you never hated your own name, did you?" What Saylor didn't say was: *you never hated yourself.*

"I guess not...but I can't believe Grandma Erika let you change it."

Saylor paused. She swore she could feel the push and pull of the tide rolling beneath the house. "Believe it or not, I was a pretty headstrong kid. From that day on, I made sure that everyone called me by my new name, and would indignantly correct them if they forgot—including my own mother." And...her father after he came slinking back after several weeks.

"When you think about it, it's pretty ironic that you named yourself Saylor."

Saylor's throat went dry; Brooke couldn't possibly know about her irrational fear of saying things out loud that she didn't mean. "Why is that ironic?" she asked, trying to keep her voice steady.

"Because..." Brooke looked at her intently. "Because your dad died by falling off a sailboat."

"That's true." Saylor turned her gaze away from her daughter and looked toward the line between sea and sky, wondering how many miles away it was, but then remembered how horizons were always unreachable. "I've never realized that before." She wrapped an arm around Brooke's shoulder. "You're very smart, you know."

"What was he like?" Brooke asked, "you never talk about him—every time I ask, you change the subject." She scrutinized Saylor with narrowed eyes and a pinched mouth.

Saylor nodded; Brooke was right—and although she was old enough to know more about her miserable grandfather, what good would it do to tell her *everything*. "Let me put it this way...my father was a complicated man—angry and insecure, mean and scared—all at the same time."

"Am I..." Brooke stared at the floor. "...Anything like him?"

Saylor hugged her daughter with all her might, hugged her harder than she'd ever done before. "Not at all, Brooke. "Not at all." She released Brooke and looked her straight in the eye. "I promise."

"Okay, okay," Brooke muttered. "I believe you already!"

Saylor held back tears. She was the same age as Brooke was now when he had died. How strange time had become. Brooke seemed so very much younger than she had been at the same age—and now, after all these years, she didn't feel that much older than her own serious fifteen-year-old self. Would it be the same for Brooke, she wondered, and then for her daughter, and down the line until Saylor herself wasn't even in anyone's memory anymore?

CHAPTER TEN

Since Brian was starting on her mother's to-do list and Devin was studying for an upcoming math test while Brooke lounged in the living room texting on her cell, and Erika was cleaning the kitchen, Saylor planned her escape.

She packed a beach towel even though she didn't plan on swimming or sunbathing due to November's chill. Still, she hoped to find Billy again, thinking maybe she'd sit on the towel under the shadowy pier with him, the place that seemed to make him feel the safest.

Just as she was about to open the front door, Erika called out. "Where are you going?"

Saylor gritted her teeth. How had Erika heard her all the way from the kitchen? "I already told you: I'm leaving for the pier." She had almost escaped—but not quite. Of course, the one time she had hoped Erika would stay on the line with Philip was the one time she didn't.

"I thought..." Erika's voice reverberated with both anger and hurt. "I thought that we'd have some mother-daughter time before you all left tomorrow."

"I'm only going to be gone for an hour." Saylor kept her voice light and friendly, hoping it would help Erika realize that she wasn't abandoning her, wasn't trying to hurt her, either. "Let's have some tea together when I get back." She quietly swung the door open, hoping to leave without any further discussion.

But Erika bellowed for her to wait, stomped out of the kitchen, and then marched toward Saylor as if she were preparing for battle. "I haven't seen you in over half a year and then you only etch out one quick weekend." She narrowed her eyes and clasped her hands against her hips. "The least you can do is spend some time with me while you're here."

Saylor stared at the floor. Her mother had a point—but still. She had to find Billy again. "Listen, Mom, I understand." She didn't dare look her mother directly in the eye, didn't dare tell her about her plans on trying to find Billy again. Instead, she reached for her mother's hand and gave it a quick squeeze before letting go. "I promise I'll be back within an hour."

"I have an idea," Erika said. "I'll go with you."

"I didn't think you liked going to the pier." Saylor gripped her keys; she didn't know how to tell her mother that she wanted to go by herself without her taking it personally.

Erika's nostrils flared as she eyed her. "I never said that I didn't like the pier; I just said that I haven't been in a long time."

Saylor nodded amicably as the familiar weight of guilt constricted her chest. Her mother wasn't just looking more subdued with time, but more vulnerable as well. She sighed, noticing just how quickly the imposing regality of her mother's body had been snubbed down by age and gravity. How odd to be almost the same height now as the once-statuesque Erika who had, by merely standing next to her daughter in the not-so-distant past, made Saylor feel hopelessly plain and squat. Saylor shrugged, figuring that she'd go back by herself later in the day. "Sure Mom." She flashed the sincerest smile she could. "We can take a stroll down the pier."

Erika's face lit up. "Yes, just like when you were a little girl."

Saylor had no memory of her mother ever taking her to the pier, but dared not argue the point.

Saylor drove her own car, explaining that the bumpy road leading to the beach wouldn't be good for Erika's tires. Thankfully, her mother agreed.

They made their way toward the parking lot, and Saylor slowed down, stealing a glance at Erika. "Mom, I have something to tell you..." For a moment, she wondered if she should backtrack, but then the words tumbled from her mouth: "I did find Billy here."

Erika's body stiffened as she took a sharp intake of air. "I don't understand...when did this happen?"

"Just a couple of weeks ago when I was driving back from Lucy's. I didn't tell you because you were so closed off about the whole Billy thing."

"Did you..." Erika asked as she clenched and unclenched her fingers, "talk to him?"

"Yes, I did." She debated whether or not to mention Billy's memories of Simon, but decided Erika would probably block it all out, or, worse yet, become defensive and angry, pushing away the truth while blaming Billy's state of mind.

"But Billy is crazy." Erika gripped Saylor's arm as if in desperation, as if she not only wanted Saylor to agree—but *needed* her to agree.

"Mom, let go." Saylor made sure to keep her voice even and low, a voice that she hoped Erika would listen to. "I'm still driving." Luckily, Erika pulled her hand away. But still, Saylor flinched as if her body couldn't trust what was coming next.

Erika let out what sounded like a whimper. A sad, little whimper that made Saylor wonder what was up her sleeve. With a sigh, Saylor pulled her Hyundai into the same spot she had parked before. Then she turned to her mother and looked her squarely in the eye. "I think any one of us could lose it if we became homeless."

"Saylor, you have to stop." Erika shook her head. "You cannot believe anything he says."

"Mom..." Saylor paused. Was it all possible that she could get her mother to agree? Probably not, but she still had to try. "I think we should help him."

"Help him?" The knotty veins on Erika's temples looked like they were about to burst. "That's ridiculous. He's a grown man. If he hasn't helped himself after all these years, then how can we ever do anything for him?"

"You said so yourself: He's mentally ill. Not to mention, he's been homeless and alone since he's been a teen. He doesn't have the resources."

Erika glared at her. "You are simply impossible, Saylor."

Saylor's stomach tightened, ready for the next blow. "What are you talking about?"

"You have no thoughts about my feelings, and yet you're worrying about this virtual stranger who is not only homeless, but crazy from drugs."

"No thoughts about *your* feelings?" Saylor swallowed, trying not to raise her voice. "It's the complete opposite. I'm always worried about your feelings."

"That's difficult to believe when I have to beg you to visit me after half a year, and then you don't even want to spend time with me."

"I'm sorry, Mom. I'm dealing with two teenage kids, an overworked husband, and trying to manage the business. It's not about you."

"No, of course not." Erika's voice rose. "It's never about me because it's always about you."

Talk about gaslighting, Saylor thought. But if she called her mother out on it, it'd only get worse. Inhaling, Saylor reached for a response that wouldn't create more animosity. After the silence became too thick, she decided to apologize again. "We should try and visit more—

The intrusive ring of Erika's cell reverberated in the space between them. With shaky hands, Erika grabbed her phone, peering at the screen. "I'll be right back." She got out of the car and slammed the door before answering.

With bent-over concentration, Erika gripped the cell against the side of her face, looking as if the call was the most important thing in the world to her. Then out of nowhere, Saylor felt the heat of impending anxiety. Quickly, she closed her eyes, chanting Billy's name. Somehow it staved off the panic, and she was now able to watch her mother without plunging into alarm mode.

With her straw-like frame straining against the wind, Erika headed back to the car and got in without any explanation. "I'm getting a headache," she said. "Please drive me home."

"Was that Philip?"

"It doesn't matter." Erika applied her pink frosted lipstick and then snapped her compact shut. "Why haven't you started the car? I told you that I'm not feeling well and you need to drive me home now."

Saylor bit the inside of her mouth. She was tired of acquiescing, tired of being bullied. "I need to ask you something."

"What?" Erika said, the blast of bitter-coffee breath emanating from her mouth.

"This may be hard for you to hear—"

"Then don't say it. I'm your mother and I don't need you to tell me anything that 'may be hard for me to hear.'" Even though her tone was harsh, her eyes were filled with fear.

Saylor was used to it. Her mother often reacted like this when she became defensive. But unlike so many other times when she decided that it was better to keep the peace, she continued, "Have you ever stopped to ask yourself if you really love Philip—if he really makes you happy?"

Erika's face flushed. "I love him—and, yes, of course he makes me happy." She let out an indignant huff. "What I do need to ask myself, though, is why I have to walk on eggshells around my own daughter."

And there was the gaslighting again. How in the world could her mother not realize how difficult *she* was? "What makes you say that, Mom?"

"Just now, Saylor," Erika hissed, her eyes narrowing with disdain.

Saylor stared at her mother. "Just now? What are you talking about?"

"Just because I wanted to take a phone call in privacy, you react as if there's something wrong with my entire life. Either that or..." Erika shook her head. "You are so insecure that you got mad just because I took a call."

"That's not what this is about." Saylor kept her voice firm, wishing she had never dared to challenge her.

Erika paused, flashing Saylor her wide-eyed, *I-do-really-care* look. "I do worry about you." She tried to reach for Saylor's hand, but without thinking, Saylor pulled away. Erika smiled serenely as if she hadn't noticed. "You are a very fragile woman, I know," Erika said, her voice now dripping with concern.

Saylor grimaced. Was she as fragile and weak as her mother made her out to be? Or was Erika merely projecting? Regardless, Saylor felt as if she wanted to tear out her hair every time Erika said it, pictured herself pounding her fists against the ground yelling at her mother to stop. Instead, she squared her shoulders and quietly told her mother that she'd drive her home.

"Fine," Erika uttered, her face now closed off and unreadable. She stared straight ahead without a word more.

Saylor revved the car more than necessary, letting the engine spew into the air what she couldn't.

As soon as she dropped her mother off, she headed straight back to Breakers Cove. She spotted Wex as soon as she got there.

"What are you doing back here?" Wex eyed her from his wheelchair, jaw set and arms crossed.

Saylor froze in mid step, feeling too battle-fatigued to answer. Erika had wanted her to go into the house with her, battering her with her same run-down speech about how short life was, how small their family was, and why couldn't they get along better. Saylor explained that she still was going back to the pier, and finally Erika stopped ranting and with a backward glance of hurt, got out of the car.

"Are you some kind of social worker?" Wex scowled, his eyes darkening.

"Like I told you before..." She smiled, hoping he could see she was telling the truth. "I'm just an old friend of Billy's."

Wex's laugh erupted, bitter and jaded. "Some friend you are; he left right after your little visit."

Saylor's hand flew to her chest. "He left?"

Wex narrowed his eyes, assessing her. "After all these years with me looking out for him, he just splits without saying a word?" He pointed a finger at her. "That's not the Billy I know. You must have said something that scared him off."

Saylor thought for a moment. Had she said something to scare him away? She did suggest trying to find a place for him to stay—but when he said no, she dropped it right away. She scraped her hand through her hair. She did also tell him that she was coming back to see him again. But why would that frighten him so much that he'd leave?

"I can see it in your face: you did," Wex yelled. "What did you say? You better tell me." He wheeled toward her.

"I swear to God, I don't think I said anything that would have made him leave." As much as she tried, she couldn't stop the tears.

"Don't do that." Wex came to a halt. "Why the God damn hell are you bawling?"

"I don't know." She yelled back so loudly, she surprised herself.

Wex put his hands up as if in defeat. Saylor tried to reign in the tears, focusing on the dirt-encrusted tops of her running shoes. Only the sound of surf and wind remained. Finally, she looked up. Wex remained on the same spot still facing her, his face no longer hostile, but curious—maybe even a tad empathetic.

"You're one crazy lady, you know that?"

"I know." The level of calm in her own voice steadied her. "I am crazy." If only Wex knew about her irrational fears. But even if he did, she had a feeling he'd laugh them off rather than judge. How bizarre that this tough-as-nails stranger made her feel safer than her own mother. How wonderfully bizarre.

"You're okay, though." He gave her an off-kilter smile. "You're okay."

"Thank you." She wiped her nose on the sleeve of her sweatshirt. "You are too." Some inexplicable truce had sparked between them, and Saylor felt as if she had finally passed his test.

A gust of wind cooled her face. She shivered and wrapped her arms around herself. "I'm sorry Billy left. Do you have any idea where he could be?" She walked closer to him.

Wex shook his head. "Nobody can find him anywhere." He paused, studying a mini whirlwind of dirt and cigarette butts on the ground before him. "It's like he's disappeared."

Saylor took in a long, ragged breath. "I'll come back and look again."

"Why are you so hell-bent on trying to get to him?" Wex's voice had grown mournful, sounded as if hope had long ago deserted him. "If you're from his old life, did you ever stop to think it's too hard for him to be around you?"

"I just want to help." Saylor glanced at the ocean, white caps streaking the surface like thick dabs of paint.

"Leave him alone," Wex uttered. "Just leave him be."

"But I told him I'd see him again." No matter what Wex thought, no matter his protective stance toward Billy, she would not betray her old friend.

"Just..." Wex said, his voice thick with warning, "back off."

But Billy was more important than fear. She put her hands on her hips and looked straight into Wex's eyes. "I know you care about Billy, but so do I."

"You need to understand." He looked at her, his hands clasped in a pleading, prayer-like gesture. "You got wheels, you got a home, you probably got a family, too. It isn't like that for Billy." Wex sighed. "It'll never be."

Maybe Wex was right. She was a fool to think she could swoop in and change a lifetime of abandonment and pain. Pausing, she looked up to the sky as if it held the answer. Suddenly, a crow flew overhead. Silent, swift, steadfast. Her heart felt as if it were suddenly floating, as if hope *was* still reachable.

"Things don't always have to stay the same," she said. Wex did not answer. She slowly walked to her car and then folded herself inside its warmth. Peering through the windshield, she held Wex's gaze. He eyed her with the sad resignation of someone who felt he knew the truth but had grown too weary to explain it. Saylor bowed her head and drove away.

CHAPTER ELEVEN

After Brian and the kids left on Monday, Saylor called Lucy straight away. Lucy was the only one who truly got the complicated relationship she had with her mother, was the only one who would let her vent without judgment, was the only one who could offer insight when Saylor was at a loss. When Lucy answered, Saylor exhaled, not realizing that she'd been holding her breath. She dove right in without any preliminary greetings, as both she and Lucy had done with each other over the years. A best friend privilege that had been earned through time and understanding.

"We visited my mom this weekend," Saylor said, leaning over her cell. "But I'll tell you about that later."

"Good morning to you, too." Lucy chuckled. "What recipe of crazy-making did you have to swallow this time?"

Saylor smiled as she began to load laundry. "Let me put it this way: I'm still dizzy with what an expert she is at turning things around."

Lucy laughed. "Oh, do share the latest guilt trip Erika tried to send you on."

"She did give me a silk blouse, though." Saylor lifted it up and made a face at the dark armpit stains. Too bad her mother never listened to her when she told her that she preferred cotton.

"She is a confusing one, isn't she?" Lucy clucked her tongue as if she were imitating Erika. "Even on top of all her weird competitive stuff, she loves you—and dare I say...even likes you—though I know it's hard to tell sometimes. But, still, the blouse thing is more about her than you."

"What are you talking about?" Neptune wedged himself into the laundry room and nudged Saylor's leg. She patted his head, waiting for Lucy's response.

"Let's face it, Saylor, you do dress..." Saylor heard Lucy inhale a cigarette. "To put it bluntly, you dress like you don't care. Your mom only wants you to look the best you can because it's a reflection on her."

"So, you think I dress like a slob?" Saylor ran the washing machine on hot, hoping to eradicate the scent of her mother's home from her family's clothes.

"I didn't say that. I just think that because your mother is so into her looks, you may have rebelled just a *tad* too much. I mean...you don't have to look all crunchy granola all the time—even if it *does* annoy Erika."

Saylor glanced down at her men's Levi jeans with the frayed holes at the knees and the faded blue T-shirt that had somehow become stained with ink on its bottom hem. "I guess you're right." Saylor threw the blouse her mother had given her into the sink and ran cold water over it with a squeeze of hand soap on each armpit. "Come to think of it, the only gifts she does give me are clothes—but at least they're in good taste."

"She wants you to look good, but never *too* good next to her. Notice how she never buys you anything revealing?" The sound of laptop keys clicked through the phone. "Still, we'll give Erika that much: She does know how to shop."

Saylor stared at the wet blouse, wondering if the stains would remain. "Listen, I need to talk to you about Billy."

"What about him?"

Saylor started right into where their last conversation had left off before Lucy had become interrupted by work. "Because of the memory Billy dredged up for me, I pretty much got the why of how my anxiety started, but I'm still working on the how-to-get-over-it part."

"Let me get this straight," Lucy said. "If I remember right, because Billy reminded you that you said out loud that you wished your asshole of a father would die the night before he actually did, you came to think of your words as weapons?"

"Yes. I believe that's why I became so afraid of blurting out the most horrible of things that pop into my head—no matter if they're true or not." She inhaled the smell of laundry detergent as she reached into a box of dog biscuits and tossed one in the air for Neptune. He caught it with a self-satisfied crunch.

"But your anxiety didn't get that bad until after you had kids. Why's that?"

Saylor leaned against the washing machine, its steady rhythm calming her down. "That's the one answer I did get when I was in therapy. When the responsibility of becoming a mom hit, the past stuff—even the stuff I couldn't remember—impacted me like it never had before. I had never fully taken that in, though...but after talking to Billy, I know it's true."

"That's intense," Lucy said, an awe-like reverence in her tone. "But it does make sense."

Saylor ambled out of the laundry room with Neptune in tow. Sighing, she entered the kitchen to clear away the rest of the breakfast dishes, the smell of burnt toast still lingering in the air. "The sad part, though, is that when I said I wanted to help him, he pretty much pushed me away, saying that I should focus on unshackling myself, helping my own family."

"He is..." Lucy paused, "right you know."

"But he does *need* help, and now he's missing. When we visited my mom this weekend, I went back to the pier to find him." Saylor tried to swallow the ever-expanding lump in her throat. "He's gone."

"You need to let this one go, Say. Billy has his own path," Lucy said gently. "And you have yours."

"So, I can't help myself if I also help Billy, too?" Saylor shoved a cereal bowl in the dishwasher. "What if I won't be able to get better unless—"

"Unless what?"

"Unless I'm able to help Billy get better, too."

"You know that doesn't make sense—"

"But he deserves a second chance, Lucy." Saylor rubbed the palm of her hand against her chest. "Of all people, Billy deserves a better life."

"How you're going to finally heal..." Lucy sighed. "Is not about becoming this guy's savior. It's the good hard work of living in the here and now."

Saylor dumped leftover coffee down the sink, not fully listening. Then, she made an excuse to get off the phone and stared out the window. After several deep breaths, she repeated Billy's name so many times that it seemed to echo in her own head, an internal beat that no one else could understand—not even Lucy.

Saylor waited in her car and inhaled the afternoon-smell of warm asphalt coming through her open window, as she stared at the closed doors of Devin and Brooke's high school. In a few minutes, teenagers would slouch out from their last classes. Because Devin was staying after school for science club, she had agreed to pick up Brooke. When Saylor had asked Brooke if she could just wait after school for her brother to give her a ride, Brooke had become adamant that there was no place at school for her to hang out. Now that Saylor was there, she felt grateful for the opportunity. Once Brooke got her license too, she'd be even less available than she was now.

With that thought, her mind went to Billy. She tried to focus on her breathing. Her ongoing thought loop about wanting to help him kept landing her from one dead-end scenario to another. But all she could think about was why Billy had disappeared from the pier, why did he leave Wex, probably one of the only people who was looking out for him, and worst of all—if it had been all her fault. If that were true, then she probably screwed up Billy's life more than it already was. She pictured him, squinting at the ocean's glare while he told her to go home and help her family. What exactly had been going on in his mind? She stared at the whispery brown and pale-yellow leaves of a nearby sycamore, and remembered how fourteen-year-old Billy had sat on her bedroom floor, his face earnest with fear. He had leaned over and whispered that he was afraid he was going to die before he hit twenty. When she asked why, he wouldn't answer, acting as if he never uttered the words. Saylor hadn't pushed him, hoping that it didn't mean anything, that it was just another one of his random notions.

She shook her head, thinking back to Lucy's advice to live in the here and now. Her preoccupation of Billy wasn't going to help anything—or anyone, himself included. Suddenly, the shrill sound of the school's end-of-day bell invaded the air. Startled, Saylor's heart raced, but she inhaled as deeply as she could and plastered on the presentable mom's expression of a bland-faced smile. Trying to locate Brooke in the crowd of kids ambling out of the now opened doors, Saylor's smile faded. When Brooke and Devin had been in grammar school, children burst out of their classrooms, running down the halls, grinning with straightforward happiness. During the middle school years, kids sauntered instead of ran out of class, their smiles worn down as if they had already become world-weary. Now, the high school kids moved even slower, a mucky sea of closed-off faces.

Finally, Saylor spotted Brooke, a lone figure in jet-black jeans and ripped sweatshirt; her tiny, stick-thin frame making her appear much younger than the other kids milling past. Then Saylor noticed a nearby group of sleek-haired beauties, heads leaning close together in the exclusive way in which popular girls are so talented. They looked much more seductive than any of the girls Saylor had known in high school with their low-cut shirts, designer jeans, and shoes more fashionable than Saylor ever wished to own. Brooke came closer, face set in full tough-girl form, her mouth, a tight line and head in defiant upward tilt. Saylor's heart ached. The girls slid sidelong glances at her, their vicious laughter snaking across the concrete and grass. Fingers clenched around the steering wheel, Saylor imagined them years ahead as vapid, unfulfilled women, whereas Brooke would be the dynamic spirit who flew miles above them. But of course, she was biased. Even these seemingly confident girls had their own secret pain and struggles. Everyone did.

Brooke slinked to the car and then plopped into the passenger seat, slamming the door with more force than Saylor thought possible for her noodle-thin arm. Saylor started the engine, seeing her daughter flexing her middle finger toward the group of girls, but just under the side window so they couldn't see.

Saylor knew it wasn't appropriate to encourage her, but she couldn't stop herself from grinning. "I couldn't agree more."

Brooke rewarded her with a dry smile.

Against the glare of afternoon sun, Saylor squinted. How she wished that she could guard Brooke and Devin from the brutality of teenage years. "Other than those horrible girls, how was your day?"

"About as boring as yesterday."

For some reason, Brooke's response made them both break into laughter. Saylor's heart lifted. Yet in the next moment, Brooke was engaged with the world inside her phone, an angry frown clouding her face, as she ignored Saylor's inquiry of what she'd eaten for lunch that day.

Mouth pressed shut, Saylor drove on. What had she done wrong? Just the other day Brooke had been so sweet while they stood together in front of her mother's living room window. And for a moment, they just shared the kind of laughter that made Saylor forget about everything else. If only she could prolong these fleeting connections, cut and glue them together to make a life free of fear and guilt.

Hands on hips, Saylor surveyed the chaos. The thought of wading through dirty dishes, folding the mountain of laundry, sweeping dog hair that collected underfoot, sorting through house bills, emptying trash, checking her voicemail, and making dinner brought on a thick exhaustion. The least she should do was start on dishes and dinner, but the dizzy fatigue from the previous night's interrupted sleep made even these two tasks overwhelming. She peered inside the fridge for leftovers, wondering if it was ever going to be possible to live without the constant sense that something bad was just around the corner.

At the kitchen table, Brooke scratched her head, turning the page of her history book. She had insisted on reading in the kitchen, leaving her laptop and cell in her room so she could 'ditch the distractions.' Since Brooke had gone into hostile retreat for the last part of the afternoon, Saylor was relieved her daughter wanted to be in the same room with her. She frowned; *how pathetic was that*? She reached for a tub of leftover spaghetti, peeled back the lid and sniffed. The slightly fermented odor made her want to throw it against the wall—now she had to toss out what she had hoped would have been an easy reheat. With head turned, she dumped the slimy mixture of pasta, sauce, and meat down the garbage disposal.

"That's disgusting," Brooke said. "Do you have to do that while I'm studying?"

Saylor ignored her. Maybe all teenage girls made their mothers feel the gamut of love, protection—and anger within one afternoon.

Brooke sighed as if the burdens of the world were upon her shoulders. "Oh, great, here's Eeyore," she said, rolling her eyes.

Saylor followed her gaze and nodded to Devin as he trudged into the kitchen. Without a word, he reached into the cupboard and grabbed a bag of chips.

"Devin, I'm about to make dinner." Saylor cleared her throat, planning to nuke the pizza she had just remembered was buried in the freezer. "Please try and save your appetite for some real food." *As if frozen pizza was real food*, she thought. *As if my words would make any difference.*

Devin shook his head and then muttered something to Brooke. Something that Saylor didn't catch, but somehow knew would rile her daughter, somehow knew would start a fight.

Sure enough, Brooke slammed her book against the table, her face distorted with rage. "Shut up, you stupid-freak-loser."

As calmly as possible, Saylor stood between them. "What's this all about?"

Devin shrugged. "All I said is that she looks as small as a twelve-year-old and should eat more."

"Why don't you just go hide in your room and stuff yourself like you always do," Brooke said, a vicious clip to her voice that Saylor had never heard before.

"Brooke, stop it," Saylor yelled. But it was too late. Underneath the mass of curly hair, Devin's round face had become exposed with hurt. Brooke's own face downturned with immediate guilt.

Devin retreated, chip bag still in hand. Saylor couldn't be sure, but she thought she heard him counting under his breath. After plodding down the hallway, he went to his room and with hardly a sound, closed the door.

Saylor's heart ached, a sadness that beat inside her chest for both Brooke and Devin. She held a hand on Brooke's shoulder. "I never want to hear you talk to your brother like that again—ever."

Brooke's mouth twisted in what Saylor knew was her way of fighting back tears. "What made you act so mean, anyway?" Saylor studied her daughter's pale face.

"Fuck off, Mom." Brooke backed away, and Saylor's hand drifted back to her side.

"Please, Brooke..." But her daughter shot out of the kitchen and slammed her door. Then something that sounded like breaking glass crashed inside Brooke's room.

Saylor ran down the hallway. After pounding urgently on her daughter's door, she called out, "We need to talk."

"Go away," Brooke screamed, her voice raspy with anger. "You'll never be able to help me."

Defeated, Saylor slumped against the door. She remembered Brooke's fits of rage when she was a toddler. With time and patience, Saylor had always been able to console her with soft words and a solid hug. Now Brooke seldom wanted any kind of comfort from her. How could she help her now? How could she help Devin? How could she help either of her children if she still hadn't been able to help herself?

For a split second, she wondered if they'd be better off without her. Then she thought about Faith and made herself rise from the floor. She pictured the lost look in Billy's eyes and knew it wouldn't help anyone if she left; it would, in fact, make everything worse. She made her way back to the kitchen just as her cell rang.

"What do you want, Brian?" she answered without bothering to say hello.

Brian didn't seem to notice. "When's dinner going to be ready?"

"I don't know." She opened the freezer, fishing for the pizza under the bags of out-of-date peas and corn. "It's been one of those days—"

"I hope..." he said, a small whine in his voice that set Saylor's teeth on edge, "that it's not frozen pizza."

She slammed the freezer shut. "Don't worry—everyone's on their own tonight. Devin's filling up on chips. Brooke's too upset to eat. And I'm too exhausted to care." She paused, hearing only a blank, empty sound. "Brian are you there?" But only dead air filled her ear. Had he hung up or was the call dropped? Either way, it was just as well. Now she didn't have to listen to what a hectic day *he* had. She shut off the ringer, hoping he wouldn't call back. She was in no mood to play the sympathetic wife.

Suddenly aware of how hungry she was, she opened the freezer again and found the pizza, but when she ripped open the box and peered through the plastic wrap at the frostbitten cheese, she shoved it back. What she really wanted was ice cream. Grateful to be alone in the kitchen, she took out a pint of pumpkin spice, sat with tablespoon in hand, and ate without thinking as she stared into space.

Half-way through the container, she heard Neptune scratch at Brooke's door and Brooke talking on her cell as she swung it open to let him in, "...I hate my mom, too. She's so crazy-worried all the fucking time that..." Brooke slammed her door before Saylor could hear the rest of the sentence. What the hell did Brooke mean? Saylor started up the hallway, thinking about pressing her ear against the door to try and hear what Brooke meant by her mother being so 'crazy-worried.' Instead, she turned back to the kitchen. With her luck, Brooke would suddenly open her door and catch her. Regardless, she knew that it was best to respect her daughter's privacy. She sat back down and shoveled in another spoonful of melting ice cream. What if Brooke had somehow heard her talk about her irrational fears? And what if her anxiety had infiltrated both Devin and Brooke, making them more vulnerable to their own emotional problems? She ate without pause, wondering what kind of food—if any—that Billy had been able to salvage for his dinner that night. After she polished off the entire pint, her gut still felt empty.

CHAPTER TWELVE

Brian's parents, Trudy and Bert Crawmore, stood side by side. Like so many decades-long couples, their looks had merged, creating a symbiosis that was somewhat quaint—yet still a tad unsettling. With their stocky builds, short gray hair and ruddy faces, Saylor sometimes had a hard time distinguishing who was who from a certain distance. She studied them now, their eyes shining with both pride and vodka, as they watched Brian carve the Thanksgiving turkey. Brian, their only son, was their prince. Trudy had made sure to tell Saylor this when she and Brian had first started dating. Even newly in love, Saylor had thought the word 'prince' was an indication that his mother favored him in such a way that it would be hard for Saylor to measure up. His two sisters, Barbara and Kelley, with their families in tow, watched him as well, fond annoyance on both their faces.

Pixie-blond Barbara lifted a Bloody Mary to her lips, standing several feet away from her gym-muscled husband, Thomas. Their twin daughters Jessica and Jackie, both varsity tennis players at Devin and Brooke's high school, were busy texting on their phones. Saylor had always marveled at what a seemingly perfect family they were, but tonight Barbara's smile was forced as she kept glancing over at Thomas, who continuously checked his cell. Even though Barbara had never been that warm to her, Saylor felt bad for her and wished that Thomas would pocket his phone already. But when it buzzed, he strode out of the room, leaving Barbara to down her Bloody Mary with audible gulps.

While quiet, doe-eyed Kelley drank from her immense goblet of red wine and her husband, Jeffrey, swigged down his micro-brewed ale, their thirteen-year-old son Michael studied everyone with unnerving intensity. Saylor wrapped her arms around herself, wondering what was going on in his head.

When her nephew started staring at her, Saylor tried to smile, wishing she could just slink away, lie down on Bert and Trudy's faux suede couch, and flip through their stack of People magazines.

Brian grinned. "This turkey smells like heaven, Mom."

Trudy nodded, her ever-present glass of vodka over ice clinking in hand.

Bert held up his own glass. "Here's to Brian: The best damn turkey-carver—and son a man could ask for!"

Trudy applauded and Brian took a quick bow before resuming the all-important task. Saylor glanced across the room at Devin and Brooke. Devin drummed his chapped fingers against each other as if he were keeping beat to some imaginary music in his head while Brooke looked on, her lip curled in disgust. Jessica and Jackie, still texting on their phones, kept their usual polite distance from their cousins.

Trudy insisted they take turns sharing what had been the biggest thing they were grateful for during the past year. When Saylor's turn came, she exhaled, trying to catch Brian's attention. He was well aware that this kind of thing sparked her anxiety, and she hoped for one quick glance of encouragement, but he wouldn't look at her. Although she couldn't help from feeling hurt, she knew what he was doing; he couldn't always be her *safe person*. So even though her heart thudded against her chest, she started talking, not quite sure how it was going to come out. "I'm grateful for..." she paused, knowing she should say something about how wonderful her husband was, or how amazing her kids were, but why not say the first thing that *did* pop into her head? Although she knew her thinking was beyond superstitious, she wanted luck on her side when it came to finding Billy again; if she voiced out loud how grateful she was for finding him once, then maybe it would help her find him again. She swallowed. "The thing I'm most grateful for was reconnecting with my old childhood friend, Billy."

Everyone stared. Trudy tilted her head as if she had heard wrong. "Your old childhood friend is named Billy? That is a man, I presume?"

Saylor nodded "It's a long story, Trudy. I'll tell you more after dinner."

Trudy turned her gaze toward Brian. After an exasperated exhale, he said, "Mom, he's homeless."

Trudy smiled brightly. "Who is next, then?"

As everyone went around the table, Saylor felt Trudy's gaze and when she looked back, Trudy gave her a disappointed shake of head. She knew that Trudy and Bert had wanted Brian to marry his old girlfriend, Dee, the one his father had drunkenly described one night as the 'gal who got away.' Brian had assured Saylor that he actually had been the one who broke it off because Dee had started to remind him too much of his mom, a good woman who worked hard, but drank even harder. But what Saylor always felt he left out—and wouldn't admit—was that his parents approved of Dee over her because Dee, in their eyes, was normal.

Saylor focused on her meal, trying to ignore Trudy's waves of hostility. She thought about glancing across the table to see how Devin and Brooke were holding up. But she knew by now that if Brooke caught her looking at all concerned, she would eat even less. And Devin didn't need the pressure of anyone's scrutiny, even if it was well meaning.

Bored with the loud table talk, which centered on Barbara's new Lexus and how many tennis tournaments the twins had won, Saylor studied Brian's face as he dived into the stuffing. What would their life be like if she didn't suffer from unrelenting fear, and he didn't live his life as if he were half-asleep? She imagined leading him away from the table and out the door to the last undeveloped field surrounding the Crawmore's neighborhood, and then without a word, making love. She reached across the table, wanting to at least touch his hand, but withdrew when Trudy abruptly asked her to pass the butter.

Saylor gripped her water glass, the first heart palpitations of an impending anxiety attack thudding against her chest. She thought about how repeating Billy's name had calmed her down before, but worried that the added stress of being with Brian's family might make her blurt it out. She bit her lip. With a cranberry-colored napkin, she wiped the sweat off her forehead and then folded it over and swiped the back of her neck. The combined odor of chestnut stuffing and cooked Brussels sprouts made her feel queasy. "Please excuse me, everyone. I need to get some fresh air." No matter what they thought of her, she needed to get out of there before the panic overtook all her senses, and she had to hold back the fear of screaming obscenities like a crazed banshee.

"You look stressed-out. I think you should have a nice glass of wine." Trudy said, and motioned for Kelley to pass the bottle.

"No, I'm fine. I just need to go outside for a little bit." Saylor shrugged, trying to look apologetic. "I'm sorry. I'll make it back by dessert." She focused on every word, making sure what she said sounded right.

"You'll make it back by dessert?" Trudy said. "Why don't you just go out to the patio for a moment?"

"I'm going to take a quick walk around the block," Saylor wiped the back of her hand across her forehead. "I'm sorry. I'll be right back." She tried to smile, hoping for some indication of understanding. But while Brian continued to eat, Brooke rolled her eyes, and Devin tapped his fork against the table in some Morse-code sounding pattern, everyone in Brian's family, except for Kelley, looked at her as if she should be committed.

"I'm sorry." Why had she said that she was sorry again? It was ridiculous to have to apologize this many times just so she could take in some fresh air. She pressed her lips together and walked as fast as she could toward the front door.

"What is wrong with her?" Barbara said in a loud enough voice for her to hear.

Saylor winced. A hint of concern would have been nice. Instead, Barbara's tone snarled with accusation. *If they only knew what was going on in my head,* Saylor thought. *But even if they did, would they care—or simply laugh at the insanity of my fears?*

Then the irritated voice of Trudy's: "It's not safe for a woman to be out by herself at night: Barbara, go with her."

Barbara was the last person Saylor wanted to be around. "I'm fine, Trudy," she yelled. "I'll be back soon." Of course, Trudy didn't suggest for Brian to go after her—and, unsurprisingly, Brian didn't make the attempt himself. She paused; even though she wanted to be by herself, it would have been nice. Barbara started to whine about how upset she was that her personal trainer was moving out of town, and Saylor escaped.

She shut the door behind her, and closed her eyes for a moment, inhaling the scent of chimney smoke and earth. She already felt calmer, but after a moment guilt wedged in. Devin and Brooke were probably embarrassed about how weird and antisocial their mother had just acted. She pressed back sudden tears. She was not going to allow herself to cry in front of the salmon-pink stucco of the Crawmore house.

Just as she was about to head down the walkway, the front door swung open. Saylor waited, hoping it was Brian. But it was Kelley, her winsome face illuminated under the porch light's glare.

"I don't mean to intrude," Kelley looked down at a flurry of dead leaves, "but I just wanted to make sure you're okay."

Saylor managed a smile. She couldn't believe that the drastically shy Kelley had drummed up the nerve to follow her out and check on her. "I'm fine—just getting some fresh air." She reminded herself not to get too stressed out by Kelley's habit of hesitating before responding. Taking a deep breath, she waited.

"Saylor..."

"What is it?"

After an agonizingly long stretch, Kelley finally answered. "I know we don't talk much, but you are my sister-in-law..." Kelley fiddled her wedding ring. "I just wanted to tell you that I'm seeing a therapist."

Saylor touched Kelley's arm, honored that Kelley had shared such personal information—and also wondering why. "I'm happy for you. I know that therapy can help a lot of people." She didn't want to tell her that it hadn't worked for her because she still believed it could help others. Others who weren't such hard nuts to crack. Saylor found herself chuckling.

Kelley raised her eyebrows in concern. "I'm not saying that you need this, but if you—or if you know anyone else who is looking for a therapist—I highly recommend him." She handed Saylor a light blue card.

Saylor immediately shoved it in her back pocket while thanking Kelley. Then for several moments they stood in silence, both facing the hush of the suburban night.

"I guess I'll go back in now," Kelley said. "You still going for that walk?"

For some reason the way Kelley tilted her head made Saylor feel a rush of gratitude. "Yeah, I'll be back soon."

With hands scrunched in pant pockets, Saylor marched down the brick path to a wide sidewalk. Stunningly quiet, the neighborhood seemed like something out of the Twilight Zone. She passed Trudy and Bert's next-door-neighbor's house. Light spilled out from the living room window, and Saylor paused, looking in. Caroline, a professional artist, who painted huge images of sky and magnified details of tree roots and branches, had divorced her husband four years ago. Saylor held her breath, watching Caroline laugh among a medley of artist-looking friends. They looked a lot happier than the house she just left. But maybe that was just her perception. Maybe everything became warped through the lens of fear. Then Caroline appeared to catch eyes with her. Not knowing how to react, Saylor stepped back then breathed a sigh of relief when she saw that Caroline nodded to someone in the room.

A gust of wind blew past and Saylor continued on. She shook her head, thinking how Trudy thought it was unsafe for a woman to be out by herself at night in this suburban order. The only cars that ever passed belonged to homeowners and their guests. Practically every neat tract house flooded the sidewalk with an outpouring of maddeningly bright light. Like the caveman days, Saylor thought, when people used fire to scare off wild animals. Only these days, the perceived predators were other people. She shrugged. No matter what kind of neighborhood she was in, she still felt more at ease under the indifferent sky than under the Crawmore's roof during a family get together. If only she could keep walking until Thanksgiving was over. Maybe if she waited long enough, though, the dishes would be done, and she wouldn't have to engage in the kitchen talk with Trudy. When she turned the corner, though, she told herself that she'd just walk around the block She didn't want to give Trudy and Barbara the excuse to dislike her any more than they already did.

Once she got closer to the house, she started to feel an odd unsteadiness, as if her feet couldn't be trusted to hold her up. She stopped in front of one of the rare unlit driveways and looked up to the sky, remembering how her mother had exclaimed that Uncle Silvio was afraid to look down at his own two feet. This was before he was gone. Her father's younger brother Silvio had never left his parent's home, never had any kind of romantic love, and only worked an odd temporary office job here and there. Over the years, Uncle Silvio became increasingly afraid to step out his parent's front door. His life had narrowed to the 1,600 square feet inside the walls of his childhood home.

When her grandparents Rosa and Frank had the family over for a Thanksgiving dinner when Saylor was eleven, Uncle Silvio sat in his same living room chair throughout the night. Grandmother Rosa had to take his dinner plate to him. On her grandmother's vinyl-covered couch, Saylor sat across from him, an excuse to get away from the big, noisy table. He turned to her. The pudding-like mass of his body looked uncomfortable, even though he sat on what Saylor had thought of as his extra, extra-large sized gingham-patterned chair. With his moon face making the blinking eyes appear even smaller, he leaned in and asked about school in a hushed tone, as if it was the most serious question in the world. Saylor knew to wait and let him ask her again. If he wasn't allowed to say something twice, he'd blink with a hummingbird's speed and have to take twenty breaths before he could continue. She didn't mind because he was always so nice; not like the other grown-ups who would ask a question and then not even listen to her answer. When she told him she was having a hard time in math, he tried to reassure her, telling her not to worry because she was going to grow up and be a brilliant artist.

Saylor had jabbed her fork into the mashed potatoes. "But I get so nervous on tests. Even when I study really hard, I never get good grades, and if I fail math, they might not let me go on to the sixth grade."

Uncle Silvio leaned in and whispered, "Saylor, you've never gotten an F or even a D, have you?"

"No, but that doesn't mean I won't"

"Don't start worrying too much—you don't want to end up like me." And, then of course, he repeated it. He smiled as if it were a light-hearted joke, yet Saylor saw that his eyes could not stop blinking.

They ate in silence after that, balancing plates on their laps. Saylor couldn't help but steal glances at her uncle's face. She imagined him as a man who no one knew had already died, and this was his ghost acting in his place. She swallowed the starchy mush, picturing how his white skin could glow in the dark with his black eyes spilling out secret tears.

Uncle Silvio did not make it through the rest of that year. When Grandmother Rosa and Grandfather Frank went away one weekend, he shot himself in the heart. They arrived home to see their son's blood seeping through the upstairs ceiling. He had locked himself in a closet that was right above their living room display of family photos. A picture of dimple-faced baby Silvio could not be saved.

Saylor inhaled the cool air, trying to distance herself from memory. She focused again on the night sky; even in this suburban sprawl, she could still see some stars. Why didn't Uncle Silvio have the capacity to look up? If he had, maybe he could have gotten out of his own head long enough to get help. Maybe it would have helped if he had kids. No matter how far down she fell into the fear and depression, she never let herself contemplate suicide. It would be the cruelest way to leave one's children—abandoning them with such finality and unwarranted guilt that there'd be an irreparable hole left in their souls. But would she have thought about it if she didn't have kids? Maybe even carry it out? Then, with a sharp intake of air, she remembered how Billy had said that her own father's death had been "an accident that he wanted to happen."

She stepped away from the driveway and trudged back to the Crawmore house, Billy's current demise haunting her more than the deaths of her own father and uncle.

CHAPTER THIRTEEN

Glassy-eyed attention on a college football game, Brian lounged on the couch. Next to the three-load laundry mound that she was folding from the other end, Saylor leaned over the four neat piles of clothes on the coffee table, stacking yet another one of Brian's T-shirts. After a commercial came on, Brian finally acknowledged she was in the room.

"Don't look so pissed off," he said. "It's the day after Thanksgiving; I'm allowed to relax."

"I didn't say anything."

"You didn't have to."

"Don't start fighting you guys," Brooke yelled from her room. She then slammed her door shut.

Saylor gritted her teeth and threw a pair of Brian's boxer shorts on the couch. She stomped off. Brian could fold his own laundry. Neptune, who'd been sitting at her side, followed on her heels. She walked by Devin's room and paused, looking in. He was crouched by his bookshelf, a stack of old science fiction books and three clean, white rags by his side.

"What're you doing?" Saylor hoped she sounded nonchalant, hoped he had enough self-awareness to know what was happening without her having to point it out.

Devin wiped his hands on his sweats and looked toward her without making eye contact. "Nothing much." He shrugged.

She tilted her head, smiling. She didn't want to be pushy—but as a mom, she needed to know. "What's the pile of books for?"

He dropped his chin to his chest. "Just organizing."

Saylor knew that he had "organized" this same shelf of books the other day. "Are you going to give those away?" *Maybe I'm making too much of this,* she thought. *Maybe he's just going through normal teenage angst and the over cleaning and organizing is a phase—a way for him to feel more in control.*

He narrowed his eyes and fidgeted from one leg to another. "I'm not giving anything away," he said with irritation, "Like I said—I'm just organizing."

Saylor leaned against the doorframe. "Have you had breakfast yet, honey?"

"I will later." He turned his back and picked up one of the rags, wiping his already spotless shelf.

"Devin?" She held back tears.

"What?" His back was still turned to her.

"Do you want to go for a walk with me and Neptune?"

"No, Mom, I have to get this done." When he finally turned to face her, she saw the all-too-familiar mix of anger and exhaustion.

"Just around the block?" She remembered when he was a little boy and how much he loved to hold Neptune's leash shouting "hee-haw," pretending he was a cowboy and Neptune, his horse. She had watched her mostly serious boy with hope at those times, telling herself that no matter how old he got, he'd never lose his joy.

Devin paused, looking over his shoulder. "Maybe later."

"Okay...maybe later then." Saylor retreated, knowing that it was his non-confrontational way of getting her to leave him alone.

A heated flash of anger toward Brian hit her in the chest. She marched back into the T.V. room and plopped on the couch. "You have to do something with Devin today." She jabbed Brian's knee, hoping he'd listen. "He's doing his obsessive-compulsive stuff again. He needs to get out of the house."

"You know every time I ask him to do something with me..." Brian paused, his attention on a commercial, where a bright, shiny family was laughing as they each grabbed an oversized slice of pepperoni pizza. "He *always* says no."

"That's because you only ask him to do things you want to do."

Brian finally looked at her. "What are you talking about?" He frowned as if he hadn't a clue.

"I know you've given up on trying to coax him into surfing." Saylor bit back her anger, trying to keep calm, trying not to burst into tears. "But you still try to pressure him into kayaking or going for long, grueling hikes with you. You have to ask him to do things he likes."

Brian shook his head. "Like going out to lunch?"

"Why not?" She couldn't stand this side of her husband. "If that's what he'd like to do with you—what's so wrong with it?"

"I thought you wanted him to get outside." Brian shrugged noncommittally, staring at the screen. "Why would going to a restaurant be any better than just eating at the kitchen table?"

Saylor's whole body tensed. "I said *out of the house*—not outside. And this isn't about what or where—it's about making time to hang out with your son." She stared her husband down, wishing he'd understand. "But all you can think about is yourself."

"I'm not thinking about myself." He gave her his annoyed look of pushed-together eyebrows that made the crease between his forehead grow more pronounced. "You don't think I want him to be happy too? All I'm trying to do is get him outside to share some father-son time."

"But you have to realize he's not Mr. Sporty like you are. You have to like him for who he is."

"I do like him for who he is." His face turned back to the T.V. "But I still think he needs to be pushed more."

"He's seventeen." Saylor gritted her teeth. "He's his own person."

"I know that, Saylor." Brian folded his arms across his chest. "But he *does* need more physical activity."

"But trying to talk him into things that he doesn't want to do doesn't help either—might in fact, make him rebel even more." Saylor knew this only too well. The more her father demanded that she stay away from sugar, the more candy bars she hoarded. "Don't you want to be there for him?"

Brian cleared his throat. "Would you just stop, already?"

Saylor stood. "Things aren't always as simple as you make them out, Brian. You need to start seeing what's happening—"

"Wait..." Brian interrupted. "You did remember to put the Thanksgiving leftovers my mom had packed for us in the fridge last night?"

She pressed a hand to her head, chiding herself for not remembering. "I'm sorry—I forgot." By the time they had pulled into the driveway, she had completely spaced out about the cheap plastic containers filled to the brim with turkey, chestnut stuffing, and Costco desserts.

"What do you mean, 'no?' You drove back last night; I figured you would have remembered to get them out of the trunk and into the fridge."

"You were there, too. You could have remembered when we got home." She had to stop herself from saying anything about him having had one too many beers to safely get behind the wheel—or to be able to remember his mother's precious leftovers.

"What a waste of good food." Saylor heard his mother's whiny inflection seep into his voice. "Where are the car keys? I bet everything is still good. It was a cold night."

"It's already ten in the morning." She couldn't believe he was actually thinking that it was okay to salvage leftovers that'd been sitting in the car for that long. "I thought you just wanted to relax and watch your game." He had remained on the sofa as she continued to stand by, her legs itching for retreat.

With an exaggerated sigh, he shook his head.

Then she did something she rarely ever did: She lied. "I'm sorry, Brian. After I realized we had left everything in the trunk, I threw it all out."

"When did you do that?"

She took a step back, avoiding his gaze. "This morning while you were still asleep."

"You just tossed out all of my mom's cooking after she had taken all that time packaging it up for us?" His face darkened.

"Don't blame me—you had every opportunity to bring it in yourself."

"You did save the containers, though?" He stood and faced her. "You know my mom wants them back."

Saylor paused, recalling his mother's vodka-induced hostility and how Trudy's departing joke hurt way more than it should have. She had stood right in front of Saylor, winking at Barbara and Kelley, and as if her daughter-in-law was invisible, said, "Poor Saylor with that wild frizz; her attempts to tame that crazy head of hair just never seem to work, do they?"

Brian clamped his hands on his hips. "Tell me where they are and I'll clean them myself."

"I've got it handled." Saylor walked away, feeling a rebellious rush. She strode out to the car, morning dew still dripping off trees and bushes. She breathed in the scent of damp stones and wet earth.

She lifted the carefully folded-over paper bag, heavy with the solid fats of Trudy's leftovers from the trunk. For a moment, she thought about dumping the whole thing in the trash, but knew Brian would flip—and, besides, it'd be wasteful. So, she unwrapped the bag, grabbed one of the containers, and turning her head so that she couldn't see, banged the plastic against the trashcan's side, listening for the thud of food hitting bottom. Although the yeasty, gone-off odor of whatever it was made her slightly ill, she took out the next container and did the same until all of them had been emptied. Since she didn't have the stomach to stand in front of the kitchen sink to clean off the remaining slime—and she didn't want to face Brian, she quietly opened the side gate and hosed them off, watching bits of grayed stuffing and stiff-white frosting settle into the blades of grass. *Let Brian return the barely washed containers to Trudy next week*, she thought, picturing how Trudy would make sure to offer him a beer while she gulped down her afternoon vodka and orange juice, the ice cubes clinking against the glass as if they were begging for escape.

Saylor threw the still-wet containers into the paper bag and wedged it behind the backseat of Brian's truck. Before she headed to the front door, she paused, glancing up to late November's pale-gray sky. For some reason, it made her think of her mother. A gust of wind swept past, and she thought about how the glamorous, social Erika she had known growing up had slowly but surely turned into the isolated older woman who still held her head up, still walked into a room as if she owned it. Although Saylor knew her mother's loneliness had to do with the ongoing obsession with Philip, she still felt sorry for her. Saylor grabbed her cell from her back pocket.

Erika answered on the first ring and even though Saylor's name would obviously show up on her mother's caller ID, she still acted as if she didn't know who was calling.

"Mom, it's me."

"So, it is," Erika answered as if Saylor had done something wrong, had done something that she'd have to amend for years to come.

Saylor drew in a deep, steadying breath. This was her punishment for daring to go to the Crawmore's for Thanksgiving. "What did you end up doing last night?" She hoped that at least one of the long-time neighbors had invited her over.

"Last night?" Erika sighed. "I watched an old Ingrid Bergman movie."

"Sounds like a better time than I had." She hoped it would make Erika feel better, but as soon as it was out of her mouth, Saylor wished that she hadn't shared. Now her mother would have even had more ammunition against Brian's family.

"Why do you say that?" Erika's voice became too bright. Saylor pictured her mother pacing her kitchen in anticipation and it made her pause. On one hand she didn't want to give her anything, but why couldn't she share with her own mother?

"Just the usual routine: too much food and drink." Saylor ran her fingers through her hair and shivered. Slowly, she made her way back into the house.

"Of course. Those people won't ever change. They are happy in their ignorance, content in their overindulgences."

Saylor felt bad, thinking how open Kelley had been and the unhappiness behind Barbara's forced smile. "Mom, Brian's family isn't bad—they're just like the rest of us: flawed people who are trying to deal with life's disappointments."

Erika clicked her tongue in annoyance. "Why don't you get in your car and come down and visit me?"

In the background, Brian yelled at the TV. Saylor edged into the laundry room and shut the door. "Do you mean right now, Mom?"

"Yes, right now. Today. By yourself. You can spend the night and leave tomorrow if you wish." Sounding as if she was heading a business meeting, Erika continued, "I cannot remember the last time you visited without family in tow."

"I know, but it is Thanksgiving weekend, and I'm not sure if the kids want to do something..." Saylor stopped herself. Her mother did sound lonely.

"Saylor, they are not babies anymore. It's not as if you're going to take them to the park or the zoo. Devin can drive himself to where he needs to go, and I'm sure that Brooke is busy with friends."

She knew her mother was right, yet it stung. "I guess I can make it."

"It will do you good." Her mother hung up with a finality that let Saylor know that in Erika's eyes, the deal was done. *But why not go?* Besides making some mother-daughter time together, she could also look for Billy again.

Without saying a word to Brian, Saylor raced upstairs and quickly packed her duffel bag, her mind playing back images of the young Billy, wide-eyed to the world but wary-faced around people. If she did find him again, how was she supposed to help him? She exhaled. She'd think of something.

She *had* to think of something. Why else would she obsess about him for all these years if it weren't meant to be?

When she came back down, she found Brian in the kitchen making a sandwich.

She placed her duffle bag on the floor. "Brian, I'm going to go—"

"I'm sorry for being short this morning." He opened the fridge, grabbing a tomato and a package of cheddar cheese. "I just hate having to lie to my mom about how much we enjoyed the leftovers."

"I left the containers in a bag in the backseat of your truck, but they're still wet; you'll have to dry them off yourself."

"Don't be mad at me, Say." He looked her in the eye with genuine remorse.

But anger still pressed against her chest. "I just wish you'd wake up."

"Wake up?" He shook his head, annoyance furrowing his brow. "What are you talking about?"

How could she explain her growing frustration with his disconnected state that most people would consider ordinary, everyday existence?

"Well?" Brian asked, tapping his foot against the kitchen floor.

"It's just that you always seem to put blinders on. You're either zoned out in front of the television, slugging down beer, or just so distracted you don't notice what's right in front of you."

He ran his fingers through his hair, sighing. "Your thinking is skewed, Saylor."

"What's that supposed to mean?"

"Just because you're always so hyper-vigilant and can never relax, doesn't mean that it's wrong for the rest of us to kick back and enjoy things."

She tried to swallow the sudden lump that had wedged inside her throat. *Was Brian, right*? Maybe her anxiety *had* skewed the way she viewed others. She touched her husband's arm. "I think we both need to work on ourselves."

"Speak for yourself." He chuckled as if it were a joke. "Right now, I'm going to focus on making my sandwich."

She watched him slice the tomato, seeds oozing onto the cutting board. The man was oblivious, but he was right about her not being able to relax—and she was envious of his ability to enjoy life without the constant intrusion of worry and concern. But would he ever be able to see things clearly? And...would she ever be able to get past her fears?

"You want some of my tomato and cheese sandwich?" He looked at her and smiled, but stopped when his gaze landed on the duffel bag. "What's that for?"

"I know this is abrupt, but I just talked to my mom, and she wants me to visit. Since she spent Thanksgiving alone, I feel like I better go."

He bit into his sandwich and answered while in mid-chew, "She should have gone to my parents with us."

"I know." Saylor didn't try to explain that even though Erika could be a snob, Trudy and Barbara often excluded her, cracking even more inside jokes when she was around and drunkenly cutting her off when she was trying to tell a story. At those times, Saylor tried to rescue her mother by linking her arm in hers and making their own conversation. But Erika wasn't stupid. "For all her bitchiness, I still feel sorry for her."

Brian's face softened. "Do you want me to try and round up the kids, and we can all go together?"

"That's nice of you, Brian—but I'm sure it will be more hassle than it's worth. Besides, my mom made it clear that she just wants me to visit—and you know how she can be if anyone tries to change plans on her."

With a knowing grin he nodded and crossed the space between them. "Can I hug you?" he said, already reaching for her.

Saylor leaned into his arms. "I wish I hadn't told her yes."

"It'll be okay." As he embraced her, his words vibrated against her chest. "Now you can take one less guilt trip off your list."

She smiled, knowing again why she loved him—and wishing that this Brian—the likable, understanding one that stood right before her—didn't submerge so often into whatever distractions pulled him away.

CHAPTER FOURTEEN

By the time Saylor found herself in front of her mother's door, it was already three in the afternoon. She shivered, guessing that the miles-thick fog encasing Breakers Point was too massive to leave anytime soon. Finally, she pushed the bell and within seconds, Erika opened the door. Her over-perfumed body and Pine Sol scrubbed house stung Saylor's nose. As soon as Saylor eyed her in her severe black turtleneck and ironed slacks, she wondered what, besides guilt and the remote possibility of seeing Billy again, had possessed her to make the trip. She really wasn't up for visiting her mother alone, and yet here she stood with the rest of the afternoon and night and next day waiting stagnant and downcast-gray in front of them. What would they do? What would they talk about? How would they not fight? She resisted the urge to scratch her neck, trying to ignore the heat of anger toward both herself and her mother.

She should have stayed home for the whole of her kids' Thanksgiving break. She could have talked Devin into a walk, maybe even ventured into his room and helped him. She could have taken Brooke shopping for some new clothes. She could have made sure that just the four of them went out for dinner. And she missed Brian. God, she felt as if she were a five-year-old again, holding back tears that made no sense.

"Well, come in already." With raised eyebrows, her mother gave her the up and down once-over. Saylor knew that in her mother's eyes, she looked decidedly unkempt and overweight. Dressed in grungy jeans, a baggy sweatshirt, and without a trace of makeup, she knew she wasn't exactly pulled together. And then, of course, there was her hair—snaky and surly-looking as it half-escaped her attempt at a bun. She hadn't stepped on a scale in years, but knew she had gained weight, all her pants—even her old, worn Levi's—had become uncomfortably tight. Erika, of course, had commented on it—more than once. And even though Saylor had told her that she wasn't interested in hearing about how to cut calories and explained that she didn't need to hear about how much better she'd look if she only lost ten pounds, Erika continued to badger her.

"Sorry, Mom, I didn't have time to doll myself up for the drive." Saylor smiled, hoping to break the all-too-early tension. "But I did bring some nicer clothes in case we decide to go out later."

Erika ignored the comment, waving her to the kitchen. "I've put on some tea. Come, let's sit down."

Tight-lipped, Erika turned on the kettle, placed a burn-scarred hot pad on the kitchen table, and set a rose-colored ceramic teapot on it. She turned to her cupboard and took down a tin of Royal Dansk biscuits. With a small napkin, she clasped one pretzel-shaped butter cookie and placed it on a dessert plate for Saylor, and then put one plain round cookie on her own. They sat without speaking while Erika placed three Earl Grey tea bags into the teapot.

Saylor squared her shoulders. Since she was there now, she better make the most of it. She was an adult. This had been her decision. Anyway, she'd leave sometime tomorrow—there was plenty of weekend left to have some family time with Brian and the kids. She nibbled her cookie, the rich, crumbly taste making her want to grab ten more. She wouldn't dare, though. Not in front of Erika.

"So, let me guess." Erika smirked. "Brian's parents were tipping it back last night...as usual?" She got up to turn off the kettle, then poured the boiling water into the teapot, tipping her elegant head just so. She settled back onto the chair opposite Saylor and waited with hungry eyes.

Saylor ignored her mother as she chomped back the rest of her cookie. What good would it do to gossip about Brian's family with her? What good would it do to stoke her mother's superior façade?

Her mother nodded as if Saylor's silence was affirmation enough. "I have to say I am glad I wasn't there," Erika continued with head-held-high assurance. She eyed Saylor as if her daughter were a mouse, and she a cat. "It was so much more relaxing to stay home, watching old movies."

Saylor felt as if she were about to burst open. The whole reason she had driven all the way down there was because she felt guilty that Erika had been alone on Thanksgiving—even though it'd been her own choice. Saylor bit her lip.

As if reading her thoughts, Erika's mouth soured. "You can't blame me for not going, Saylor. It hasn't been very fun for me in the past, you know."

Saylor looked past her mother toward the menagerie of old photos that had accumulated on the fridge, focusing on a faded picture of her mother and father standing stiffly by her long-dead grandparents. "I thought about Uncle Silvio last night." Even though her mother was visibly taken aback, Saylor continued on. "I was only eleven at the time, so I can't really remember exactly how Dad had dealt with his brother's death." No one spoke of Uncle Silvio after his suicide. But Saylor had never forgotten him, had never stopped wondering if there was something she could have done, something she could have said that would've stopped him.

Erika smoothed her knotty fingers over her already flat placemat. "Your Uncle Silvio was a very troubled man, you know."

Aren't we all troubled? Saylor thought. Suddenly afraid she might have said it out loud, Saylor looked at her mother. But Erika merely poured a small amount of tea into each of their cups. Relieved, Saylor exhaled. It wasn't nearly as bad as some of her other thoughts that she worried might have slipped from her lips, it was, actually, quite an ordinary thing to say. But Erika would *not* have appreciated it. Erika, in fact, would have *hated* it.

"Well," Erika narrowed her eyes and barked, "aren't you going to ask for more? Keep digging at me until every detail is turned over?"

Saylor flinched. Erika couldn't stand her inquisitive nature—especially when she was trying to piece together something from the past. "Okay, Mom..." Saylor reached for a second cookie, and dunked it in her tea, watching the liquid slowly rise. "Since you mentioned it, I am curious—Dad never talked about Uncle Silvio after he died—didn't even seem that upset..." she ventured, hoping to nudge her mother's memory. "He was his only brother."

"I only know that your father was very angry after Uncle Silvio died." Erika's face darkened. "He didn't cry, but he was angry."

"What do you mean?" Saylor wasn't surprised by her father's response—Simon was a very troubled man himself, and anger always did seem to be his go-to reaction. Still, how could anyone *not* cry after losing their brother?

Without a word, Erika poured more tea into their cups. At first Saylor thought she was trying to evade the question, but then Erika leaned in. "I know he blamed his mother," she whispered as if guarding her words.

"He blamed Grandma Rosa? Why?"

"Your Grandmother Rosa..." Erika gazed into her teacup. "I had never shared this with you before, but I know you're going to keep at it and I am too tired today to—"

"What, Mom?" Saylor squeezed her mother's hand. "I'm not a child. You can tell me."

Erika sighed, shaking her head. "Your father had confided to me that your Grandmother Rosa was a bit off. She thought your Uncle Silvio had been possessed."

"Possessed?" Saylor knew her grandmother had always been superstitious with her whispers to Grandfather Frank about whether or not someone had been giving her the evil eye and how she always crossed herself with furious intent whenever she entered their house, but she had no idea that her grandmother harbored such an insane notion about her own son.

"Yes. According to your father, because Silvio had developed so many nervous tics when he was little, she became convinced that her youngest son was possessed."

Saylor's hand flew to her chest. "That's way beyond being *a bit off*. I don't remember Grandma Rosa acting *that* unbalanced." Although Saylor had never felt comfortable around her grandmother—whenever she thought of her, she pictured the big, square face spouting out criticisms about what Saylor happened to be wearing or what she'd been doing, and then there were those fiery eyes that always looked both furious and terrified—she was still surprised to hear of her grandmother's strange delusion.

"You weren't around her that much to have seen it. Your father limited our time with them—and we saw them even less after your uncle died. Then they passed away within a year of each other after Simon's accident."

"But what a devastating way to grow up, having your own mother think that you were possessed by some evil spirit."

"It was." Erika's voice had grown shaky. "It was horrible for both Silvio and Simon." Erika bowed her head as if she had taken on her mother-in-law's shame. "She conjured up this insane theory that if she kept feeding Silvio, she could somehow coax out the bad spirit. But she never believed it left, so year after year, she insisted on stuffing that poor boy with more and more food. From what your father told me, your Uncle Silvio never rebelled; he just wanted to placate her and show her that he was okay—so he ate as much as she gave him, plus more."

"But what about Dad?" Saylor reached for another cookie. Erika's eyes widened as she stared at her daughter—but Saylor went ahead and crunched into its buttery goodness. After several moments of silence, Saylor repeated her question, "Mom...how did she treat Dad?"

Erika threw her head back as if she had just been jolted from a deep sleep. "Your father..." Erika sighed. "He learned to stay out of her way the best he could—but for some reason that woman also hated Simon as if he were the devil himself. You know that father of his, your Grandfather Frank, he was simply a weak puppet of a man that couldn't make a difference."

"What do you mean she hated him? I never noticed her being any worse to Dad than anyone else in the family."

Erika smiled, her eyes glancing sideways into the past. "He told me that she was nicer to him after he married me."

"She introduced you two, didn't she?" Saylor studied her mother's face. There didn't look to be a hint of regret, only the proud shine of accomplishment.

"Yes, she did. She had never approved of his former girlfriends—but she took to me right away. I had met her while working at Saks, and within fifteen minutes she made sure to get my number. Despite her issues, she still knew I'd be good for her son."

Saylor stared at the table. For all the unhappiness he had caused her, she now felt sorry for her father, was able to understand his own pain more. "I finally get why Uncle Silvio and Dad had so many problems."

"Your Uncle Silvio was the sick one, but your father worked hard." Erika nodded as if trying to convince herself of her own words. "But your father was a good man."

Saylor's stomach twisted. "How was Uncle Silvio *not* a good man—and Dad was?"

Her mother patted her mouth with a napkin for nonexistent crumbs. "Your father loved you and he loved me—that's all you need to remember."

Saylor gritted her teeth. Uncle Silvio had loved her, too. There was no use, though, in arguing that point with Erika. "But don't you remember how controlling Dad was?" She didn't dare mention his strange mood swings, his dark bouts of depression. Or...how very mean he could be—and, then, of course, there were the multitude of affairs.

Erika scowled. "Define controlling, Saylor." Her mother was challenging her, trying to make it seem as if she were exaggerating. But she wasn't going to back down this time, wasn't going to let Erika's take on history dissuade her own memory.

Saylor tried to look her mother in the eye, but Erika would not meet her gaze. "For starters..." Saylor said, trying to keep her voice steady. She cleared her throat, feeling the spike of adrenaline, the pounding heartbeat of fear. But she took a deep breath and continued on, "For starters, he made us both feel that if we weren't thin enough—then we weren't *good* enough." Saylor exhaled. She had finally said out loud a simple, but undeniable truth, a truth, she knew Erika was going to refute.

And, sure enough, her mother shook her head as if Saylor had gotten it all wrong. "He just wanted us to be healthy, Saylor."

"You don't remember the way he used to scrutinize our food, the way he threw tantrums if he caught us eating something that he considered 'poison'?" Even the diet-conscious Erika liked an occasional treat, and would become sullen-faced and tight-lipped when he caught her eating something he didn't approve of. Yet, Saylor didn't go into the night before he had died, the night he pelted ice cream at her, because she knew her mother hadn't witnessed it. As usual, Erika had kept her head in the sand, had tuned out his insane yelling as she continued chatting and laughing with their guests in the living room.

Erika sipped her tea, her body rigid with hostility. Saylor continued to stare her down, but still, Erika's eyes would not meet hers. "Mom, don't you think that Dad might have been suffering from some form of mental illness?" This was the first time Saylor had said it out loud, never quite sure herself.

Erika set her cup against the saucer, the clanking sound of restrained anger. Except for the refrigerator's hum, the kitchen became hard with silence. Saylor didn't know what to say.

Finally, Erika looked at her. "Even though he had gone through hell as a child, your father," she said, "was *not* mentally ill. You need to respect his memory, understand that he did the best he could."

"The best he could?" Saylor had to stop herself from shouting. "He was my dad. If he wasn't mentally ill, then he sure as hell should have tried harder."

"I don't know why you do this, but you have always overdramatized things." Erika heaved out a huge sigh as if, once again, Saylor had badgered her to the point of exhaustion.

"I overdramatize things?" Saylor heard her own heartbeat, a loud echo inside her head. "How about that you've always been blinded by the men in your life? That you've always let them come first before your own daughter?" Saylor's stomach tightened, a strange mix of relief and dread swirling in her gut. Finally, she was confronting her mother. But what, ultimately, was to come of it? Erika's eyes watered, but all Saylor wanted to do was shake her.

"Your memories are convoluted," Erika said, her voice cracking as if she was having a hard time believing herself. "Yes, your father had his issues, but he wasn't half the cruel, awful man you like to think he was. He was just complicated."

And you are as lost as lost can be. Saylor bit her lip; the words had just slammed into her mind without any conscious thought. She searched her mother's face for any kind of clue, praying that her thoughts had not escaped.

"What is wrong with you?" Erika asked.

"What is wrong with me?" Saylor's heart raced even faster. "What do you mean?"

"You were staring at me with the oddest expression. Are you on meds?"

Saylor squeezed her eyes shut for a moment. "No, Mom, I'm not taking any medication." Then it came again: *Lost, lost, lost...* "I just don't feel well..." She stood on shaky legs, and feeling as if she really might become sick, ran into the living room.

Her mother called after her, "Saylor, there *is* something wrong with you. Why are you being so strange?"

Saylor couldn't answer, the nausea making her feel as if she'd lose everything in her stomach if she dared utter a word. She pressed her forehead against the window, wondering how her mother could have plastered down reality. Did Erika love Simon so much that she couldn't allow herself to see how sick he was?

Saylor backed away from the glass and stared at the wall of fog, which obscured both ocean and sky in an unrelenting realm of flat gray. Now that she knew about her grandmother's probable mental illness, she wondered if not only was her father doomed, but herself as well...and what did this mean for Devin and Brooke? She hoped that genetics weren't as strong as she feared. But when she heard her mother slamming one of the kitchen cabinets, she knew without a doubt that Erika's ongoing denial and claims that her own daughter's memories weren't real had contributed to her anxiety. No wonder she had trouble trusting her own mind.

She thought of Billy and what he had remembered. How she needed to see him again, hear what had happened to *him*, be able to share with each other whatever memories would help. Compared to the maddening line of communication with her own mother—the one person in the world who she should be able to turn to—rootless, wounded Billy understood.

"Saylor!" Her mother called from the kitchen. "Stop acting so silly and come finish your tea." When Saylor refrained from answering, Erika stalked into the living room. "You just need some more tea," she said, her gaze less severe. "Come back into the kitchen."

Saylor followed, swallowing down the lump of frustration, hurt, and anger.

After scanning the empty parking lot, Saylor ventured under the pier. But this time, there were no smoke trails from a cigarette, no elbows jutting out from a piling, just damp, cold sand and a rising tide.

She listened to the far-off call of a gull, not knowing what to do next. She was too exhausted to make the trip back home tonight, and the thought of staying at her mother's seemed to magnify everything else that felt stuck and wrong with her life. Now hearing the gull's cry overhead, she made her way to the topside of the pier. Holding back tears, she reached for her cell. As she waited for Lucy to pick up, she stepped over the wooden planks and breathed in the odor of gutted fish and sea.

As soon as Lucy answered, Saylor let out a sigh of relief. "Thanks for picking up." She strolled over to the side of the pier so that the random passerby wouldn't overhear their conversation.

"So," Lucy said, "did you survive Thanksgiving?" She chuckled. "I guess you did or you wouldn't be calling."

Saylor smiled into the phone. Only Lucy could immediately break up the gloom. "Oh, I survived—but now I'm visiting my mom—"

"You're visiting your mom?"

Saylor knew that Lucy was shaking her head at that very moment. "She seemed down...and I felt guilty that she was alone, but what I need to talk about is what she shared about my Grandma Rosa—"

"But your grandma died a long time ago."

"She did, Lucy...but my mom finally told me about how totally out-there she was—she actually believed that my poor Uncle Silvio was possessed as a kid, and thought that she could somehow get rid of whatever demon was inside him by stuffing him with food." Shivering, Saylor pulled the hood of her sweatshirt over her head, hoping that Lucy wouldn't make a joke out of it.

"That is one of the most insane things I've ever heard..." Lucy lowered her voice, "He was the one who committed suicide, wasn't he?"

"He was." Saylor ambled over to the pier's railing and stared at the gray-blue water below.

All of a sudden, Lucy laughed, which made Saylor cringe. "What about Simon?" Lucy asked. "If she thought Silvio was possessed, then she surely must have known your dad was!"

"Very funny." Saylor's stomach tightened. Lucy meant well—and, yes, she appreciated—even liked—her friend's snarky humor, but sometimes it was too much. Saylor took a deep inhale, and continued on, "According to my mom, she didn't think Simon was possessed. She *just* hated him. Does explain a lot, though, about why my dad had so many problems—"

"Don't start making excuses for the man." Lucy paused. Saylor waited, knowing what was coming next. "There's no excuse for the way he treated you," Lucy declared as she had so many times before.

"I know," Saylor said, sensing Lucy's frustration. "But I still feel sorry he had to grow up that way." A long silence filled Saylor's ear. It was time to change subjects. "So, how was Thanksgiving at your sister's?"

Without missing a beat, Lucy dived in. "Same old, same old: her husband eyeballed me all night, her three kids were cute but annoying, and all she did was complain about how old she's looking while making cutting remarks about how young I dress."

"Sounds stressful," Saylor said, laughing. "Maybe we should trade families next year. I could go to your sister's and you can hang out with my relatives. I bet we could put them in their places." *And...*Saylor thought, *we wouldn't be triggered because there'd be no history, no ongoing resentments that could fray the moment.*

"Not a bad idea..." Lucy made an exaggerated smacking of lips sound. "I'm just getting over it all by lounging around in Felix the Cat pajamas and eating pumpkin pie leftovers, and you're getting over yours by...*hanging out with Erika?*

"You have a point." Saylor straightened her back. Next time, she'd think it through before succumbing to the trying-to-please-Erika knee-jerk reaction. "Though, I'm already taking a break on the pier."

"Don't tell me: Even though Erika chose to be alone, she still made you feel guilty, so now that you made the trek down there to visit, you already need to get away from her."

"I *did* miss her." Saylor frowned. It was actually true. She did miss her mother on Thanksgiving—or at least, she missed the thought of having her mother there. "I thought it'd be nice to connect with her after feeling so depressed last night with Brian's family, but it just turned into another fight."

"Oh my, you're already taking a long walk on a short pier." Lucy began to hum the tune to the song, "Crazy."

"It does feel that way." Saylor leaned her back against the railing and watched a pelican waddle ahead, surveying two fishermen on opposite sides from one another as if he were mayor.

"I wish..." Lucy said, her voice taking on a more serious tone, "...that you didn't let her affect you so much."

Saylor stepped away from the railing and continued walking toward the end of the pier. "The irrational stuff really rears its ugly head more often when I'm around her."

"That's sad. Moms are supposed to be our refuge." Lucy's sigh echoed into the phone. "Even though my mom was quite the drinker, at least she was nice to me."

Saylor didn't dare mention all the times Lucy had called her complaining about what a selfish wreck her mother, Irene, was. She was dead now—what good would it do? Besides, Irene had been Lucy's mom—for better or for worse, she'd always be Lucy's mom. "You must miss her even more during the holidays."

"Holidays are the worst." Lucy paused, and just when Saylor was going to fill the silence, Lucy cleared her throat. "But enough about that—what did you and Erika fight about?"

"She called me overdramatic again." Saylor clenched her teeth, wondering if it were true. "Do you think she's right?"

"Your mom said that whenever you tried to stand up for yourself. Remember when she wanted to throw you a huge sweet sixteen party, and you said that you'd rather just go out to pizza and a movie with a couple of friends, and then she blew up saying how silly and overdramatic you were for refusing to have a party?" Lucy chortled. "As if *not* wanting a big party is being overdramatic—when it's actually quite the opposite."

"I remember that day..." Saylor pressed a hand against her throat. Lucy was right; Erika did turn things around whenever she dared to stand up for herself. Why had she not seen that before? As if searching for an answer, she looked toward the end of the pier, and saw a man in a wheelchair, his back to her as he overlooked the water. She stepped up her pace, hoping it was Wex.

"She really knew how to head-trip you." Lucy munched on what Saylor guessed was her second—maybe even third—piece of pie. The way Lucy managed to stay so lean while eating whatever she wanted—whenever she wanted—was both charming and annoying. "I guess," Lucy continued, "you're still letting her do it."

"I'm *not* letting her do anything, Lucy." Even as the words left her mouth, though, Saylor wondered if she was. "Anyway, I don't think she means to *head-trip* me...she just wants everything to be just so—"

"So much so that she's mean to you?" Lucy's voice had grown sharp, accusatory, even. "I don't know why you even put up with her anymore."

Saylor stopped in her tracks and breathed in the damp air. Even though Lucy was usually spot-on, the bossy attitude and black and white thinking made her wonder about Lucy's own triggers. No matter how close they were, no matter how much her best friend understood, Saylor reminded herself that no one person had all the answers. "Lucy, she's in her seventies now, not to mention...she *is* my mom. I can't just write her out of my life. Besides, we did kind of make-up after our fight." Saylor kept her eye on the man in the wheelchair, a figure of wound-up tension who was still staring out to sea

"All I can say..." Lucy said, interrupting her thoughts, "...is that you'd be a lot better off if you put up more boundaries."

Saylor nodded, even though Lucy couldn't see. "I get it," she said, eyeing the man, who she was now sure was Wex. She could tell by the straight black hair jutting out from under the faded baseball cap and the narrow shoulders, alert and determined-looking, even at a distance.

"Don't be pissed off, Say" Lucy said, her voice softening. "I just want you to realize you have choices."

"I'm not mad, Lucy—I know you're right." Wex turned and looked at her. She wasn't sure what his blank-faced expression meant. Without hesitation, though, she walked toward him.

"So," Lucy demanded, "what are you going to do about it?"

Saylor kept her gaze on Wex. "Sorry, but I'll have to call you back—I just ran into an old friend." She hit the end button before Lucy could ask who it was and continued toward Wex. When she was about ten feet away from him, he gave her a two-fingered salute from the rim of his baseball cap, and even though his face remained solemn, she sensed it was okay to approach.

"You still looking for Billy?" His eyes felt as if they were burning into her. She opened her mouth to answer, but he held up a hand. "No, you don't need to tell me. You haven't found him, have you?"

Saylor ducked her head. Why did she feel so nervous around this man—and so inept? "The only time I went looking for him since I last saw you..." she began to answer, hearing a brittle crack in her own voice, "...was just now under the pier—and he wasn't there." She bit her lip, studying the raised burn scars running down the undersides of both his arms. She wondered how he got them, how long they'd been there, and if they were still painful to the touch. "You haven't seen him?"

"No, but the guys tell me he's doing okay—"

"Where did they see him?"

He grimaced. "Slow down, lady."

"I'm just wondering if he might still be there." She forced herself to hold his gaze, even though his eyes had narrowed.

"You talk too fast—and you ask too many questions." He wiped his brow. "It gives me a God damn headache."

"I'm sorry," she said, taking a step back.

Wex shook his head. "You shouldn't apologize when someone's being rude to you." He finally smiled. "I won't bite, you know." He turned his attention back on the ocean. "Anyway, he'll be back. He just needs time."

Right at the horizon, a line of open sky glowed through the grayness. Saylor widened her eyes to the burst of approaching sunset lighting through the band of leaden atmosphere. "How do you know he'll be back?" Then, realizing she asked another question, she pressed her hand to her mouth.

But he acted as if he hadn't noticed and slowly answered, his tone calm and even. "Just a hunch. I know I blamed you at first, thinking it was something you said—or that he was running away from seeing someone from his old life. But now I'm guessing he just needs time to figure out what he's doing next."

"How'd you guess that?"

"I put myself in his shoes. I get it."

"But what do you mean: 'What he's doing next?'"

"Look," Wex said, pointing to the horizon, "turning out to be an actual sunset after this shit-gray day."

"It has been..." Saylor said, "a really murky kind of fog, hasn't it?"

He turned to her and paused, then squinted in a way that made Saylor wonder if he was trying to figure her out. "If you don't mind me asking; you're a nice lady with, what I'm guessing is, everything you need. Why, I wonder, are your eyes so damn sad?"

"My eyes are sad?" Taken aback by his scrutiny, she looked away.

"So, what is it?" he asked.

He was just as inquisitive as she was, just as needy for the truth. Was that why he made her so nervous? "What are you asking?"

"It's simple...why are you sad?" He cocked his head, a look of concern etched on his weather-beaten face.

She studied him, trying to read what lay behind his expression and words—but only saw a person who cared enough to ask. She nodded. "Remember how the last time I saw you—you called me crazy?"

"I didn't mean," he said, trying to cover up a smile, "that you were *literally* crazy."

"I know, Wex." She clasped her hands together. "But in my own way, I am. I know how lucky I am to have everything I have, yet I'm still afraid. I battle fears, Wex, that don't make any sense." She grinned. "That's why I am kind of crazy."

Staring at her, Wex didn't say anything at first, and Saylor worried that she had somehow offended him. "You really are okay, you know that?" He nodded his head in what looked to be approval.

"So are you," she said, relieved. After that, he began to laugh, and she did too.

CHAPTER FIFTEEN

"Mom?" Saylor entered Erika's unanswered front door. "You home?" She called out again, and then several times more. Why didn't her mother answer? Saylor calculated that she had only been at the pier for an hour at the most—hopefully not long enough to make her mother so mad that she had left. Saylor shuffled through the darkened hallway to the kitchen and then living room, turning on lights as she went. Finally, she paused in front of her mother's bedroom. The door was open a crack, but she didn't see any light. Then she heard her mother whispering to someone and caught the last part of what Erika said before she hung up her phone: "Philip, I need to see you as soon as she leaves. I miss you fiercely."

Annoyed by how relieved she felt about her mother actually being home, Saylor pretended she hadn't heard anything and knocked on the side of the door. "Mom? You in there?" She had worried that Erika might have decided to punish her by leaving the house and going off to an early dinner by herself as she'd done in the past. Yet beyond today's initial frustration, Saylor had felt scared that something bad had happened to her mother, something that would have been her fault because they'd fought. Now that she knew Erika was okay, all the disappointment and guilt turned into the need to make things right.

"I was just taking a nap," her mother's voice hesitant—Saylor guessed—due to the fact that she couldn't be sure if Saylor had heard her talking to Philip or not.

In the most cheerful tone she could muster, Saylor chirped, "Can I take you to dinner?"

When Erika didn't answer, Saylor tapped the door again. "Mom, I'd like to take you out for a nice dinner. Maybe at that fancy restaurant you had wanted to go to before?" She tried to make her voice sound happy and light, acting as if they'd been getting along, acting as if their relationship was as loving and smooth as the sentiments on a Mother's Day card.

"I'm very tired," Erika slowly replied. "Please just open yourself a can of soup. I have several in the cupboard."

Saylor paused. If she said what she wanted to, she'd run the risk of her mother turning things around. Damn it, though, why the hell should she worry how her mother would react? No matter what, Erika was going to find fault with her. Saylor pushed back her shoulders and inhaled deeply. "Mom, I drove all the way down here to see you, even though I was looking forward to hanging out with the family this weekend. So, no, I don't want to sit alone in your kitchen and eat canned soup. I'm sure you can pull the energy together for me to take you out to dinner." Saylor now exhaled, not knowing what to expect. She'd never been this assertive with Erika. It was both liberating—and frightening.

Finally, Erika opened the door wearing her pink bathrobe. Even though she still had a full face of make-up, Saylor noticed how red the rims of her eyes were and hoped that it wasn't from crying. "What am I, if I am not your family?" Erika questioned her, her face so sorrowful that Saylor's heart hurt.

"You know I didn't mean it that way, Mom—"

Erika shook her head. "I really am not up for it tonight."

"Please, let me take you out to dinner." Saylor inwardly winced at the desperation in her voice.

After a long, hard stare, Erika finally answered, "If it means that much to you, Saylor..."

The host already knew her mother and seated them at a quiet table—but one where Erika could still be seen. Saylor settled on the padded seat, noting the old-school elegance of the restaurant's dark interior with its linen tablecloths and cream-colored candles flickering inside hurricane glass holders.

"I can see why you like it here." Saylor opened the leather-bound menu, determined to get along with her mother. "What's your favorite dish?"

"The shrimp cocktail is quite fresh. Or you may want to try their sea bass and request steamed vegetables instead of the wild rice; it tastes like it's drenched in butter." Erika gave her the first smile of the day.

"I'm glad you're feeling better," Saylor said without thinking.

Erika's mouth puckered into what Saylor used to picture as her mother's soured-milk expression. "There wasn't anything wrong with me before. Just because I told you I took a nap—doesn't mean I was feeling ill."

"I wasn't even thinking of your nap." Saylor wondered how she went wrong again. "I was referring to you saying that you were too tired to go out—and now you seem to have gotten your energy back." Saylor flashed her mother the most benign smile she could, hoping to put her at ease, wishing that *she* could feel at ease.

Erika sniffed. Before Saylor could say anything more, a busboy showed up with a basket of sourdough rolls and whipped butter.

"We don't need any, thank you," Erika said in her crisp, curt way that made Saylor cringe.

Before he could whisk it away, Saylor tapped his forearm. "You can put it on my side of the table." She gave him an apologetic smile, and he nodded back with professional neutrality.

"Honestly, Mom, Dad's gone." Saylor grabbed a roll and buttered it. "He's been gone for decades now. It's safe for you to eat those *forbidden foods* every now and then."

"You have to stop this, Saylor. You're not only wallowing in the past, but it's a false past full of things that you are exaggerating beyond recognition."

Saylor chewed her roll. Even if she did remember things correctly—why *did* she bring up the past? And why did she so often focus on the bad recollections and not the good?

Suddenly ravenous, she slathered on even more butter and proceeded to devour the rest of the roll, remembering how Erika used to take her out for Chinese food when she was little, while Simon was away on his many business trips. In a low secretive voice, her mother would order the forbidden sweet and sour chicken and fried egg rolls—dishes that the two of them could only indulge in when he was gone. Although Erika always made sure not to eat too much, she still seemed to enjoy herself more than she did now. Seemed, sometimes, to act so much softer, as well. Saylor recalled how they'd come home, and Erika would let her pick out a picture book. Nestled against Erika's side, Saylor had been so comforted by the ebb and flow of her mother's gentle story-telling voice that she'd fall asleep before the last page was turned. What a confusing mother Erika had been: harsh and judgmental one day, tender and kind the next.

Saylor now reached for her mother's hand. "Mom, I do have lots of good memories about you. I'm sorry I don't mention them more often."

Erika squeezed Saylor's hand back, and, for a moment, an unguarded flash of love softened her mother's face. But then fear flickered in her eyes, and all too quickly, she withdrew her hand. "I am tired." She glanced at her watch. "I'd like to get home early. Let's figure out what we want to order before the waiter comes back."

Slumping in her seat, Saylor nodded. "Of course, Mom."

They studied the menus, and Saylor peeked at Erika's gaunt, yet elegantly beautiful face. What a puzzle her mother was and what a confusing maze of mother-daughter relationship she still had to navigate. But it couldn't *all* be Erika's fault—she had to take responsibility, too. And maybe part of that responsibility was to acknowledge the happier times. Yet just as she decided to start right here and now, she glanced at the menu's signature steak section and remembered a night when she was six years old. It had been one of the rare occasions when her father had taken them out for dinner. At the red-carpeted steakhouse, Saylor sat at the edge of the banquette, catching the cruelty in her father's profile. He glared at a family waiting to be seated as if he were a hawk eyeing its prey. The parents were obese. The father's close-set eyes and overbite made him look like an overstuffed rat, while the mother, with her immense white face, resembled Humpty Dumpty. Their little girl, who was about Saylor's age, had inherited both her parent's physical attributes. Saylor remembered the dread. Would her father purposely blurt out something cruel? She guessed that he would. And sure enough, Simon put his hands behind his head, leaned back, and sneered. In a voice loud enough for the other family to hear, he announced, "There ought to be a law against ugly people having children." Although Saylor had heard him say this line plenty of times before, she still recoiled in embarrassment, still wanted to disappear under the stiff white tablecloth.

But she remained stuck, a girl too scared to rebel, a girl too young to flee. Her stomach in knots, she watched the father from the other family stare at Simon, his lips so tight they had turned white. Saylor caught the hurt in the man's eyes. Then she noticed Simon's smirk while the mother said to her teary-eyed daughter, "No, honey, he's not talking about us. He's making a mean joke about someone else." The woman distracted her daughter by letting her reach for a mint, and then glared at Simon, her fists clenched at her sides. For a moment, Saylor thought the woman might come over and sock him in the face and almost hoped she would. But the family was led away by the hostess and seated at a different section. Simon went back to cutting his sirloin into small, dried-out pieces, which he then chewed with grim and methodical precision.

She had studied her jagged fingernails, wondering how her mother could sit there and trill on about how wonderful her veal tasted as if she hadn't heard a thing. Saylor had to stifle the urge to yell at her but instead said nothing, feeling trapped between her parent's different kinds of wrongdoing.

"I'm going to have the shrimp cocktail," Erika now chirped, bringing Saylor back to the present. "What have you decided on?"

"I'm not sure yet." Saylor wouldn't look at her mother. She knew it didn't make sense, but she still felt more upset with her than she had with her father. Although he was the one who had been cruel and inappropriate, it was her mother who made her feel as if she would explode.

"Why don't you just order the bass with vegetables, then?"

"Because, Mom..." Saylor sipped some water, trying to keep her cool. "Because I don't want the bass." She looked at the menu again. "The eggplant lasagna looks good, though—"

"Are you sure, Saylor? It is awfully rich."

Before Saylor could answer, a young, somber-faced waiter strode up to their table. He bowed slightly after greeting her mother. What the hell was it about Erika that caused people to act so damn deferential? Erika nodded to him as if she was giving him permission to speak.

Saylor let Erika order her shrimp cocktail first, and then asked for eggplant lasagna, ignoring Erika's tongue clicking.

For the rest of the meal, she forced herself to engage in small talk and half-listened to her mother's gossip, all the while inwardly obsessing about the Billy who'd been there for her from the past and the one that she hoped to help in the future.

Back at her mother's house, Saylor sat in the darkened living room. Erika had whisked out her cell as soon as they got in, retreating into her bedroom like a secretive teenager. Saylor stared out the window, barely making out the sheen of nighttime ocean.

Then with a strange sense of calm, she grabbed her keys and left. She knew it was a long shot because Wex had just told her that Billy hadn't been around, but remembered Billy saying something about how he liked it better at night, as if being out in the open was somehow safer then. Maybe he hung around there after sunset, and for whatever reason, Wex still felt the need to protect Billy's whereabouts.

With hands clenched around the steering wheel, she drove toward Breakers Cove Beach. When she got there, the unlit lot was empty. She stood watching sparks from a beach bonfire sail upward then burn out in midflight. Two people huddled around the fire and one person was leaning back on something, all three faces glowing in the light. Saylor walked toward them and before she stepped onto the sand, saw the empty wheelchair.

Wex was the first to notice her. "Hello there." He motioned her over with a wave of hand. His back propped up against a large log with an indented hole dug in for him to sit and mounds of sand under the crook of his knees, Saylor could see that his friends knew how to take care of him. She looked over at the same two young men that she'd seen the first time she'd met him and imagined them carrying him across the beach in a joined-hand kind of forearm chair. "Join us," Wex said, grinning.

Saylor edged toward them, and then sat between Wex and the guy with the baseball cap. She took off her tennis shoes, pushing her feet into the layer of cool sand. "This is nice," she said, meaning it. She breathed in the smell of burning driftwood, enjoying the warmth on her face, and then looked toward the pier.

"No, he's not back yet," Wex said, shaking his head. "Just like I told you earlier today."

"I thought that maybe he'd be around at night."

"He's good, ma'am," said the guy next to her. "He'll be back when he's ready."

Saylor nodded, listening to the crackle of burning driftwood and the muffled sound of waves rolling in. "I'm Saylor, by the way."

He pulled off his hat and ran his fingers through sandy brown hair. "I'm Dustin." He cocked his head toward the even younger guy next to him. "And this is Jack." Jack gave her a fleeting smile and then stared at the fire as he scratched his scraggly beard. "He doesn't like to talk," Dustin said.

"That's okay with me." Saylor nodded as Wex lifted a bottle to his lips.

"You want some?" Wex tilted his head, studying her. "It's Sailor Jerry Rum."

"Sailor Jerry?" Saylor smiled, feeling an uncustomary sense of ease. "With a name like that, I have to try some."

She reached for the hula-girl labeled bottle and sniffed the opening, then held her head back, swallowing down the rum's spicy burn. "That's good." She passed the bottle to Dustin.

Wex eyed her. "You said before you have fears that don't make any sense. What are they?"

Taken aback by Wex's sudden probing, Saylor cleared her throat.

"Come on," Wex prodded, "we won't judge you...I just want to understand your pull toward Billy."

"My pull towards Billy?" Saylor's mouth went dry.

Wex looked her straight in the eye. "I know you're old friends, but I'm feeling like there's something deeper there, something that connects you two...?"

Saylor slowly nodded. "I am connected to him." She held back unexpected tears, wishing she could envelope Billy in her arms, wishing she could let him know that everything would be okay. "He's one of the kindest people I've ever known."

Dustin and Jack nodded in unison. "That's our Billy," Dustin said.

"So," Wex pressed his hands together. "Tell us about your fears?"

She shrugged, embarrassed. "They *really* don't make sense." She looked at all three men, thinking that Dustin and Jack were barely in their twenties and wondering what hardships lead them here. Surely, they all had endured too much to be able to stomach her neurosis. "I don't think you guys want to hear a middle-aged woman go on about her ridiculous fears."

"I do," Jack blurted out, his voice high and squeaky sounding as if he was just emerging from puberty.

Dustin let out a sharp whistle and exchanged wide-eyed looks of disbelief with Wex. "Jack, how come you've never said anything before?"

Jack shrugged, but didn't utter a word.

Dustin turned to Saylor. "You better answer the man."

"It's silly..." Saylor smiled at Jack.

"Please," Jack said, quietly this time. So quietly, she wasn't sure he'd even spoken again. "I want to hear," he whispered.

"Okay." She motioned for them to pass the bottle back to her and took another sip, readying herself. "I'm afraid..." she ventured, watching them watch her, "I'm afraid that I'll blurt out crazy, horrible stuff without meaning to." She exhaled. It was done. Now, these three virtual strangers held her irrational fear in their hands, could throw it back in her face, could make her want to climb back in her car and never look for Billy again.

Wex let out a whoop of a laugh. "Sweetheart, that's a good one. I think you should run with it."

Perplexed—but also relieved, she gave him an incredulous stare. "What do you mean?"

Both Dustin and Jack watched him, nodding in solemn agreement as if whatever he was about to say would be something she'd better listen to, something they all could learn from.

Wex squinted at the fire. "There's a power in shouting out anything that comes into your mind," he announced loudly as if to a large audience. "It makes other people scared."

"That's true," Dustin said, grinning. "I've seen plenty of crazy dudes do it, and I'll tell you: people leave them alone." He winked at Saylor. Without a word more, he then tilted his head back and howled.

Jack laughed and joined in, and then Wex did too. Saylor took in the three men's upturned faces, their coyote calls sounding remarkably like the real thing. She threw her head back, but hesitated. What was she doing? And how would this help?

"You can do it, Saylor," Wex said as if reading her thoughts. "Just go for it."

She bit her lip. *Why not*, she thought. *Why the hell not*? She grinned, tossed her head back again, and then howled. Loud and strong and fierce. Tears streamed down her face, but she didn't care, didn't even try to hold them back. Then without even thinking about it, she shouted out all the swear words that popped into her head. The men continued to accompany her, intermittent high and low baying that seemed to make a song out of her crazy cursing.

Moments later, as if there was an invisible conductor signaling an end to their cacophony, all four of them abruptly stopped. In the red-orange light of the dwindling flames, they looked at each other and burst out laughing. Next to that dying bonfire with the three homeless men by her side, Saylor had never felt so free.

CHAPTER SIXTEEN

The next morning Saylor opened the bedroom door and listened; she didn't hear Erika's usual early morning clattering in the kitchen. Grateful to be alone, Saylor crept out and made coffee in such a quietly measured way that she had to remind herself to breathe. She exhaled with relief that Erika hadn't emerged from her room yet. Seated in the living room, she allowed herself to do nothing else but sip from her mug and gaze at the ocean. She smiled at the thought of howling around the bonfire last night with Wex, Dustin, and Jack. She was just about to go into the kitchen to pour more coffee and indulge in some of her mother's Royal Dansk cookies when Erika marched into the living room, pink robe tied so tight around her waist that it looked painful.

"What are you doing up so early?" Erika's mouth tightened in irritation. Saylor got the distinct feeling that her mother didn't like being caught without her armor of make-up—even if it was by her own daughter.

"I'm sorry." Saylor got off the couch and stood. "I was just about to brush my teeth." She wasn't about to admit that what she really was going to do was start her morning off with cookies. Or, of course, where she'd been the night before. Saylor fidgeted her weight from one leg to another as she fought back the urge to flee. The flush of red on Erika's face made her nervous, the old fisherman's saying popping into her mind: Red sky at night, sailor's delight; red sky in morning, sailor be warning.

Ducking her head, Saylor began her retreat to the bathroom. But before she had made it half-way across the room, Erika cleared her throat.

"Come back here, Saylor."

With a sinking heart, Saylor turned around. "What is it?"

"We need to talk." Erika was perched on the edge of the couch, too rigid and alert for having just gotten up.

"What about?" Saylor sat back down on the opposite sofa, wishing that she had snuck more coffee and some cookies to her bedroom before her mother had emerged.

"I'm tired," Erika said, her voice as dry and prickly as a tumbleweed, "of being your whipping boy."

Saylor gasped. "Your whipping boy? What are you talking about?" Her mother's language could be so over-the-top, especially for someone so quick to accuse others of being overdramatic. And, how in the world, was her mother in any way, shape, or form, her *whipping boy*?

"It's quite obvious." Erika shook her head as if Saylor was a mere child. "First, you manipulate me to go out when I really didn't want to. And then after we get home, you disappear."

Saylor balled her hands into fists, trying not to scratch her neck. But the itch was too intense, too hot and angry to ignore. She scraped her nails against the raised edges of her rash. "Mom—"

"Don't try to apologize. It's too late." Erika narrowed her eyes. "I know you don't like me...in fact, I'm not so sure you even love me."

Saylor pinched her lips to keep them from trembling. "I love you, Mom—"

"But I know you don't like me." Erika's face flushed a darker red.

Saylor pressed her palms against her eyes. How did her mother expect her to like her when she acted the way she did? Sighing, Saylor let her hands drop to her lap. "I want to get along with you, Mom. Really, I do." Was there anything she could say or do to make this right? Anything that would stop her mother's downward spiral?

Erika stood. "You've never liked me, Saylor." Her head drooped and eyes watered, a sorrowful woman who looked as if she'd been deeply wounded—a wound, she was claiming, that was caused by her own daughter. "Even when you were a little—I could tell you didn't."

Saylor opened her mouth to speak, to let her mother know that it wasn't true, but Erika held up a hand. "I cannot bear this any longer. It hurts my heart."

"Please, Mom." Saylor bolted from the couch and rushed to her. Hoping to convince her that she cared, that above all else, she did, indeed, love her, Saylor tried to hug her. But Erika's arms remained at her sides. "Please, let's make up," Saylor pleaded. "I love you—and I like you." Saylor's own heart ached. She hadn't meant to hurt her mother, didn't even understand what had set her off.

"Please stop," Erika said, "I want to be alone now." She looked past Saylor as if Saylor had suddenly become invisible. "Go ahead and get back to your family."

"Let's please work this out." Saylor tried to grab her mother's hand, but Erika withdrew. Without a backward glance, her mother stalked off and slammed her bedroom door behind her.

Standing in the middle of her mother's living room, Saylor held a hand across her throat, holding back rage, pushing down hurt. She didn't think she'd done anything wrong, but guilt still burrowed inside her chest, still made her wish that she could have found the right words that would have brought Erika back. Still made her want to push her mother's door open, fall on her knees, and apologize all over again.

And even though she knew it wouldn't help, she still walked up to her mother's door and knocked. "I'm sorry, Mom." She waited. But, no answer. Only the sharp hush of blame.

The same old frustration and hurt and anger biting her heels, Saylor turned away and went back to her room. What else could she do? As quickly as possible, she threw her clothes in the duffel bag, brushed her teeth and made her bed, hoping Erika would get over this sooner rather than later, but at the same time afraid: what if this really was it?

At the front door, Saylor paused. She *had* to try again. She dropped her bag and ran back to her mother's bedroom. Pounded on the door with all her might. Finally, Erika opened it without a word. Saylor entered her room and then stood as her mother stared past her with arms crossed.

"I'm sorry, Mom. I just want to get along, and I feel so bad that it's come to this." The air congealed with Erika's continued silence. Saylor wasn't surprised, knowing her mother's pattern of having to punish her before they could make any kind of amends. Not knowing what else to say, she looked at her own reflection in the mirror above her mother's vanity. *I look like Medusa,* Saylor thought, with *all these snaky-looking curls. Hell, I feel like Medusa.*

She was about to make a joke of it. Maybe it would pull Erika out of her mood. But when she caught her mother's glare, she froze. Lowering her gaze as quickly as she could, Saylor fought back a sudden nausea. In that one flash of a moment, she saw something that she had never believed before—despite

Lucy having had commented on it years ago: Her mother was jealous of her. She wasn't sure how she knew this from just one look, but there it was—the air so thick with it that Saylor could almost taste its bitterness brewing in the space between them.

Remaining behind her wall of silence, Erika turned away. Saylor held back from crying. Slowly, she left her mother's room, gently closed her door. Heading to the kitchen, she concentrated on finally tying her hair back and heard herself whisper the words: "She *is* jealous." Saylor gasped, surprised she had uttered out loud what she was thinking. Just a month ago, she would have broken into a cold sweat if she heard herself say something without meaning to. Then she smiled, thinking about how great it had felt to yell obscenities into the night sky. Telling herself that Erika would come around in a couple of days, she poured herself more coffee and helped herself to a stack of cookies. She took her time sipping and nibbling while vacantly staring out the kitchen window.

Still hungry, she knew she needed something more substantial besides sugar and caffeine. She went to the fridge, thinking that she'd cut up a grapefruit and toast some whole wheat bread—foods her mother always made sure to keep stocked in her refrigerator's top shelf. Before Saylor pulled the handle, something made her pause. So used to the photo her mother had displayed all these years under the yellow and black bumblebee magnet, Saylor never took notice of it. She leaned forward, taking in the picture as she had never really done before. It had been part of Saylor's wedding day photographs. Erika had insisted that the photographer take several mother and daughter shots minutes before the ceremony was to begin. Saylor had been annoyed and nervous, but of course, didn't argue. Smiling, she now studied her younger, smoother self, who was squeezed into a wedding dress with monstrous puffed sleeves and enormous shoulder pads.

But when she gazed at her mother's image, her face fell. Standing next to Saylor, Erika's hand was clenched on her own forearm while her other hand was drawn in a fist. Her smile looked forced and her eyes did not face the camera. Instead, she looked sideways at Saylor, a slicing kind of rivalry narrowing her gaze. Saylor's breath caught. Why had she never noticed her mother's jealousy before? Even when Lucy had commented on it, she still didn't take it in. She stared at the picture and thought about the dinner party she had thrown years ago for Erika's birthday. Afterward, Lucy had told her how she had noticed Erika eyeing Saylor with such a "dark envy" that it took her aback. At the time, Saylor just thought it was because Erika was mad at something Saylor had said or done. Now, she thought, Lucy was right. How odd. It wasn't as if she was wealthy, glamorous or beautiful—traits she knew made her mother envious of other women. And even if she were any or all these things, why would one's own mother be jealous? If anything, a mother should be happy for her daughter's good fortune.

Saylor backed away from the fridge. Her appetite having suddenly vanished, she stowed the cookie tin back in the cabinet and methodically washed her mug, taking her time to rinse out the sudsy green dish soap. Before picking up her bag she paused. She was still reeling with the familiarity of hurt and confusion, but the dead silence inside her mother's house made her feel even more sorry for her. Saylor tapped on her mother's door. "Mom, I'm going now." No answer. "I love you." Still, no answer. Could her mother really be that resolute in her anger? Saylor sighed, turning. She grasped the front door's handle, hesitating. Had she just heard a faint "I love you, too" trailing down the hall? She called again, "Mom?" But now all she heard was the running water of her mother's bath.

By the time she drove away from Erika's house, the midmorning sky had cast an even murkier gray. After several miles, she noticed the fog seemed to be following her, and it grew even denser the farther she traveled. Within half an hour it became so thick that it turned to an annoying drizzle; the in-between stuff that made her wish for real rain and brought on an even thicker depression. Almost everyone in her family of origin suffered from some kind of mental health issue: Grandma Rosa, Uncle Silvio, her father—and, obviously, her mother as well. Saylor sighed. She herself wasn't exactly the paradigm of mental health. And how much could she blame her problems on her parent's behavior—especially if those parents had been tormented by their own mental health conditions? Yet...where was the line between one's struggle with emotional torment and ultimate responsibility as a parent? That was a question, she was sure, that she'd never ask Erika, one that she'd have to answer for herself.

Through the drizzle, Saylor continued to steer with straight-backed concentration. In just another hour or so she'd be home, but it felt too soon. She needed a break between being a daughter and a mother. She needed a break between the two roles she had become so lost in, not to mention, so inept at. So, when the faded sign for Found Hills Café came up, she slowed down. After all these years of wondering about the place, should she finally give it a try? Someone honked behind her, and that was all she needed. She turned onto the exit, rolled down the window, and clicked off the radio, wanting to smell and hear everything that passed by. She wondered about the place: Being miles from any town, who would work there? And with no visible signs of its existence, how long would it take to reach it on this winding road edged through sagebrush? As far as Saylor could tell, there weren't any other buildings. But right after she guessed that it must have been out of business for years now, she came around a bend and saw that it was still open.

Found Hills Café stood with its graying shingles and stone chimney chugging out smoke, looking like a storybook illustration. It sat on an oasis that she never imagined could exist between all the miles of low-lying brush. Shaded by a mini forest of oak trees, a canopy of soft green light filtered from overhead, and yellow hills framed the distance behind it. When she emerged from her car, she heard the sound of a running creek and noticed a hiking trail sign. No wonder a good number of trucks, cars, and motorcycles were parked out front of the small structure. A weak beam of sunlight glimmered through the trees. Through the silhouette of leaves and branches, the sky was clearing.

She walked up to the café's wooden porch and breathed in the welcoming smell of a wood-burning fireplace combined with the breakfast scents of waffles, apple bacon, and coffee. Her stomach growled. She pulled on the screen door's handle and stepped inside. A couple of trucker guys, their wide, beefy backs straining white T-shirts, sat at the counter hunched over plates heaped with bacon and eggs and thick, brown hunks of some kind of homemade looking bread. At the end of the counter sat a lone man with skin the texture of cracked leather. Roosted on the edge of his stool, he looked both comfortable and skittish at the same time, like he enjoyed being there, but his body, tense and alert, was ready to bolt without notice. Saylor couldn't stop watching him; he had the scrappy vibe of a stray cat, while the weakness of his chin made her think of her Uncle Silvio. She glanced away when they locked eyes, embarrassed that he had caught her staring.

She scanned the room, finally noticing just how small the café was. The only thing against the farthest wall was the fireplace and in the middle of the room, just three short picnic-bench style tables stood, with two cramped pinewood booths by the window—and they were all occupied. Groups of bikers, hikers, and horse-folk gulped coffee, wiped up egg yolks with the dark bread, talking and laughing without paying any notice to Saylor. She looked around, trying to figure out if she should wait for a table to clear or sit at the counter. Since no one looked like they were ready to leave any time soon, she started toward the bar stools. The lone man seemed to be waiting for her, and as their eyes met again, his hesitant, yet earnest smile took away some of the meekness from his face. She smiled back and made her way over, settling on the chipped green stool next to him.

He nodded, his gaze darting around like a vigilant animal's, zigzagging from her face to the rest of the room and back to her face, but still appearing as if he was taking everything in. "I hope you don't mind me saying so, but you sure look like someone's put you through the ringer." His words came out in a surprisingly rich baritone, way deeper than she expected from such a reedy man.

At first Saylor wasn't sure how to answer. She hadn't anticipated that big of a voice—or that much of a candid observation from this nervous-looking soul. She turned to him. "You could say that." Then she wondered how this stranger could tell just by looking at her.

He focused his attention back to his mug, the Lipton tea tag hanging cheerfully over the side. "I'm Lenny," he said. "I live right beyond the hills." He pointed out the window and grinned. "You visiting for the day?"

She nodded. "I'm Saylor—and I've seen the highway sign for so long now, that I finally had to check it out."

"Saylor? That's the one of best names I've heard in years," he said. "Maybe the best name I've ever heard." Lenny dipped his head as if he was giving her a sit-down bow, and they shook hands, his callused palm and fingers making Saylor wonder what he did for a living.

"Thanks." Saylor shrugged, bewildered. No one had ever told her they liked her name. "Most people are confused by it, thinking that it's actually the word sailor—like sailor on the sea—but the spelling is really S-a-y-l-o-r." She grabbed one of the laminated menus pinched between an old-fashioned metal holder and sighed, the pent-up tension from the fight with her mother slowly releasing off her shoulders.

Lenny chuckled. "I hope you live up to your name, and you aim to say what's on your mind, then."

If he only knew what her fears were, he'd be laughing a lot harder. "Oh, I'm working on it."

"That's the best you can do." Lenny nodded to a young waitress who had just emerged from the kitchen carrying a load of plates, grinning in her plaid shirt and Lee jeans, the tips of her brown braids grazing her belt loops. *The epitome of a cowgirl*, Saylor thought. As the girl whisked by, she called to Saylor, "I'll be right with you, so be thinking about what looks good."

"I recommend the avocado-mushroom scramble-up," Lenny leaned over. "They've got the same thing in an omelet, but scramble-ups are always better."

Saylor nodded in whole-hearted agreement "That's so true. Omelets are too neat. You always seem to get more of the good stuff in scramble-ups." Although Lenny was different than anyone she had ever met, it seemed as if she had known him forever.

His smile reached to the corners of his eyes, their earth-rich shade so dark that she couldn't see his pupils, a deep, bottomless color that matched the depth of his voice. "You're not the usual little sparrow, are you?"

With an internal cringe, she thought about how she acted with her mother and how much she had kept saying how sorry she was instead of standing up for herself. "What do you mean?"

"What I mean is that you're not going to be satisfied pecking away at the small stuff." He cocked his head as if he himself were a bird. "You've got bigger fish to fry."

"Bigger fish to fry? But is that a good thing?" she asked, smiling, not sure where this guy was going with the bird and fish analogies.

Lenny laughed. "Of course, it is. It's way better than good, it's the greatness of character." He waved his hand toward the room while everyone else ate and talked and laughed as if there were no other world but the one inside the café.

"Everyone you see has pain, of course," he said, his eyes staying more focused on her than before. "But it's what you do with it that counts...and I can just tell from that furrowed brow that you're aiming to fix it."

Before Saylor could answer, the waitress sped past them and popped behind the counter. "Sorry I'm the only one here," she said breathlessly. "And you don't even have a cup of coffee or glass of juice in front of you. What can I do you for?"

"Don't worry, I've had my fill of coffee today." Saylor felt her stomach churn. "I'll just order the avocado-mushroom scramble up with some of that bread." She pointed to the remaining crust on Lenny's plate.

The waitress grinned. "Good choice. That's Lenny's favorite. Our Lenny won't steer you wrong." And then she was off, her tan cowgirl boots clipping against the dilapidated wood floor.

Feeling as if this stranger could somehow see her better than family and friends—even seemed to understand her more than her own mother—she turned to him, gently pressed her hand on his forearm. "You can tell that I want to change?" She exhaled. "But how do I start?"

He threw his head back, raspy laughter escaping his lungs. "You don't think I'm some kind of psychic, do you?"

"No." She laughed with him, trying to make him think that she'd just been kidding. *I'm way too porous*, she thought, *and too gullible*. But, still, she felt a connection, still felt that he offered a wisdom that couldn't be ignored.

"You know what, though?" he asked, without waiting for an answer. "You know how I said that you weren't the usual little sparrow?"

She leaned in, hoping to catch every word. "Yes?"

"You're more like a crow, I'm guessing." He squinted at her. "You like crows?"

"I'm like a crow?" Saylor laughed again. "Most people complain about crows—but they've never bothered me."

"Crows and ravens, pretty lady, are the smartest birds on this earth, not to mention, loyal, funny, and highly communicative. They've learned to adapt to our crazy world. But, still, they remain wary, intelligent enough not to trust anyone who has ever tried to harm them." He tapped his temple with two fingers. "It's been researched they're even able to teach their young to stay away from any human who ever tried to shoot them—and somehow they're able to pass that knowledge from generation to generation." He sipped his tea, scanning the room. "I think their communication skills are better than a lot of humans I know."

Saylor smiled. The man was right. "Do you study birds for a living?"

"That would be a dream job, but no. I just respect the misjudged creatures of this world that most people don't take a liking to. I've got a stack of books on all sorts of animals at home, especially the corvids. They're beautiful birds, really." He tucked his head down, looking embarrassed. "Sorry for going on. I have such a big place in my heart for these birds that I forget how I sound."

"It's okay. I actually think crows are kind of cool." Saylor thought about how her neighborhood crows dropped walnuts from the highest tree branches, waiting for them to crack. After noticing this on a walk one day, she always made it a point to crack open what they couldn't and carry it over to the side of the street so that they could eat without the fear of approaching cars. She knew it was silly, but it always made her feel as if she had made one little connection between her world and theirs. Somehow, it always made her feel better.

Lenny grinned. "Have you ever noticed the way the sun makes their black feathers shine blue? And the way they fly, sometimes playing in the wind as if they're tumbling down a wave?" He glanced up to the wood-beamed ceiling as if he could see them flying overhead. "Sometimes I wish I could be up there with them. In the evenings, I watch them flock, gathering in the same direction so they can roost someplace high and safe together."

"They are survivors, aren't they?" Saylor found herself whispering.

"That's what I mean." Lenny tipped back the rest of his tea. "They are survivors. But not only that, they have grace."

"Grace? I've never heard the word grace attributed to crows." Saylor thought how grace was one of those words that actually sounded just like the attributes it was meant to convey: ease and beauty, thankfulness and blessing.

"The grace of crows is the kind of grace that's straightforward and honest," Lenny said, the low bass of his voice reverent-sounding. "It's not the superficial stuff that so many people think makes them look good. It's the steadfast strength to carry on."

"The steadfast strength to carry on," Saylor repeated. "You're right, Lenny; that is grace, isn't it?"

"Damn straight." He nodded to the waitress, who was walking past them with a pot of coffee. "Bella, I got to get back...when you get a chance, I need my bill."

Bella stopped, shaking her head no. "It's on the house. I finally took your advice—and it worked!" She looked over at Saylor, smiling. "This man here is the best advice-giver I know. If he offers any to you, grab it!" Bella tilted her head at Lenny. "The least I can do for you is to comp you one measly breakfast."

"But that was no work at all for me."

Bella smiled as if she didn't hear him and went to refill waiting coffee mugs.

Saylor looked at him. "You seem to have the magic touch, don't you?"

"No magic involved." Holding his hands up, he looked as if he were making sure to convey that there weren't any tricks up his sleeves. "Just understanding." He pulled his wallet out of his back pocket and took out a twenty, slipping it under his plate. "I liked talking with you, Saylor. You're good people."

"Thanks, Lenny. I feel lucky to have met you." She wished she could have talked to him more. She liked this odd man who was so passionate about what he called the misjudged creatures of this world.

"Likewise, darling, likewise." He slid off the stool and stood. He wasn't much taller than she was, Saylor noted—and she was considered short, even for a woman. She knew that it couldn't be easy for a guy and guessed that he had certainly been through his own trials.

"I got a suggestion for you," he said.

"What is it?"

"After you're done with breakfast, you might want to go for a hike before you head on home. The creek is running and there's still a lot of green." He winked. "I think it's way more truthful than any church I've ever seen."

"Thanks. I just might do that." Not exactly life-changing counsel, but it did sound like a nice idea.

Lenny nodded. "You continue on, Saylor—and keep finding people you can trust. Let them understand and let them help." He tapped his temple like he had done earlier when he'd been talking about the crows. "Then you'll see that one day you'll be getting closer to where you want to be." He turned to the door and squared the shoulders of his slight body in such a way that it looked as if he was preparing for something important. After several moments, Saylor heard the roar of a motorcycle.

She stretched under the now-bright dapples of sunlight streaming through oak branches. Her breakfast still warm in her belly, she glanced over at the trailhead. Already it was past twelve-thirty, there was still enough time to hike for a couple of hours and start the drive back before dusk.

She reached the trailhead and smelled the stream's mossy rocks before she could even see water. She quickened her pace, a kind of visual hunger engulfing her as she took in the wild grass and tiny purple wildflowers growing between rocks on the side of the trail, the blanket of oak, aspen, and sycamore trees on either side of her; even the fallen decay of leaves looked beautiful. It was as if she were moving through a work of art, with her tennis shoes' rhythmic thud a steady drumbeat against the trail's compact dirt.

Mesmerized by the momentum, it almost came as a shock when she finally made it to the creek. But as she stood off the path, it became the most natural, comfortable place to be. She remained still. She closed her eyes, feeling a slow breeze on her face and arms, and listened to the sound of traveling water. With the kind of shiver that felt like an electric discharge had released from her body, she opened her eyes, a clear moment of non-thought.

She went to sit on a nearby boulder, pulling off her shoes and socks and rolling up her jeans just under her knees. She jumped down and strode into the creek, the water, an icy rush across her feet and ankles. Pebbles pressed their water-smoothed surfaces against the bottom of her soles. She smiled.

When she heard the rise and fall of voices, Saylor reluctantly walked back to the boulder and shook out her socks before peeling them back on her damp skin. Two young couples passed by and said their hellos. Without hesitation, the women, with the men following, took turns rock-hopping their way across the creek. Saylor watched their sure-footed maneuvers, wondering why she had lost so much of her own self-assurance since the time she'd been a young twenty-something woman. After giving them a good five minutes to get ahead, she hesitantly stepped onto the closest rock, waiting to stabilize both feet on it before continuing to the next. Eventually, she made it to the other side.

The trail wound upward, trees giving way to a lower brush line. From the unrestricted sky, the sun shone full-force. Trickles of sweat rolled down Saylor's back. She stopped, hands on knees and looked up, noticing how the trail's switchbacks lead to a mountain's peak, and even though she was already out of breath and her calves, stone-hard sore, she knew that she would make it. She loved this world of rocks and sun and sky. The earlier world, the foggy, murky one surrounding her mother's house and stalking her up the coast, seemed thousands of miles away. She straightened up, took in a deep breath and continued on. She used to hike Dune Beach's backcountry trails before she had Devin and Brooke. Slowly, but surely, she had lost her sense of adventure, had narrowed her world to home and office. For the last eighteen years, this was all she had been focusing on—except, of course, for the anxiety. *Not good*, she thought. *Not healthy*. And it seemed that the smaller her world had become, the more the fear had expanded.

She peered at the line of yellow hills that she had first noticed behind the café and saw now they were a lot farther away than they had appeared. Hand across brow, she tried to view the highway and then the road that she had taken in, but couldn't see either. She couldn't even see Found Hills Café. She shrugged and continued up. After some time, the trail narrowed so much that she had to look down at her feet to make sure she wasn't too close to the edge. Her only thoughts were how to maneuver the path and how long it would take to get to the top. She continued on this way—hot, determined, focused. Then she saw something that made her heart jump: across the trail about ten feet away was a snake.

Panicked, she froze, not sure if it was just a gopher snake—or could it be a rattler? Mottled brown with a dark, triangle-like pattern covering its scaly body, it was hard to tell. She knew that rattle snakes had more of a diamond shaped head, were thicker and, of course, sported rattlers on their tails. She didn't want to get any closer to try and discern these differences. The snake, looking as if all it was made out of was one long, slimy tail, didn't move, dead-set on soaking up the sun's heat.

Instinct made her back away. She was disappointed in having to turn around, but really, what was she supposed to do? Risk her life just to get to the top? About to backtrack, she shook her head, but heard someone running down the trail.

Feeling foolish, she yelled, "Look out for the snake."

The foot pounding continued without missing a beat, and she had to shout again. "Snake on trail."

"I hear you," yelled a male voice.

The man appeared, red-faced and sweaty. He nodded to her before he slowed down, walking just a few feet away from the snake. After a brief inspection, he jerked his head up, grinned in Saylor's direction. He then jumped over the still-reclined reptile. "Just a gopher. Nothing to worry about," he said, coming toward her.

She edged her body against the mountainside. "Don't you think you got kind of close? What if it had been a rattler?"

He stepped around her and laughed. "Trouble ain't going to bite you unless you provoke it."

He jogged away and she eyed the snake. If only she could view danger with such nonchalance. Then, steeling her shoulders, she decided to continue forward, hoping that the man was right about it being a gopher snake. She pounded her feet as hard as she could while she moved ahead. It didn't budge, so she stomped even harder against the dirt, willing it to leave. And just as she got within a few feet from it, the snake finally slithered off. Relieved, yet also guilty, she stopped. She leaned into the bushes and spotted the snake coiled under a bush. He looked at her and she realized he was scared. Stepping away, she thought about Lenny's fondness for misjudged creatures and felt her eyes sting.

Then, even more determined to make it to the top, she slid her watch around so the timepiece was sitting on the inside of her wrist and began making the trek up again. She wouldn't stop until she was there.

After an indeterminate amount of time, she made it. Her feet planted on a flat boulder, Saylor held her arms up, Rocky Balboa-style and grinned. And then, taking in the jumble of foliage below, she realized how far she had climbed and sat down. The boulder's sundrenched warmth permeated through her jeans and an overwhelming exhaustion overtook her. With face to sun, she laid flat against the rock and fell asleep.

What seemed like hours later, but by the angle of the sun had only been about twenty minutes, a determined-sounding caw woke her. Two crows glided in the sky above, the tips of their wings outstretched like fingers. One of them had several feathers missing from their right wing—a beautiful ragged creature who still soared. Slowly, Saylor sat up and watched the black silhouettes against blue sky, taking in the grace Lenny had talked about. And she knew it was her grace, too. Yes, she was wary and afraid—but like the black-winged creatures above, she realized that she *did* possess the strength to carry on. She watched the crows' upward flight, and under the hot, quiet sky, Saylor was struck as if by lightning: There would never be the perfect antidote to fear, yet she could still rise above it.

In that flash of reality, she found freedom. Freedom in knowing that she could get better, while still accepting that it was okay to be who she was—that it would be possible to feel scared sometimes while still finding courage, still experiencing joy.

CHAPTER SEVENTEEN

She arrived home without remembering the last miles of her drive as she re-lived the bonfire last night, the side trip to Found Hills Café, and how the afternoon hike had felt like a dream. In fact, it all felt surreal, so separate from both her everyday reality—and the irrational fear. In the middle of her walk-way, she paused in the yellow path of light, thinking about her anxious life within the walls behind the blue front door, about her mother's bitter loneli-ness inside her weather-beaten house, about Billy's life of paranoid homeless-ness. She stepped forward and unlocked the door, hoping the flash of free-dom she had felt on top of the mountain could be regained.

She sighed. Soy sauce-stained Chinese takeout boxes greeted her on the kitchen table and dirty dishes filled the kitchen. Overwhelmed, she wished she were back on the trail with a daytime sun warming her face. Beyond the dinner's—and probably lunch and breakfast's—immediate mess of dish-es and food, she noticed how the grout joints around the sink had become even darker with mold, that the cabinets were marked with more impossible-to-get-out grease stains, and worse of all, how piles of paperwork and var-ious junk scattered on tables and shelves in the adjoining living room had grown even more monstrous, an exhaustive organizational process that she couldn't imagine tackling. How could things look so much worse in just one day? How could she feel so down within minutes of entering her own home?

"Hey, is anyone here?" she yelled, wishing she could just throw every-thing out, including the dishes—and the dirty kitchen sink while she was at it. "Anybody home?" She slogged down the hallway and saw that Devin and Brooke's doors were shut. The upstairs TV blared, and she knew Brian was most likely sprawled on the bed watching the screen, his face vacant.

She knocked on Devin's door. He answered with a science book in hand.

"Hi, Mom. Sorry I can't really talk right now. I have a big test next week." He clenched his jaw in the same way Uncle Silvio used to.

Saylor noticed the red sores around his cuticles. "I'll let you get back to studying—just wanted to say hi." He started to close the door. "Wait," she said, wishing for even the tiniest of connections with him. "How were the last couple of days here?"

"Mom, it's Saturday and you only left Friday. Nothing monumental has occurred."

"I missed you guys, though." She smiled, wishing she could pat his head like she did when he was little. "Maybe we can all see a movie tomorrow night."

"It'll be the night right before my test. I'll be having to study," he said. "Sorry."

"I understand." Of course, she did...but still. Even though Devin and Brooke were teenagers, even though they all lived under the same roof, she missed them. "Maybe we can all go out to brunch, then."

"I doubt Brooke will want to," he mumbled, flipping his book open.

Her heart lifted. He hadn't said no, which in teenager speak, meant he was game. "I'll check with her."

He nodded, his attention on the condensed print interspersed with complicated-looking equations.

Even though the book was upside down to her, Saylor knew that she'd never be able to understand what it all meant. "I'm proud of you, Devin, you're really working hard," she said, willing him to look at her. He glanced at her for one nanosecond, and she smiled. "Don't study too hard."

"I won't..." He shrugged as if he didn't really mean it.

Though his gaze fell right back onto his book, she noticed that his face still had an openness to it, a soft vulnerability that flooded her heart with tenderness. She could still see the little boy who used to call her mommy, who would run into her open arms, who would nuzzle his head into the crook of her neck. "Love you," she said, wishing she could have kept the wispy sound of nostalgia out of her voice.

"Love you, too." Devin slowly closed his door. Even though the words were mumbled in typical teen obligatory tone, Saylor exhaled with relief.

She wandered down the hall and paused in front of Brooke's bedroom, thinking how separate everyone in her family had become. Lightly, she tapped on her daughter's door. When there wasn't any response, she called out that she was home and knocked again.

Finally, Brooke swung the door open, eyebrows scrunched in annoyance. "What's up?"

"I just got back from my mom's. How is everything?" She saw Brooke's laptop glowing on her bed.

"Fine." Brooke looked over her shoulder, clearly wanting to get back to the screen.

"I was wondering if we could all go out to brunch tomorrow?"

"Brunch?" Brooke looked at her as if she were crazy. "With just you guys? I've already made plans with friends to go shopping."

"You can have breakfast out with us first. It would be nice to do something with just the four of us—"

"We'll see. I might be sleeping in late."

We'll see my foot, is what Saylor wanted to say, but knew it would make Brooke more rebellious. "I'll check brunch times for Sunday. I'm sure I can find one that runs on the later side."

Brooke rolled her eyes before she turned away, but at least she didn't argue.

Saylor watched her daughter pounce back on her dark purple comforter. Brooke began to click away, seemingly oblivious to the fact that Saylor was still standing in the doorway. "Brooke..." Even though she often told Devin and Brooke that she loved them, it felt especially important tonight. Having been alone with her mother made her feel even more of a need to be close to her children. "I love you."

"I love you too, Mom," she answered in the same mumbled way Devin did. Then without looking up from the screen, she waved one hand in the air. "Now could you please shut my door?"

"Of course." Saylor reached for the handle.

"Thanks, Mom." Brooke looked up, rewarding her with a small smile.

Saylor smiled back. Brooke's voice lacked the usual sarcasm, had even sounded—dare she think—*friendly*. She closed the door and stood in the hallway, Brian's shouts at whatever game he was watching booming down the stairs. She figured that since she hadn't seen Neptune, he was curled up on the bed with Brian. She headed out the back door, hoping to breathe in a moment of peace before heading back in the house again. In the damp evening air, she walked onto the lawn, wet grass already soaking the sides of her tennis shoes. She heard the metal clang of Neptune's dog tags and walked over to the side patio where the gray outline of his body huddled on his outdoor dog bed. She shook her head, angry that no one had remembered to let him inside before dark. When he finally saw her, he rose on stiff-looking legs, but still wagging his tail as he nudged his muzzle against her knee. Her back ached from the combination stress of dealing with her mother and the long drive home, so she carefully kneeled down to pet him. "We're both getting old, aren't we?" He looked straight into her eyes as if in agreement.

By the light of the fog-obscured moon, she then glanced down to see the faint outlines of Devin and Brooke's childhood footprints embedded in the cement slab. It seemed like such a short time ago that Brian had helped them mush their squiggling feet in the wet cement. Baby Brooke had giggled at the stickiness on her little corn-kernel toes and soft-tummied Devin squatted with wide-eyed wonder while Brian engraved their names with a stick. After he was done, Brian patted Devin on the back. "Someday your feet will be so big, you'll think this footprint looks like a kitten's paw compared to the pad of a grown-up lion." Devin looked at his own feet and then at Brian's.

Saylor recalled how he stretched his neck to look up at his father. "Will I ever be as big as you?"

Brian smiled back, the happy father who was right there in the moment. "Bigger."

Saylor remembered how she had felt like an outsider to their simple joy, her anxiety on high that day due to what had happened earlier that morning—something that she couldn't explain away. When she had gone grocery shopping, a dark-eyed man made her do a double-take: if she hadn't known any better, she'd swear that he could be her father's proverbial long-lost twin. The man looked as if he were in his late sixties, about the same age her father would have been if he were still alive. Following him in line, she held her breath when he asked the cashier if they'd honor a coupon for another store. Even his slow, somber voice sounded like her father's. When he had turned toward her, a strange nausea hit. A nightmare-like memory—one she couldn't be sure had really happened or had only been a bad dream—flashed by. It was an image of her father laughing at her mother, the threat of violence permeating inside their kitchen walls.

When the man glanced at her, the memory vanished, replaced by the words *I will kill you*, thudding in her head. The man looked like he winced—but she couldn't be sure if she had imagined it—and then he quickly turned his attention to loading his groceries onto the conveyor belt. She made herself breathe, reminding herself how one of her self-help books had described irrational fear as *false evidence appearing real.*

After he left, the older, pink-rouged Maureen, who usually gave Saylor a friendly, "How are ya doin' today?" greeted her with only a perfunctory nod. Saylor pulled the cookie-dough ice cream out of her cart and as Maureen scanned it, Saylor leaned forward. "You ever try this flavor, Maureen?" Saylor kept her voice light.

Maureen shrugged, the usual gap-toothed grin missing. "I don't much like sweets."

Saylor studied Maureen's face. Did she look sad? Was the woman merely tired? Why was she so much less exuberant today? Or was her subdued de-meanor a reaction to Saylor's blurting out those awful words? It became yet another one of those times when fear took over.

Saylor now ran her fingers over her children's footprints. All too often, her crazy anxiety had intruded into what should have been her happiest and sweetest of times during Devin and Brooke's childhoods.

But instead of crying about the past, she stood and pictured herself back on the mountain, recalling the freedom in realizing she didn't have to be per-fect in order to change. She closed her eyes and saw the two crows gliding above her in the daytime sky. She would get better. It wasn't just for herself. Her children—even if they were now teenagers—needed her as well...and so did Billy.

CHAPTER EIGHTEEN

By the time Saylor trudged upstairs, the T.V. was silent. On her way to the bathroom, Saylor stared at Brian's jeans, T-shirt, and dirty socks littering the floor. Brian, standing in dark blue boxers, brushed his teeth with an up and down vengeance that made him look as if he was trying to scrub away a bad taste in his mouth. He hadn't seen her yet, and she had the impulse to sneak back downstairs. But he spied her in the mirror and spun around before she had the chance.

"You just got back?" he said, foamy-mouthed. Saylor looked at him for a moment, wondering at what point, if ever he would have called to see if she was okay. He turned back to the sink, spitting with bull's-eye aim into the drain's center.

"No, I've been home awhile. I just finished cleaning the kitchen." She stopped herself from complaining about what a mess she came home to. It would only would lead to a fight—and she was already battle fatigued from having to deal with Erika. "How did everything go here?"

"Nothing much, I hung out, did a little surfing. The kids—I don't know...they just did their typical thing." He rinsed his brush, flicking off the extra water.

Behind him, Saylor peeked into the mirror and winced. Even though she still had her hair back in a ponytail, a mass of unattractive frizz had escaped, not to mention the unhappy looking wrinkles around her mouth and dark circles under her eyes. "Crap, I look awful."

When Brian didn't respond, she figured that he was either not in the mood to feed her the compulsory compliment—or worse yet, silently agreeing with her. "How was your mom?" he asked without missing a beat as he squeezed by.

Saylor rolled the bottom of the toothpaste, pressing out the last, small squirt onto her flayed brush. "She was her typical self—but even worse," she said over her shoulder. She was too tired to supply him with all the details, too sad to relive it. But, still, she wished that she could share her afternoon. Yet Brian would probably laugh at her conversation with Lenny and tune out what she had experienced on the hike. And then he'd think she had *really* lost it if she told him that she had been sitting around a bonfire the night before, drinking rum and howling into the night sky with three homeless men. She smiled at the memory and splashed cold water on her face, foregoing her usual cleaning routine. But she couldn't leave her hair alone. She squirted anti-frizz oil from roots to ends and then braided the curly mass as tightly as possible with the hope it would compress its unruly snarl into something more subdued by morning.

She entered the bedroom and peeled off her clothes. Even though Brian wasn't looking at her, she wrapped herself in her robe and made sure to slide under the covers before wiggling out of it. Brian turned off his bedside lamp and reached for her.

Her body tensed. "I'm sorry." She pressed her hands over her eyes. She really was sorry; really did wish she could feel the same way. "I'm just not in the mood."

"When are you ever in the mood anymore?" Abruptly, Brian turned from her, switched on his light and reached for his latest mystery novel.

Saylor blinked. He was right, but she still couldn't force herself go through the motions when she felt less than nothing. "I'm sorry. I don't know what's wrong with me. I'm sure tomorrow night will be better." She laid her hand on his chest, fearful that if he hadn't already, he might soon have an affair. God knows he had plenty of opportunity with all the women designers and homeowners he worked with every day. And the man, damn him, was just as much his outdoor-handsome self—if a bit older and a tad bloated—as when she first met him, hair still thick and dark, skin still appealing brown, and body strong.

He patted her hand in a half-hearted way that made it hard to tell if it was because he wanted to reassure her, or if it was annoying him, and he really wanted her to move it. "Part of the reason I fell in love with you was because of what a sensitive and caring woman you were."

"Were?" She pulled her hand away.

He closed the book, looking at her. "You still are, Say. But the constant fear has made you—"

"You don't have to say it," she snapped. "It's made me irritable and depressed." She exhaled. "And hard to live with."

"You know I still love you," he said, but his eyes looked sad, a demoralized gaze that made Saylor shiver.

"Do you?" She clenched her jaw. "You still love me even though I'm a bitch who doesn't put out?" She had to make a joke of it because it was all too real.

"I still love you." His voice was more than weary. It sounded downright exhausted. "The question," he whispered, "is do you still love me?"

"I do, but..." Saylor scolded herself. Why didn't she just say that she loved him and leave it at that? But, somehow, she couldn't.

"But what?"

"Brian, you're not perfect either. I feel like you're always trying to escape from me...from us." She exhaled, not realizing that she'd been holding her breath.

"Escaping? How can you say that? I work hard. I come home to my family every night."

"I know you work hard—and I appreciate that," she said. They were sliding into their standard fight—but, still, she wasn't going to stop. "You have to admit, though, that you do sneak off on surfing trips more than you ever vacation with me. And just as I was trying to explain before I went to my mom's—when you *are* home, you're so disconnected that it's hard to get through to you." She paused, purposely enunciating her words so he'd listen. "But the saddest thing is that you're not trying hard enough with the kids—I think they can feel it."

"Here we go again." Brian rolled his eyes. "I'm just a terrible person because I like to surf, and when I get home, I actually want to relax."

Saylor shook her head in frustration. If Brian's mother was there, she'd be nodding in agreement with her son, clucking away about how much the *poor dear worked* and how much he deserved his time off, with the unsaid notion that Saylor didn't work nearly as hard as he did. Saylor eyed the door, making sure it was properly shut before she continued. "Brian, have you even noticed your own kids lately?"

"Yeah, they're teenagers." He shrugged. "They want to be left alone."

"Don't you see that Brooke's not eating enough? That she's looking bone-thin? And we can't ignore Devin's obsessive-compulsive stuff anymore. It's getting worse."

"Brooke is naturally skinny, you know that, and Devin is just the genius type who has his own idiosyncrasies." Brian flipped his book open again.

A rush of anger heated Saylor's cheeks. "Do not." She sat up and stared at him. "And I mean it: Do not put your head in that book right now."

"So, what are you saying?" Brian scrunched his face as if he were in pain. "You want to send our kids to a so-called professional who'll stick some label on them?"

"Not all therapists are like that—"

"But don't you think that once a kid gets pigeonholed it can actually create problems, or at least make any so-called problems worse—problems they'd probably outgrow without someone having to overanalyze them, make them think they've got issues when they don't?"

"Are you saying you're afraid that if a professional thinks that Brooke may be heading towards an eating disorder that it will make her have one if she doesn't already? That if Devin is diagnosed with OCD, then it will make his symptoms worse?" Saylor dug her fingernails into her rash, the itch too intense to ignore. What was Brian so afraid of? And now that she thought about it, why had it taken her so damn long to voice her concerns?

"All I'm saying is they're teenagers." Brian spoke in a slow, calm voice—the kind of voice that put Saylor's teeth on edge. "They're going to have problems. It comes with the territory. They'll get through their stuff, if we give them the space to do it."

Saylor shook her head. "I wish you would face reality and stop that I'm-so-mellow-surfer-dude kind of thinking that makes you act like everything's fine—when it clearly isn't."

"Have you ever stopped to think," Brian said, "that it *is* fine?"

"You're wrong. If Brooke loses any more weight, she might become anorexic. Plus, my poor Uncle Silvio, who suffered from horrible OCD, didn't get any help when he was younger—and look what happened to him."

"Like I said; it's all a phase. Brooke will be fine. And Devin isn't anything like your uncle. You know that." An inpatient sneer escaped his lips, a sneer that made Saylor's eyes water. "I can't believe you'd compare your son to him."

"You didn't even know him." Saylor felt her throat close up. If only Brian understood that just because someone suffered mentally, didn't mean that person was in any way *less than*. In fact, it oftentimes meant they were even braver than the average person. It took a lot to carry on with life, regardless—even more so when fighting an invisible battle. "He happened to be my favorite relative—"

"How can you say that? The man killed himself for God's sake."

"Just because he had problems, didn't mean that he wasn't a good person, Brian." She pushed down the quilt, hoping to ease the pressing heat of what she knew was her upset mixed with the hormonal fluctuations of perimenopause. "I just learned from my mom how twisted my superstitious Grandmother Rosa was with him. She convinced herself that he was possessed as a kid because of his nervous tics—and thought that if she stuffed him with enough food, then whatever demons were possessing him would leave."

"I don't believe that." Brian cocked his head and laughed. "You must be exaggerating."

"I'm not. You can ask my mom. She also said that my grandmother hated my dad as if he were the devil himself."

"Your mom's probably remembering wrong."

Saylor grabbed her robe, quickly wrapping it around herself.

"Where you going?"

"Nowhere." She got up, tightened her robe's sash and yanked the quilt off their bed.

"Saylor, what are you doing?" Brian stared at her as if she were insane and for some reason, it made her feel more powerful than she had in weeks.

"I'm getting rid of this old thing. I can't sleep another night with this on my bed. My Grandmother Rosa made it, and it's time to get rid of it."

He shook his head. "I thought you liked the fact that your grandmother had made it."

"Did you not hear what I said about what a horrible mother she was? Oh...that's right, you don't believe it." Saylor began to fold the quilt, not sure what to do with it. Even the thrift store wouldn't take it due to the stains from years of midnight snacks, morning coffee spills, and pet mishaps. She pushed it under the bed, figuring that she'd throw it away sometime next week when Brian was back at work.

"It's a family heirloom," Brian said, taking on his mother's annoyingly cloying tone. "You should at least store it in a box for Brooke. Maybe she'd want it for her own home one day."

"I doubt that very much." How could he not remember that Brooke eschewed anything she deemed as too *old timey*? "Besides, I don't want our kids to be wrapped up in my family history."

"You do realize..." Brian cleared his throat. "That you sound pretty superstitious yourself."

"Maybe I do. But I don't want to have any more reminders—"

Brian scowled. "It's wasteful to throw it away."

"I never said that I was going to throw it away." Had she blurted out her thoughts without knowing it? "What made you say that?" She stood, hands on hips.

"I know you better than you think I do."

Now he was sounding way too much like *her* mother. "Then you should know that I need a change," she said. "You have to stop making such a big deal out of this." She sighed, wishing he'd listen. "Please."

"Can't we just put it back on for tonight?" Brian hugged his arms around his body as if he were playacting. "I'm cold."

She could tell he was lying, knew that he ran hot. *Why*, she thought, *did he even care about the damn quilt*? Was it only to irk her? And if so, what good would that do him? "I'll go get some extra blankets from the hall closet."

"Why are you being so stubborn?" He frowned. "Just put it back on."

She had to stop herself from screaming that *no*, she wasn't going to put the ratty quilt back on their bed. Then realizing they had completely gotten off track about Devin and Brooke, she paused. Straightening her back, she looked straight at him. "We can't ignore our children's problems anymore."

Brian yawned. "You're just tired. Everything will seem better in the morning."

She knelt, pulling the quilt from under the bed. "I'll be back with the extra blankets."

"You aren't actually going to throw it out." He made it sound like a command rather than a question.

Saylor pressed her lips together; she didn't owe him an answer—or any further explanation. The quilt was a relic from her family—not his. A burden of memory that affected her—and not him. "I'm going to make myself some tea." Without a word more, she tromped downstairs with the quilt. Quietly, she opened the front door and slipped outside. She gritted her teeth. The cold cement against her bare feet made her shiver, but she continued on. Heart racing, she lifted the trash bin's lid and placed the quilt under as many trash bags as she could reach. She then stood in the dark, slapping her hands together in self-congratulations.

Back upstairs, she slid under the covers. Brian was already asleep. Curled up on the edge of the bed, she wondered if Brian was right about labeling the kids. Would Devin and Brooke buy into having something "wrong" with them and act out even more? Could the wrong therapist make them worse? And if she didn't get either of them professional help, what would happen then? Could Brooke become anorexic? Would Devin's obsessive-compulsive tendencies worsen to the degree that he'd become like Uncle Silvio?

Her mind would not shut down. And when she finally did doze off, she fully awakened within an hour. She bit her lip. She'd be slogging through the day tomorrow as if she were wading chest deep through sludge. The more she fretted about it, the more sleep eluded her.

She watched the rise and fall of Brian's chest. How had their lives become so marred? Remembering how they had met, she mused at how much happier their younger selves had been. She was living in Santa Monica, working in an art gallery for minimum wage, and in her free time, painting acrylic landscapes in colors and combinations that pleased her: cobalt blue for earth, emerald green skies, pyrrole orange mountains. She and Lucy were waiting in line for a movie at Third Street Mall, and she noticed how the guy standing in front of them had that solid kind of physique that made her feel safe and reassured. Of course, Lucy noticed her noticing him.

In a too-loud voice, Lucy jabbed Saylor in the side, saying, "Looks like you sure could hang a tool belt on that one!"

He turned around with a friendly eyebrow raise and smiled. With his dark brown eyes and rugged good looks, his face was amazingly close to what she had envisioned from behind.

"You must have heard me, sorry." Lucy laughed, grabbing her wallet. She handed him the card where Saylor worked—Lucy always kept a stash of Saylor's business cards in case she wanted to fix her up with whatever attractive guy she predicted would be a "good fit." Lucy grinned. "You have to call her; you two are just too cute not to be together."

Saylor felt like stuffing a sock in Lucy's mouth. "I'm sorry about her—"

"Don't be," he said, his smile even wider. "The funny thing is—I am a carpenter."

He had called her the very next day and they went out to dinner at a popular seafood restaurant packed with tourists. After only ten minutes of talking with this stranger again, Saylor felt disappointed that he lived all the way north in Dune Beach—and that he was only in town for a couple more days. He had made the trip to visit his favorite cousin whose wife had just given birth to twin baby girls. "How strange it is," he had said, "I didn't even feel like going to the movies last night, but I wanted to give them some space." He tilted his head and grinned. "But I'm sure glad that I did."

The restaurant was so noisy, Saylor wasn't sure if she had heard him right and since she didn't want to assume anything, she said the only thing she could think of: "So you're glad you saw the movie you did?"

He winked at her, "Yes...and you?"

After some time, it became their inside joke to ask each other if they were glad about picking the movie that they had, a joke that endured after all these years, a joke that reminded them how grateful they were for finding each other.

Saylor closed her eyes and pressed her palms over her lids. Neither of them had uttered it for a long time now. As Brian's slow breathing of perfect sleep continued, she couldn't help but wonder what her life would have been like if she had never met him. What would his life have been like? And how in the world had the seemingly simple outside of their lives become so increasingly difficult to live with from within? Here she was, a housewife in a solid marriage with two kids living an ordinary existence in a typical—if rather messy—tract home. She rolled onto her stomach, blaming herself. If she had been able to control her fear, she'd be able to enjoy the everyday comforts of life. If she was happier, then Brian's stuff wouldn't bother her so much, and her children wouldn't have the problems they had. That's what upset her the most: Devin and Brooke. It wasn't fair to them. Whether they ever heard her talk about her anxiety or not, they still had to grow up with a mother who was constantly worried, always stressed. It had to have affected them. There was no way it hadn't.

She couldn't stay in bed any longer. She had to do something. Anything that could elicit change. She tiptoed to the bathroom and shut the door. She turned on the light and seized her scissors. Maybe if she chopped off her hair—gave herself a radical new look. Maybe external change could somehow bring about an internal shift. But she placed the scissors on the counter. "Real change takes time," she whispered. She nodded at her reflection, Lenny's words at the café coming back to her: "Everyone you see has pain, of course. But it's what you do with it that counts."

Sunday morning's sky was what Saylor thought of as heavenly blue. She turned on the album *Wavelength* by Van Morrison, fed Neptune, and cleaned house while Devin and Brooke slept in. Brian, in his navy-blue robe and white-socked feet, drank coffee behind the newspaper (which he still subscribed to, even though he read the bulk of his news online). After her night of guilt-ridden ruminations and waking up from a string of dreams she couldn't remember, she sat in bed, tired and stiff, stared out the window and told herself that it wasn't too late. Since she now understood what had sparked her irrational fears, she should be able to control them.

Today would be the start: she would be both the person Lenny had sensed she could be—and the person she hoped to be, the one who could become stronger because of her fear. And with this, she'd become a better role model, and her kids would have a better chance for happiness. It was possible.

At nine-thirty, she tapped on Devin and Brooke's doors, reminding them about their brunch at Ocean Dunes Hotel. Saylor smiled, thinking of the many celebratory meals they had enjoyed there and how they used to take the hotel's trail down to the beach, exploring tide pools and collecting pieces of broken abalone and empty hermit crab shells. Despite her anxiety, they were a good family—and continually feeling guilty about her challenges wouldn't help Devin and Brooke get over theirs.

"Come on, guys I don't want to be late," she yelled from the kitchen, pouring another cup of coffee.

No one responded. Brian folded the front page he was reading and picked up the business section.

Saylor set her cup on the table. "Aren't you even going to try and help me?

He peered over the top of the paper, placid irritation on his face, an increasingly common expression of his that she had grown to detest. In fact, she had learned over the years that the more composed his face was, the more animosity brewed beneath. "I'm fine with just having a bowl of cereal here," he said.

"But you agreed it would be a good idea when I made reservations—and you know I wanted to try and get us to do at least one thing together—"

"We did: we all went to my parents for Thanksgiving."

"You know very well that I meant just us as a family."

His gaze was back on the paper. "That was family."

"You're not listening."

In baggy jeans and jet-black shirt pulled over to expose a bony shoulder, Brooke slumped into the room. She headed straight for the coffee pot. "I don't want to go," she said. "I'm not hungry for a big buffet. I'd rather spend the money on clothes."

"But I already made reservations, and you already agreed that if I gave you fifty dollars to go shopping—"

"Like fifty bucks is so much money." Brooke rolled her eyes. "It hardly even buys a shirt."

Saylor looked at Brian who didn't look back—and who didn't say anything either, ignoring Brooke's rudeness as usual. Saylor turned her attention back to her daughter. "As a matter of fact, fifty bucks is a lot of money, Brooke."

"Maybe for the work-clothes look you've got going on."

"Very funny," Saylor replied, looking down at her olive-green slacks and white rolled-up sleeved blouse. She had purposely dressed in what she had thought was a nice outfit for going to brunch. She pressed her lips together. *I will remain cheerful,* she told herself. *Even if it kills me.*

She heard Devin shuffle down the hallway and could tell by the long pauses that he was obsessing about something. When he finally entered the kitchen, she noticed how red his eyes were and wondered how much sleep he had gotten, if any. With his disheveled head of greasy curls, Devin sat at the kitchen table, his grungy sweat pants and T-shirt giving off the unwashed stink of weeks-long wear. Saylor turned, guilty how disgusted she was by her own son's odor. How could someone who was so afraid of germs not bother to shower for days on end? How could he walk around in such grimy clothes without smelling himself?

Brooke pinched her nose. "Gross, Devin. Have you ever heard of the soap and water concept—I mean, beyond the perimeters of your wrists?"

"I've been studying," he said, sounding unaffected. "Something that you should think of doing from time to time yourself."

"You are just so weird," Brooke said. She slinked into the adjoining living room and plopped on the couch next to Brian, reaching for the comics.

Saylor stood mute, her bare feet sticking to the floor. It was only morning and the day had already gone sour. "Do you still want to go to brunch, Devin?" She finally found her voice and hoped it sounded half as chipper as she intended.

"I guess," he answered, shrugging. "But only if everyone else does."

"I know I do," Saylor said. She looked over at Brian and Brooke's oblivious newspaper-in-face postures, and pleaded, "Come on you guys. Remember how good their waffles are?" Brian grunted something back that she couldn't make out, and Brooke merely turned the comics to the back page. Saylor continued, "Remember how beautiful their view is?"

Brooke sighed. "Enough with the guilt trip. I'll go already, but I can't stay that long. Remember that I have to get back to go shopping with friends."

"I know that—"

With a loud exhale, Brian interrupted, "I hope their brunch hasn't gotten even more expensive."

"Screw expense," Saylor retorted. "Life is short."

"Yeah," Brooke said, "Screw expense!" She gave Saylor a sly smile. "Remember that when you give me money for shopping today, okay, Mom?"

"What I really should do is remember that when I take myself out to go shopping, don't you think?" Saylor raised an eyebrow at her daughter.

Of course, they were going to be late because Devin, once he got coaxed into taking a shower, took forever to get out. And, of course, after he finally did get out and announced that he was ready, Brooke decided that she needed to change her outfit, skirting into her room before Saylor could try and stop her. When Saylor rapped on her door to tell her they had to leave soon, Brooke shouted not to pressure her. Saylor had to refrain from yelling back to get it together already. She knew from experience, though, that it would only make Brooke move even more slowly. Since Brooke was capable of changing outfits at least ten times, Saylor trudged back into the kitchen and vented her frustration by scrubbing grout joints.

Brian, dressed in T-Shirt and jeans, sauntered in with keys in hand. "Where is everyone?"

"Devin is waiting in his room. He says he's ready now, but Brooke is doing her frustrated-with-how-everything-looks routine."

"Remember when she didn't care how she dressed? Seems like just a couple of months ago that she thought it was stupid when people worried too much about how they looked."

"She'd probably tell you the same thing today," Saylor lowered her voice, not wanting Brooke to hear. "I think maybe—"

"That maybe..." Brian interrupted, in a voice Saylor knew was purposely loud enough for Brooke to hear through her closed door, "She's trying so hard to appear like she doesn't care what other people think, that it takes her near-to-forever to figure out how to look dark, depressed, and angry all at the same time?"

Saylor shook her head, knowing he was only making things worse, and also wondering if Brooke's behavior was stemming from a wholly different reason than he thought. She stepped closer to him and whispered, "Did you ever think that maybe it's because she may be suffering from a kind of body distortion and truly does not like how she looks in the mirror?"

"No," Brian said, crossing his arms. "You have to stop overanalyzing everything and realize your teenagers are just that: teenagers."

"Yeah, Mom, we're just teenagers," Brooke said, sarcasm dripping. She had somehow appeared in the room without either of them noticing.

Not knowing how much Brooke had heard, Saylor tried to laugh, but knew it sounded forced.

"See, Brooke agrees with me." Brian smiled and went to sit on the couch, picking up the paper again and settling back into the cushions.

Brooke wore the same exact outfit she had on before, but Saylor didn't say a word. She called down the hall, "Okay, Devin, let's go."

When they were finally all in the car, Brooke's cell rang. "Yeah, I'm stuck with them for now." She clicked off and tapped Saylor on the shoulder. "We're going to need to eat fast. Penelope's mom will be at our house by eleven-forty-five."

"Didn't you tell her where we're eating?"

"What does that matter?"

"If Penelope's mom knew that I had planned a family brunch at the Ocean Dunes Hotel, then she'd understand to make it later—no matter what time you and your friends had planned on." Saylor missed the earlier child-hood days when parents talked before the kids did—when parents could check in with each other, help each other out. Now that Devin and Brooke were teenagers, she was lucky if she even knew the names of their friend's parents, let alone had ever talked to them on the phone, or met them in person. No one came to the door anymore when they dropped off or picked up their kids either. Thanks to the cell phone age, parents just texted their kids, remaining anonymous entities waiting inside their cars. "If I could talk to Penelope's mom, then I'm sure she'd understand and make it a little later—"

"I don't have her mom's cell," Brooke said. "Even if I did, don't you think that would be obnoxious?"

Brian slammed on the brakes. On impulse, Saylor hit her foot on the floorboard, wishing for control. Why hadn't she driven? As usual, he was pushing past the speed limit and tailgating, acting annoyed that all the other cars on the road were in his way. "Brian! You were way too close to that car ahead of us."

"Stop overreacting, Saylor."

I hate you. I hate you. I hate you. The words screamed in her brain louder than anything around her. Louder than Brian's voice asking if she was okay. Louder than the blaring horn behind them—louder than Brooke and Devin's bickering in the back seat.

She swallowed. "Did you just ask me if I was okay?"

"Yeah." Brian stepped on the gas, still following too close to the sporty Fiat ahead. "Are you? You look sick. Your face is all flushed and sweaty."

She was surprised her anxiety showed, especially enough for Brian to notice while driving. "So that's the only reason you asked if I was okay?"

The back seat went quiet. "Why are you asking him that?" Brooke sounded too interested. Saylor turned around and shrugged, trying to act as if nothing was wrong.

"Damn!" Brian honked his horn. "There's always traffic here. They really should step up with the times and make this road a two-laner. Dune Beach isn't the homey little beach town it used to be."

Saylor wiped her forehead, disappointment mixing with the anxiety. This was supposed to be the day she vowed that she would finally control her fear. It was still morning and panic had already grabbed her, already making Brooke wonder why her mother was acting so weird.

By the time they were seated, Saylor had talked herself down, remembering something important from one of her anti-anxiety podcasts: Just because a day starts out badly, doesn't mean it can't turn around. She took in the view and smiled at her family. "Look how blue the ocean looks today—it seems like you could swim forever."

Brooke nudged her elbow. "Can we go line up at the buffet now?"

"Sure," Saylor answered. "I'm starving." She looked over at Brian and Devin. "You guys ready?" They nodded. No one liked to cross Brooke when she had a time agenda.

As they made their way to the buffet, Brooke glared at Saylor, her thick eyeliner making her eyes appear even more intense. "Why are you acting so happy all of a sudden?"

"What do you mean?"

Brooke shrugged, then pulled her cell out of her back pocket and checked for messages.

"Can you please shut that thing off until we're done with brunch?"

"Calm down, Mom."

They had just gotten in line. Saylor looked around, embarrassed at how condescending her daughter sounded. Before the kids had turned into teenagers, she never thought they'd ever talk to her like that. A young family stood in front of them. The mother held her little girl's hand. They sang some made-up sounding song about ice cream while the father was busy patting the back of a gurgling baby boy. The baby nestled his chin on the man's shoulder and stared at Saylor, wide blue eyes unblinking in that same wise-looking preverbal stage that her babies had entranced her with. She envied the parents. Although their days most likely felt long, they had no idea how fast the honeymoon phase of being a young family would pass. Beyond that, she envied the mother, guessing that the woman could enjoy these small moments without any fear. If she could only go back in time...but she reminded herself not to think like this. It did no good to get caught up in regrets. Besides, who knew what the woman was going through? One of her children might have a debilitating disease, or her husband might be cheating on her. The woman may even have some form of anxiety herself. Saylor stepped back.

"Cute baby," Brian said. "You miss those times?"

Saylor nodded and Brian cradled his arm around her shoulder. "I miss them too," he said.

She leaned into him, appreciating the unexpected closeness.

"You guys don't think we're cute anymore?" Brooke glanced back with a scowl.

"Of course, we do." Saylor looked at Brooke and then at Devin who stood off to the side, his focus straight ahead as if he didn't know these people who claimed to be his family. "We love you guys more than ever."

"Yeah, right," Brooke said, rolling her eyes.

The mother and daughter had stopped singing, and the woman turned back to give Brooke a look of disdain, then glanced at Saylor with the kind of superior empathy that made Saylor want to say, "Just you wait."

After they loaded their plates at the buffet, Saylor steered everyone to a window table. Sighing, she wondered why she hadn't learned that any family outing was most probably going to be a clash of desperation on her end and lets-get-this-over-with-already sentiment on Devin and Brooke's. She took a bite of her syrup-drenched waffle and looked around the room, noticing re-laxed-looking couples, parents doting on infants and toddlers, and boisterous groups of extended families. No other mothers and fathers had dragged their teenagers out for a solo family brunch. Somehow, everyone else had got the memo but her. When you have teenagers, you have to let go. She bit her lip. From now on, she had to be more realistic.

Brooke cleared her throat, glaring at Saylor. "Will you please..." she said, cocking her head toward Devin, "Please tell your son to stop eating so loudly. It's grossing me out." Devin looked up momentarily, but then continued to shovel in his food, ignoring his sister's nastiness.

Saylor paused, noticing the thin slices of pineapple and small circle of scrambled eggs dotting Brooke's plate. "Brooke, let him enjoy his food—that's why we're here."

"Yeah, Brooke." Brian slurped his coffee. "You're wasting money eating so light. Try to get some more bang for our buck."

"You guys are disgusting." Brooke pushed her plate away.

Saylor went back to the comfort of waffles and strawberry syrup. If only she could transfer her appetite onto Brooke. She tried to think of something to say that they could all talk about. If she distracted her enough, maybe Brooke would relax and eat again, but nothing came to her. She waited, hop-ing Brian or one of the kids would chime in with something. But amidst all the surrounding chitchat, their table remained silent. She studied her fami-ly, trying to figure out what was going on in each of their minds. Although Devin ate with gusto, she could tell by the tap of his foot and the once-every-few-second drum of fingers on the table that he was barely keeping his OCD under wraps. Dour-faced Brooke, having pulled her plate in front of her again, allowed only the tiniest forkfuls of egg to enter her mouth. Obliv-ious as usual, Brian focused only on the stuffed croissant with crab salad in front of him. She wondered where they all were headed. Then catching eyes with the young mom from the line, she smiled, knowing how utterly depressed she must have appeared. But the woman only looked away, which made Saylor feel even more foolish.

Brian, Devin, and Saylor ambled to the parking lot, holding their stomachs in post-indulgent bliss while ahead of them, fast-paced Brooke furiously texted on her cell.

And then Saylor saw him. The wretched man from the bookstore was walking toward her, his sunken eyes focused on the pavement, as if he was searching for something lost. He wore the same running shorts and workout shirt she had last seen him in. Trailing behind him was his daughter and his plump—but certainly not fat—wife, a slack-faced woman in an unflattering maroon velour pantsuit. Saylor paused in mid stride.

"What are you stopping for?" Brian asked.

"I'm coming," she said, grabbing Brian's hand, wishing she could explain. She kept her face turned away from the man's direction. If they didn't make eye contact, maybe he wouldn't recognize her. But when he came closer, she couldn't stop from looking at him. He stared at her, but she couldn't read his face, couldn't tell if he remembered her from the bookstore or not.

Then just when she thought she was in the clear and he passed by, he whispered, "Bitch."

She froze. He kept walking.

"What's wrong?" Brian said. Luckily, Devin was now behind them, and Brooke remained paces ahead.

"Didn't you hear him?" Saylor said, her throat constricting.

"Hear who? What are you talking about?"

"Shh." She squeezed Brian's hand as hard as she could as the wife and daughter came closer. When they passed, she averted her eyes, but not before she saw the girl's same conspiratorial smile that she had flashed in the bookstore, the smile that made Saylor think she really had blurted out her thoughts about the father being a bastard.

"I think I'm going to be sick." She let go of Brian's hand and ran toward the hillside shrubs. He followed. "No, please, go back, Brian…I just need a minute." When she heard Devin's nervous call for Brooke to wait up, his voice breaking in mid-yell, she inched farther into the bushes. Brian was still on her heels. She sucked in air, trying as hard as she could from getting sick. "I'll meet you guys at the car."

"I don't want to leave you," Brian said. He reached for her, but she pushed his hand off, the brush of his fingers on her shoulder making her even queasier.

"I'm sorry, but please just go…"

With a dejected sigh, Brian backed away.

After he finally left, she bent over with hands on knees, gulping for air, staring down at the waxy leaves of a white-flowered shrub. She couldn't understand why the thought of throwing up terrified her. Eyes stinging, she focused on the scent of ocean air and eventually straightened up, weak but whole. Flooded with relief that she stopped herself from getting sick, she decided that if there was any time in her life to take control, it was now.

She marched back to the parking lot, wondering if she still had the therapist's card that Brian's sister, Kelley, had handed her on Thanksgiving.

CHAPTER NINETEEN

When Saylor woke, the room was too light, the house too quiet. She checked the clock. How could it be after eight in the morning? She pushed her feet onto the floor, wondering how she could have slept through her family's rackety morning routine. An odd sense of loss hit her at not having been in the middle of cereal boxes, coffee mugs, even Brooke's snarky irritability and Devin's nervous fumbling. She saw that Brian had left a note on her bedside table and read it with blurry eyes. His pencil-scrawl said that he had tried to wake her but she wouldn't budge—and that he hoped that she was feeling okay. She hazily remembered his voice trying to coax her awake, and then rolling onto her stomach to bury her head under the pillow. On the downstairs floorboards, Neptune's nails tapped impatiently. She knew he was wondering why he hadn't been fed yet. Calling him up, she tried to stave off the disconcerting loneliness. She couldn't remember ever sleeping through her family readying themselves for the day, and it made her think about how empty her mornings would be when Devin and Brooke moved on.

She bent down to pet Neptune and noticed the film over his eyes had grown even hazier, wondering if it made it seem as if his whole reality had blurred—and if this bothered him or had he merely adjusted to it without noticing? He was growing old without any of them wanting to admit it. Saylor swallowed. By the time Devin and Brooke left home, Neptune may be gone too.

She straightened her back, telling herself that she'd better get out of this melancholic mood before the whole day became washed in regret. She tried to think about the everyday tasks ahead: dishes, office work, grocery shopping. But when she tromped downstairs, the odd nightmare from last night intruded. In her mother's kitchen, the man in the bookstore was pulling his wife's hair. Venom in her eyes, the woman glared at Saylor while her crazed skeleton-faced husband grinned like a maniac. With her back to them all, their daughter was leaning over the kitchen sink. An unnamed panic sweeping over her, Saylor had pulled the girl away, but just as they were fleeing toward the front door, she bolted awake.

Neptune nudged her calf with his nose. "I better feed you already," she said, talking out loud to fill the stillness of the house.

After plopping the dog food in his bowl, she searched through the junk drawer, hoping to find the therapist's card Kelley had given her. She couldn't remember if she had tossed it in the drawer before washing the jeans she wore on Thanksgiving, or did she throw it in the recyclables because she was so sure that she'd never use it? She didn't want to have to call Kelley and wasn't about to contact one of her old therapists or take a chance on some random name from the phone book. Hoping that she hadn't chucked it, Saylor dumped everything on a towel and sifted through useless receipts, old sticky coins and throat lozenges. After several frustrating minutes, she turned from the metallic-mint smell, knowing that she had to call her sister-in-law. If only shy, sweet Kelley knew that her longer-than-average response time escalated Saylor's anxiety. It was worse over the phone, but still Saylor reached for her cell.

After they said their hellos, Saylor told her that she had misplaced the therapist's card and hoped that Kelley wouldn't mind giving her the info again. True to form, Kelley paused for so long before answering that Saylor thought she might have been angry at her for losing it. But finally, Kelley responded.

"Hold on a minute and I'll look it up for you," she said without a trace of judgment in her voice.

Saylor waited, relieved.

After Kelley got back on and slowly recited his name and number, she drew in a delicate sounding breath. "I'm not going to pry, but I know you're going through something. I just want you to know that Nathan Greenberg has really helped me."

Saylor felt her face flush, but then realized that Kelley was admitting that she had problems of her own. "Thank you, Kelley. I appreciate this." She held the phone tighter to her ear, knowing what a private person Kelley was, especially compared to the rest of Brian's family. "I hope we can start sharing more. It's nice to know I'm not alone."

After a moment, Kelley answered, "Yes...I would like that very much, Saylor."

The second after she hung up, Saylor dialed Nathan Greenberg's number before she had a chance to change her mind.

"You made an appointment for a family session without talking to me first?" Brian honked his horn at the driver that dared a too-close lane change in front of him. He swore at the lineup of cars ahead and hit the brake with too much force.

From the cracked windshield, Saylor stared at the stone-gray clouds perched on the horizon and wished that she had asked someone else for a ride to her mechanic.

"I bet you didn't even find out how much this therapist charges."

Sensing danger, Saylor turned to see that the grid of a semi was edging too close behind and hoped whatever was creating this traffic jam would soon be fixed.

"Well, did you?" Brian said, the profile of his face rigid.

"He's going to charge us a sliding scale fee."

"What price does that start at? Two hundred dollars for fifty minutes of over-analytical gibberish?"

"I didn't ask." She knew this was going to lead to a fight, knew he'd be upset. Still, she had hoped he wouldn't be *so* combative. "Remember," she said, "it *is* a sliding-scale fee—and I doubt your sister would recommend him if she didn't think we could afford it."

"But you know that I don't think the kids even need therapy." He shot her a pained expression that made her stomach churn. "Why can't *you* just go?"

"I don't want to get into what I think is happening and what you *don't* think is happening with the kids again." She rolled down the window, trying to cool her frustration. "I believe a family session is worth a try."

"But you said so yourself that therapy didn't work for you."

"That was before."

"Before what?"

She hesitated, not sure if she could explain. "It's just that..." She closed her eyes for a moment, recalling the epiphany she had when she was on top of the mountain watching the crows. "I know this sounds simple, but I used to think that I had to completely banish my fear in order to get better. Now that I've become more realistic, I'm ready to let someone help. I know there's no perfect cure, just like there's no perfect therapist."

The car grew silent. Then, after several minutes, the traffic jam had untangled itself for no apparent reason. They sped forward, the sound of the truck's engine and rush of wind through the window blending into a rumbling white noise that seemed to subdue the tension. Brian nodded. "Looks like rain's coming."

Saylor touched his forearm. "It'll be okay."

By the time they got to her mechanic, the sky had grown dense with cloud cover and a few heavy raindrops had already thudded against the windshield.

"I told you it was going to rain." Brian smiled at her.

"I know." Saylor hopped out of the truck, the expectant smell and electrified air of an impending thunderstorm making her skin tingle.

CHAPTER TWENTY

Saylor was relieved to see that Nathan Greenberg's space wasn't the drab off-white and beige color scheme of her earlier therapist's offices. His was a high-ceilinged loft, the walls bold shades of cadmium yellows and cobalt blues. And Nathan, himself, seemed a lot different too. Instead of the strained, over-contemplative dourness that made her think that the people who were trying to help her were actually more screwed up than she was, Nathan's deep smile lines made his wonderfully weathered face look relaxed and happy, his clear brown eyes making him appear as if he was more than ready to laugh at the absurdity of it all. Smiling, he greeted them wearing jeans and a crisp, emerald-green shirt.

Although Saylor trusted the man, not much happened the first several sessions. Tight-lipped Brian and withdrawn Devin didn't say much, while the usually forthright Brooke clammed up. But to Saylor's surprise, no one resisted going and it was a hell of a lot easier getting the whole family to each session on time than she thought possible. In his respectful, calm way, Saylor imagined that Nathan Greenberg was helping to cultivate whatever was about to bloom.

Yet Christmas and New Year's passed, and still no one was able to open up enough for things to budge past the point of talking about day-to-day frustrations. Then on a gusty afternoon in late January, Saylor wondered if anything was ever going to really happen. But she pictured Billy's intent words telling her that she should unshackle herself and help her own family. She drove everyone to the appointment, silently willing for a breakthrough.

Saylor was the first to sit, picking one of the middle seats in the semi-circle of chairs. She gestured to Brian to sit next to her. Brooke and Devin, still acting as if they were cats in an unfamiliar territory, gingerly sat on the cushioned chairs with Brooke sitting next to Brian with Devin next to Saylor.

"Welcome," Nathan said. "Today, I would like for each of you to tell me again why you think you and your family are in counseling." He had already asked this during the first session, but they hadn't gotten past the *because our mom thinks we need it and my wife is worried about nothing* routine. "I'll start with you, Devin."

"You want me to start?" Devin began to tap his foot against the oak floor as Nathan nodded.

"Why do you think you and your family are here?"

"I guess we're here cause my mom is concerned."

"Your mom is concerned," Nathan repeated. He looked at Saylor. "Do you agree with Devin?"

"Yes." She didn't elaborate, waiting to hear what everyone else was going to say.

"And you?" Nathan looked at Brian.

"That about sums it up." Brian crossed his arms. "But things are as bad as she thinks they are—"

"Let me save you some time, Doc," Brooke said. Surprised, Saylor leaned forward, watching Brooke's face.

Nathan held up a hand, smiling. "You can keep calling me Nathan," he said. "But go ahead, Brooke. Tell me how you can save me some time."

"If you haven't figured it out over these past couple of months..." She glanced over at Saylor, but then faced Nathan. "This is why we are here: First of all, my mother has big-time anxiety."

Saylor's heart felt like it was going to explode. How on earth had Brooke known about her fear?

Brooke turned to her, as if reading her thoughts. "Mom, you think Devin and I don't know you have problems? We've heard you crying to Dad about them when you thought we weren't around," she said matter-of-factly. "And even if we hadn't heard you, it's pretty obvious. You always look like you're about to jump out of your own skin"

"I'm so sorry." Saylor wondered what, exactly, they had heard her say. "I didn't want you to be burdened."

"It's harder not knowing." Brooke shrugged as if it wasn't any big deal, but by the look on her face, Saylor knew it was.

"You're right, Brooke, it is harder when you don't know. I should have explained to you guys—"

"Anyway, it's not just her." Brooke looked at Nathan again. "My brother has OCD." She rolled her eyes. "And my dad is just plain oblivious."

Regret and relief, both, swept over Saylor. Now, she finally knew she was doing the right thing in getting her family into counseling. If fifteen-year-old

Brooke understood her father walked around with blinders on, her brother had OCD, and her mother suffered from anxiety—then it was obviously time—way beyond time.

Nathan nodded as if this was the stuff of normal, everyday life. "Thank you, Brooke. Very succinct and helpful." He paused, tilting his head as if to listen even more intently. "And how about yourself?"

"Me?"

"Yes, you've summed up everyone else in your family. What would you say is going on for you?"

"I'm..." Brooke ran her fingers through her hair. "I'm just angry."

"Just angry?" Nathan's eyebrows shot up.

"I know my mom thinks that I have some kind of eating disorder. But my real problem is that I'm so pissed off, I can't deal sometimes. I know that no one will take this seriously, but it makes me lose my appetite."

"So, you don't feel like eating when you're pissed off?"

"Right."

The room grew silent, a charged hush that felt as if it were electrified with hope. Saylor stared at her daughter's delicate profile, waiting.

"What makes you angry?" Nathan asked.

Brooke paused for so long Saylor wasn't sure she was going to answer. Nathan waited, his hands folded-calm in his lap. Then Brooke spat out her words without pause: "I'm mad at my mom for always acting as if something horrible is going to happen, I'm mad at my brother for always acting so weird, I'm mad at my dad for always acting as if there's nothing wrong."

"That's a lot of stuff you're contending with," Nathan responded. "Stuff you can't control."

Brooke's gaze fell to the floor, her eyes watering.

Nathan went on in a gentle voice, "But you can pretty much control what you eat and what you don't."

Brooke gave the smallest of nods. Saylor glanced at her daughter's black combat boots turned pigeon-toed, witnessing what she hoped was the first crack in her armor.

Nathan turned his attention on Devin. "Devin, what do you think of what Brooke said?"

"I don't know." Devin edged forward on his seat, looking as if he wanted to bolt right out the door.

Nathan didn't prod, and again an electrified silence surged through the room.

Then, Devin exhaled, sitting back. "I mean—sometimes," he stammered. "Sometimes I can just tell by the look on my mom's face that she's afraid of something really bad, and I don't know what it is—and it makes me feel even more nervous."

Saylor tried to swallow down the lump in her throat. Her anxiety *had* affected her children. "I'm so sorry, Devin," she whispered. "I'm sorry, Brooke." She held back the tears she was saving for later when she could be by herself. How would she ever make this right?

"It's not your fault, Mom," Devin said.

"No, I should have been stronger. This isn't fair to you guys."

Nathan held up his hand. "Your son is right, Saylor. Your anxiety isn't something you asked for. But we'll talk about that later." He looked at Devin, "What I'm interested in right now, is how you feel about what your sister said about you."

Devin shot a sideways glance at Brooke, but didn't answer.

"She said you have OCD. Do you know what that is?"

"It's obsessive-compulsive disorder. I've done some research on it..."

"And?"

"I like to keep my room clean and, yeah, I like to tap my feet a lot, but I don't think I have OCD."

"Okay," was all Nathan said, and then waited.

"And I don't have any kind of problem with food," Brooke piped in. "I just can't eat when I get stressed."

Nathan nodded. No one spoke as the wind howled through the slender birch trees outside his office window creating a kind of yearning sound that made Saylor feel both sad and hopeful.

"You haven't had a chance to say anything, Brian." Nathan said. "What do you think about what your daughter has laid out?"

"I think everyone is too quick to label these days." Brian nervously twisted his wedding band. "I believe Devin when he says that he doesn't have OCD, and I believe that Brooke is doing fine as well."

"I'm interested in what you think about Brooke's remarks regarding you," Nathan said.

"What remarks?"

Nathan uncrossed his legs. "She said that she feels you're oblivious to what's happening around you."

"Do you really think that, Brooke?" Brian averted his eyes from Nathan Greenberg's gaze. "Or is it just what you've heard from your mother?"

"Mom hasn't said anything."

Brian shook his head.

"Dad..." Devin's voice was quiet, but firm. "You and Mom are at the opposite ends of the spectrum. She's always hyper aware of everything and too stressed out, and you're so in your own world all the time that I'm not even sure you really see me."

Saylor bit her lip, surprised Devin was able to speak up.

"What are you talking about?" Brian asked.

"Devin's right," Brooke said. "Mom's not the only one who has a problem. You both need to change."

Brian exhaled, looking both astonished and defeated.

"What do you think of all this, Saylor?" Nathan asked.

"I think..." She paused, telling herself that it wasn't the time to challenge her kid's resistance to their own issues. "I feel that Brooke and Devin are right about me and Brian. I'm ready to work on getting over the anxiety, and I feel that Brian would be a better husband and father if he learned to tune in more."

Fidgeting in his chair, Brian looked at Nathan. "So...what happens next?"

"Each one of you may very well be feeling a lot of the same emotions right now: fear, vulnerability, anger. But with time, each of you can learn better coping skills."

Brian grimaced; discomfort written all over his face. "Do you want us to keep seeing you?"

"I recommend seeing a family therapist—whether you continue with me or decide to go with someone else," Nathan said. "However, I also recommend some individual therapy for Brooke and Devin. And when you two are ready for it, couples counseling."

Brian visibly winced and Nathan Greenberg smiled at him.

"I want you to know that I understand how the cost of all this therapy must seem overwhelming. But please don't think that it has to be something that will go on and on. In fact, sometimes I think the best counseling is short-term," Nathan said.

"And for you, Saylor, I know from my own struggles that anxiety can be a long, arduous trek to overcome," Nathan added. "What have you tried?"

She inhaled the clean scent of his office, amazed that he had battled anxiety too. "I've tried everything." She felt Devin and Brooke's eyes on her. "Individual therapy, medication, hypnosis, self-help books, you name it."

"What has worked the best?"

"What has worked the best?" She asked this out loud, hoping that it would help her to come up with a response. She closed her eyes for a moment, knowing that her answer wasn't just important to her, but to Brooke and Devin as well. Oddly, it came to her in an almost snapshot kind of way. Picturing Lucy, Billy, Wex, and Lenny's faces, she answered, "It's really a mixture of being conscious of my past, knowing that I'm not alone—and trusting that other people can understand and help." She looked at her family. "But most importantly, it's realizing that things will never be perfect—least of all, me." Then without even thinking about it, she said, "I just have to work on being able to say how I feel without letting fear get in my way."

"Sounds like a good start, Saylor," Nathan said. "Whatever you're working on, just remember some days will be better than others. And some days, old thought patterns and habits may very well sneak up on you and bite you on the you-know-what." He chuckled. "But this is what each and every one of you needs to remember..." Looking as if he wanted to make sure his words were being absorbed, he sat up straighter. "When you're consciously working on change, you'll get there." He nodded. "I promise you can all get there."

Saylor exhaled, believing.

When they exited through the waiting room, she walked up to a Van Gogh print that Nathan Greenberg must have put up since their last session. Although she knew it had been one of Van Gogh's last paintings, the crows flying in a stormy sky over a robust wheat field appeared more like a flight toward trust rather than despair.

"I'm needing ice cream," Brooke gripped her fingers on the back of Saylor's seat just like she used to do when she was little and wanted something right then and there.

"Sounds good to me," Saylor said. "You guys want to go to The Sugar Cove?"

"I am craving something sweet," Brian said and Devin agreed.

They were greeted by the smell of baked waffle cones and chocolate syrup. "I don't think we've been here since you guys were kids," Saylor said. "It's been way too long."

They stood in front of the case, gazing at the tubs of ice creams and sherbets. Saylor strolled up and down the pink and turquoise tiled floor, noting the name and color of each flavor.

"Would you like to sample something?" An older woman, whom Saylor remembered from years past, smiled.

"If I had my way, I'd have a taste of everything," Saylor answered.

The woman grinned, patting her belly like a cartoon bear who had devoured a whole beehive of honey. "That's why I'm so pleasantly plump myself." She winked. "I think life's too short not to indulge in happiness."

Saylor nodded. "What's your favorite flavor?"

"Hands down, it's the Chocolate Rip Current." The woman had a way of enunciating every word so that it made it sound even more appetizing.

"Then I'll definitely have a scoop of that."

By the time they were seated in a corner booth, Saylor's ice cream was nearly level to the cone.

"Like your ice cream much?" Brooke asked, a bemused smile making her face look both young and wise at the same time.

"I know...I couldn't help it. It was just too good." Saylor studied the brazen pink of Brooke's Shore Break Berry, the calm green of Devin's Pacific Pistachio, and the sunny yellow of Brian's Lemon Wave, realizing that her desire to "feel" the colors was something that she hadn't experienced since her painting days. She licked a drip off the side of her cone and told herself that she'd better check out adult ed's next session of painting classes before they filled up.

Brooke bit into her ice cream. "It does taste better when you really chomp into it," she said.

"Doesn't that hurt your teeth, though?" Brian shivered.

Brooke squinted at him as if she was inspecting something that was too elusive to understand. "Dad, you are going listen to the therapist, aren't you?"

Brian paused, looking less upset than Saylor had guessed he would. "Is it that important to you?"

"Isn't it to you?" Brooke stared at her father as if she were daring him into honesty.

Saylor touched his forearm "It's important to us all."

He glanced up with a mixed expression of embarrassment and humility. Saylor mused that it wasn't a bad thing to finally see these emotions on his face.

Then Brooke smiled. "Doesn't Nathan remind you guys of the 'Wizard of Oz'?"

Devin nodded. "He did. The 'great and powerful' wizard behind the curtain who promised everyone that they could achieve what they already had: the scarecrow, brains; the tin man, a heart; the lion, courage."

"What about Dorothy, though?" asked Saylor, knowing that Brooke had purposely changed the subject to take the heat off Brian. "Didn't he help her too?"

"Don't you remember?" Brooke said. "The wizard tried. They were about to launch off in his balloon to get her back home, but Toto leapt down to the ground, and she had to climb out to get him."

"Because the balloon was already floating away, she wasn't able to get back in," Devin added.

"That's right. It was really the good witch who reminded her that she always had the power to get back home," Saylor said. As a kid, Saylor had always wondered why Dorothy hadn't taken the good witch's word from the get-go, but now it made sense: The girl would never have appreciated all she had if she hadn't gone through all the trials and tribulations that helped her understand both herself—and others.

Brooke smiled slyly at Saylor. "You remember the message, Mom. Dorothy had to learn it for herself."

"She did," Saylor answered. "I remember."

CHAPTER TWENTY-ONE

By the time Saylor had finished coding March invoices for Brian's business, it was already one in the afternoon, and she had to race to her one-fifteen hair-cutting appointment. So, when her phone rang, she didn't answer. Whoever it was, it could wait. Still, as she shut the front door and ran to her car, the sticky heat of unnamed dread burned the back of her neck.

When she arrived at Dune Beach Hair Salon, she was able to shrug it off, attributing it to the nonsense of low-level anxiety. She reminded herself that they had a family session next week with Nathan and wondered if she should mention it—maybe share with the kids that she was learning to let things go more.

"So...you're finally going to do it?" Lindsey smiled, dimples gracing both her cheeks.

With just-washed hair wet against her neck, Saylor sat in the salon chair looking up at her stylist. For twenty years now, Saylor had been going to Lindsey for nothing more than the much-needed trim every three months or so. "Yes. It's time, Lindsey. I want you to finally do with my hair as you see fit."

Lindsey clapped. "Miracles of miracles, wonders of wonders, at long last!" She combed Saylor's hair and then tilted her head, pausing. "Your rash is clearing up!"

Saylor turned the side of her neck so that she could check it out in the mirror. "I knew it was getting better..." She touched her skin. "It is almost gone, isn't it?"

"Yep. It was looking pretty ugly there for a while. I'm glad it's in remission."

"Me too." Saylor settled back and closed her eyes. "Just do your magic, Lindsey. I'm not even going to watch."

Listening to Lindsey's careful snipping, she smiled, glad that she hadn't chopped it off herself. She peeked down at the white squares of linoleum; the frizzy curls looking like electrified snakes.

After Lindsey brushed away the snippets of hair from around Saylor's neck and shoulders, she smiled. "Close your eyes while I blow dry," she said. "Don't open them until I tell you."

Saylor obeyed, feeling the hair dryer's warmth on her face. She couldn't remember the last time she felt this happy and relaxed. As the comforting drone of dryer continued, she realized her anxiety was definitely getting better. In fact, since she had driven away from her mother's house in November, there was only one incident when she had worried about blurting out her thoughts, the time she had been thinking *I hate you* about Brian when he'd been aggressively driving them to brunch. Since then, she hadn't struggled one moment with the fear that her intrusive thoughts would burst out. Even seeing the horrid man from the bookstore didn't throw her off for as long as it would have in the past, especially since Nathan Greenberg had explained that she probably hadn't blurted anything out. A man like that, he pointed out, would very likely react with hostility at a woman challenging him with the slam of a book and disapproving look. And the daughter was probably smart enough to catch all that, and that was why she flashed Saylor a knowing smile. After all her prior attempts, therapy was finally helping.

Even the dread that she had felt earlier today had been fleeting. But most of all, seeing Devin's OCD diminishing through his work with a cognitive behavioral therapist, and Brooke's eating habits and mood improve through her sessions with a therapist who specialized in nutritional counseling, made hope expand past the fear. Saylor smiled, thinking how resistant Devin and Brooke had first been to individual therapy. Yet, after she shared more about her own emotional challenges, they finally relented. Two unfinished things, though, still made her stomach drop: how was she going to patch things up with her mother and the thought that she may never find Billy again.

Lindsey turned off the dryer. "Okay Saylor, you can open your eyes now."

Saylor touched her hair, the odd sensation of not fully recognizing her own reflection made her feel as if she were floating. Instead of the mass of long frizz weighing down her face or the pulled back constraint of a ponytail, loose ringlets now framed her face. It looked both pretty and unrestrained.

"Well?" Lindsey said, her eyes scrunched with concern.

"I love it. I feel like it's made me look, well...more like *me*!"

Lindsey grinned and exhaled loudly as if she'd been holding her breath. "I was worried cause you've always fought me about making changes—and this was a big one. I wasn't sure if you were going to freak out or not...but I had to do it for you." She unsnapped the plastic apron off Saylor and dramatically whipped it in the air.

Saylor shook her head back and forth, feeling the ends of her hair tickle her shoulders.

"Do you like how I gave you a more up-to-date look, but still made sure it was natural?" Lindsey said. "I wanted to bring out that fun, wild side of yours that I know is bursting to get out."

"You are..." Saylor said, smiling at both their reflections. "You are brilliant."

Lindsey bowed. "Thank you for recognizing my genius." She smiled; her dimples even more pronounced than usual. "Now, my dear Saylor, it's time for you to go out in the world and recognize yours."

After Saylor got in the car, she grabbed her cell and texted Devin and Brooke, to tell them that she had errands and to make sure that Devin gave Brooke a ride home. Then she headed to a new clothing boutique she had seen advertised in Dune Beach's weekly paper.

Saylor entered the store and paused, inhaling its new carpet smell. She ran her fingers over the brightly hued shirts, purposely ignoring the lower rack of blues, blacks, and grays that constituted most of the colors she already had in her closet.

A silver-haired woman in fashionable navy pedal pushers and a scarlet jacket smiled at her and asked if she could help her.

Usually, Saylor didn't want any input from salespeople. She knew her own taste and what would fit her chunky body. But after her experience with Lindsey, she was ready to let go and see what someone else came up with. The clear-eyed woman with bright silver hair looked like she knew what she was doing. "I'd love to find some clothes that my daughter won't say makes me look like I'm working on a farm."

The saleswoman dipped her head with what looked like empathy as Saylor watched her take in the outdated jeans and coffee-stained shirt. "I'm Pauline," she said, extending her hand. "I'd love to help you get a whole new look."

They shook hands. Saylor hoped Pauline wasn't *too* disgusted with her disheveled self. "You have a great sense of style," she said. Was it possible that she could look as pulled-together and fresh and happy as Pauline? "I really like it."

"Thank you. I've worked retail for most of my life and finally decided to go out on my own." Pauline threw her hands up and smiled. "Since I'm a grandmother now, I figured it was about time!" She grasped the red-framed glasses that had been holding back her hair and settled them on her nose, studying Saylor's face. "So, tell me what you're looking for."

"I want to get out of my rut." It wasn't much to go on, Saylor knew, but it summed up what she was looking for.

Pauline patted Saylor on the arm with the kind of warm reassurance Saylor wished her mother would be able to provide. "I don't want you to say yes or no to anything I find for you until you try it on," Pauline said, "and then if you'd like, I'll help you decide."

Saylor's phone rang, an intrusive shrill in the otherwise quiet boutique. She smiled apologetically. "Excuse me for a moment." She thought it might be one of the kids and wanted to make sure everything was okay. But when she pulled it out of her purse, she saw it was Erika. At first, she felt compelled to answer; it might be an emergency. Yet she hesitated. It'd been four months since she had driven away from her mother's house on that foggy November day. Four months in which Saylor had tried to discuss what had happened, had tried to talk her mother into spending Christmas with them, had even tried to set up a weekend visit with Devin and Brooke. Yet, her mother continued to push her away—evading Saylor in her short, curt way before abruptly getting off the phone.

Saylor knew without a doubt that her mother continued to withdraw because Saylor hadn't participated in the usual dance of swallowing it all down for the sake of getting along. In fact, Erika was probably furious that Saylor hadn't begged her for forgiveness, even though she had nothing to be sorry for. Some years ago, her mother had divulged that she had tallied on her calendar how many times Saylor had called her. According to Erika, she had discovered that over a year's time, she had "reached out" to Saylor more often than Saylor had to her—even though Saylor was sure it was actually the opposite way around. When Saylor dared to refute it—dared *not* to get down on hands and knees for forgiveness—Erika wouldn't return Saylor's calls, texts, or emails for over two months. It was only after Saylor finally bit out a false apology that Erika finally responded.

Saylor now turned off the ringer and didn't bother to wait and see if Erika had left her a voicemail or not. With a sigh, she shoved the cell to the bottom of her purse. She then turned back to Pauline. "Sorry for the interruption. I'm ready now."

"Good. I already have a couple of things in mind I want you to try on." Pauline took hold of Saylor's hand and showed her several fitted shirts. Although Saylor would never have picked them out herself, she couldn't wait to try them on. Pauline led her to a rack of pants and held several pairs up to Saylor's hips, either shaking her head as she whispered 'no' or nodding as she whispered 'yes', her lips otherwise pursed in determination. Saylor liked how Pauline made her decisions with such thoughtful-looking authority. It made her feel taken care of. Before she knew it, Pauline had a good amount of clothes waiting for her in the dressing room. "Now follow me and I'll get you set up."

Saylor trailed behind, admiring the older woman's no-nonsense confidence. It made her even angrier with Erika and brought on a sudden desire to share her transformation. "Right before I came here, I got a haircut. I had kept my hair the same style for over thirty years, and it felt so good to finally let go and make a change."

"Yes," Pauline replied, "and now you will be dressed for the occasion as well."

"The occasion?"

"The emerging-from-your-rut into who you are really meant to be."

Pauline glanced over her shoulder. Her wonderfully arched eyebrow made her look like she knew what she was talking about. "I think women sometimes feel it's superficial to put energy into how they look because so many people go overboard these days. But my philosophy is that it's okay to take the time to think about how different styles and colors best compliment you. In fact, it's like an art form—art that lets the world see you as you see yourself." Pauline laughed. "And why not make the world a more beautiful place?"

Saylor nodded. Pauline's theory made sense. Even Lucy would agree.

Smiling, Pauline pushed back the curtains to the first dressing room, and then carefully hung the skirts, shirts, and pants on separate hooks. She winked. "Give everything a chance—but remember to only choose the stuff you really like."

Saylor closed the door behind her and slowly but surely tried on every piece of clothing. Triumphant, she finally emerged from the dressing room in her favorite outfit, a pair of flattering black women's Levi's and a kiwi-green blouse.

"Superb," Pauline said. "See you can still wear Levi's, but they don't have to be so old and ragged that people see them without seeing you."

Saylor beamed. "Can I go ahead and wear these out?"

"Yes, of course. I'm not letting you walk out of here in the old clothes you came in with. You've got to show off that new hair cut with an all-around style!" Pauline raised her arms as if her favorite team had just won.

Saylor rushed out of the shop with her old clothes at the bottom of a glossy black bag, the rest of her new garb resting on top in artistically wrapped hot pink tissue paper.

She glanced at her watch. It was time to hit the grocery store and figure out what to make for dinner. But once she got in her car, she found herself heading for the adult ed office. She didn't want another day to pass where she got too busy or worse yet, talked herself out of it because she felt intimidated by not having painted for so long.

A young, dreadlocked man behind the front desk was talking on the phone, and when he noticed Saylor, he raised a finger and mouthed "one moment." She leafed through the schedule and saw that three different art classes were starting soon: a beginner's watercolor, a figure drawing class, and a landscape painting class that would meet at various outdoor locations for eight consecutive weeks. She started filling out the form, in the hope the landscape class wasn't already filled.

The young man finished his call and swiveled in his seat. "What class are you wanting to sign up for?"

Saylor inhaled. "Landscape painting."

"That one's mega popular. People sign up for it as soon as the schedule's out. Let me see if there's any openings." He wore a T-shirt with a band's logo that said, "The One Connection," and as he clicked away, Saylor felt a flutter in her belly. Now that there was a good chance that she couldn't get in, it seemed even more important that she take it.

He looked up and smiled. "Quick—get your credit card out: someone just canceled—and there's only that one spot left!"

Saylor gave him her information as quickly as possible as he inputted it into the computer with his lightning-speed typing. After he was done, a surge of gratitude coursed through her. "Thank you so much for helping me," she said, "it means more than I can say." *If only this young man knew,* she thought, *just how much his everyday kindness mattered.*

"No problem." He shrugged. "That's what I'm here for."

Saylor wanted to fling herself over the counter and bear hug him, but instead, just smiled and thanked him again. With a copy of the class confirmation tucked safely in her purse, she walked out to her car, her heart lifted, and then stopped for a moment to look up at the cool dome of gray sky.

Then she remembered her phone. Gritting her teeth, she fished it out from the bottom of her purse. Her mother had left a voice message. She readied herself and listened.

Erika's words played back in what Saylor thought of as her mother's lean, mean voice. The voice she reserved for when she was beyond angry and had crossed into the territory of cold reserve. "It's been months now without any apology—and I'm beginning to think that something is very wrong with you." There was a quick pause. "But on a more pressing note, you need to call me right away."

Saylor deleted the message. How could her mother turn things around like this? Had she forgotten that she had told Saylor—her own daughter—that there were many things she disliked about her? Had she forgotten that she was the one who walked away from Saylor and locked herself in her bedroom, ignoring Saylor's calls of *good-bye* and *I love you*? And how could she not acknowledge that Saylor had been calling her at least once a week since their fight, begging for connection?

"Something very wrong with me?" Saylor whispered to herself. "More like something *seriously* wrong with you."

Back at the car, Saylor tried to guess what was going on. Whatever it was, it couldn't be good. Just as she opened her door, the cell rang again. Relieved, Saylor saw that it was Lucy.

"Thank God it's you," Saylor said before Lucy had a chance to say hello.

"I'll take that as a compliment."

Saylor collapsed into the car, a sudden exhaustion making it seem impossible to drive. "It's so good to hear your voice, Lucy." She leaned back. "How are you?"

"Listen, I'm fine, but your mom is flipping out."

"Why do you say that?

"She just called asking if you've visited me since Thanksgiving and when I told her you hadn't, she asked me if I had run into Faith Underhill again. When I asked her why, she started acting really over-the-top saying what a crazy alcoholic Faith was and not to believe her lies."

"That's weird." Saylor wondered why her mother would worry about anything Faith would say. "She also just left me a voicemail to call her—"

"Something is definitely up, then," Lucy said.

"Do you have any idea what could be going on with her?" Saylor wanted to prepare herself, wanted to figure out the best possible strategy to calm her mother's nerves.

"Who knows?" Lucy answered. "All I do know, though, is that I've never heard your mom sound so distraught."

Saylor gripped the phone. "I guess I better call her now."

"Let me know what happens."

Saylor sighed. "I wish I knew what it was before I had to talk to her—"

"Saylor," Lucy said, her tone on the edge of irritated. "Don't let the woman scare you so much. She's just an insecure bully."

Saylor rubbed her forehead. "It's more complicated than that; she *is* my mom."

"Well, good luck, regardless."

"Thanks—I'll need it." With a loud exhale, Saylor hit the end button. She adjusted her rearview mirror and touched her hair, and for a moment wondered what it would feel like to just move forward with her life, brushing away Erika's demands like meaningless crumbs. Yet before she knew it, she was calling. Waiting would only make it worse.

Erika answered on the first ring with an urgent-sounding intake of air. "Saylor?"

"What's going on?"

"When was the last time you saw Faith?" Saylor heard both anger and distress in her mother's pressured speech.

"When you and I saw her at that restaurant in Malibu...why?"

"You do understand that she's a complete drunk?" Erika made it sound more like a statement than a question.

"What is this about?" Even though her mother sounded out of her mind, at least she was finally reaching out to her. Finally wanting to talk—even if it was due to some outlandish misunderstanding with Faith Underwood.

"The woman is a liar, Saylor."

"Mom, just tell me what happened." Although the late March afternoon was gray-cold, sweat trickled down the back of her new shirt. She rolled down the window and breathed in the outside air, hoping that Erika wasn't going to somehow lay the blame for whatever had happened with Faith onto her.

"Philip was supposed to visit me last night, but he texted that he wasn't feeling well..." Erika's voice broke, but her breathing was so ferocious that it sounded like she was hyperventilating. "So, I decided to take myself out for a glass of wine, but then I saw his car in her driveway."

"Her driveway?" Saylor was brought back to the time when she spied her father's car in another woman's driveway. A woman who also happened to be one of Erika's friends.

Erika grunted into the phone. "Don't you remember how I told you that Faith Underwood decided to move down the street from me?"

"And?" Saylor gripped the phone to her ear, knowing how hard this must have been for her mother. Although Philip was a married man, Erika considered him to be *her* married man.

"And then" Erika said, "I knocked on her door. She opened it without hesitation and then draped her arm around his neck and stared at me. Did not say a word to me, just stared at me like a cat who stole all the cream. But Philip was worse. He only gave me a limp hello as if we were merely acquaintances."

"Mom, he is a married man, you know—"

"He and I are best friends, Saylor—and, as you know, we've been together for years. He's never treated me like this. I know that horrible woman must have influenced him against me."

Saylor could tell that her mother had been crying. "I'm sorry, Mom—this must be really hard for you." She paused. Why did Erika feel the need to share this with her when she had been so busy pushing her away for the last four months? "But why did you need to know if I had run into Faith?"

"After all these years..." Erika suddenly coughed as if she had something stuck in her throat. "After all these years, I finally told her what I thought of her—and it backfired. I should have known better. I should have remembered what a horribly vindictive woman she could be."

Saylor shook her head. Faith was selfish. And petty. And, of course, vain. But she seemed too self-consumed to be *horribly vindictive*. "What," Saylor ventured, "did you say?"

"She had whispered something in Philip's ear—and they both laughed at me. Both of them *laughed* at me." Erika sounded as if she were choking back tears. "So...I finally told her what I wanted Philip to know: that she is a shrew who hurts people for sport—and that *no one* will *ever* truly love her."

"Why would you say such a thing?" Even if Faith was now entwined with Erika's man, what in the world did she mean by Faith being horribly vindictive...or that she hurts people for sport?

The silence on the other end made Saylor want to shriek. Instead, she got out of the car and paced the empty parking lot. The lampposts had been turned on, their orange luminescence against the gray sky making the afternoon look even darker than it already was. "Mom, you still there?"

"I can't believe the nerve of that Faith. Do you know how she reacted? She threw her head back and laughed at me again."

"Is that all that happened?" Saylor felt her mother's anger bristle over the line.

Finally, Erika answered. "No, that's not it."

"Well, what is it, then?"

"I will tell you, but you need to listen to me." Erika exhaled as if emphasizing her point. "After she had finally stopped laughing in my face, she spat out such an outlandish lie that if it weren't so awful, I would have laughed right back at her myself. It's not only mean, but downright cruel to twist the truth so much that it tarnishes my dead husband's memory."

"It tarnishes Simon's memory?" Saylor rolled her eyes. Thank goodness they weren't on a video call.

"Let me give you a little history, Saylor." Her mother paused to blow her nose, and then continued, her words sounding as if they were spiked. "That woman had tried to seduce your father. She had led him into my bedroom at one of our parties, telling him that she couldn't find her purse and would he please check under the bed. Of course, your father didn't want to be rude, so he went with her. But what she really wanted to do was get him to have an affair with her—and when I walked in on her kissing him, he was relieved that I had inadvertently got him out of an embarrassing situation."

Saylor circled a lamppost, shaking her head at her mother's denial. How could a smart person like Erika have allowed herself to swallow so much of Simon's crap.

"Anyway, I know she's a liar. She never got her claws into your father. He even shared with me that she had been trying to seduce him for a while, but that he had repeatedly pushed her away." Erika gave a short, mean-sounding chortle. "She didn't love your father. She just wanted to try to wreck what I had because she was jealous of me. I know that's true because your father told me so."

Saylor pinched her lips together. Her mother would never be able to take in the truth. "Is that why you were so worried about me running into Faith? Because you thought she'd tell me that my father had flirted with her?"

Erika paused for so long that Saylor thought the call had dropped. But finally, she answered. "You need to prepare yourself against her lies, Saylor..."

"But you just told me everything."

"There is more—something I wish you never had to hear, something that will only make you obsess more. But I want to tell you before she ever does. You have to be prepared to know that it's *not* true."

Saylor stopped in her tracks. "What is it, Mom?"

"You do promise me that you know she's a liar?"

"Okay...I'll take your word for it; she's a liar." Saylor held her breath, waiting.

"That crazy woman actually went so far as to say that *I* was just jealous of *her*. And, Saylor, she came up with this theory because she is claiming something that never, ever could have happened."

"What's she claiming, Mom?"

Her mother paused again, and just before Saylor was about to repeat the question, Erika finally answered, "That she and Simon had a son together."

Saylor's heart beat so fast that she felt her knees go weak. "A son with Dad?"

"Yes, she taunted me, telling me that she's going to let you know that Billy is your half-brother."

"Billy is my half-brother?" Saylor pressed a hand against her chest, sudden tears blurring her vision.

"No, of course he isn't. You are not to believe her. She's a sick woman. Your father would never have betrayed me. That crazy, homeless man is certainly not in any way related to you."

CHAPTER TWENTY-TWO

After Saylor plopped a salad and microwaved lasagna on the table, she checked her watch and called Brian. "You coming home soon?" She needed to talk with him more than she could say, more than she wanted, even, to talk to Lucy.

"I'm just turning down our street."

"Good, I have to tell you something."

"Is it that you're glad you picked the movie you did?"

Saylor smiled. How long had it been since either one of them had uttered their inside joke about how they first met? "Yes, I'm glad I picked the movie I did. And you?"

"You don't need to ask."

Neptune pricked his ears up, sensing Brian's arrival before she could even hear the truck's engine. Life appeared to be as normal as usual, even though her whole world had shifted.

After hearing about the possibility that she and Billy could be half brother and sister, Saylor had forgotten about her afternoon makeover. Instead, all she could do was focus on whether Faith's supposed lie was the truth or not. So, after Brian walked through the front door and Devin and Brooke emerged from their rooms for dinner, she was surprised by their stunned faces. "What?" she asked.

"Your hair...your clothes!" Brooke exclaimed. "Mom, you actually look kind of good."

Saylor couldn't help but grin. Coming from Brooke, that was a huge compliment. "Thank you." She turned to Brian, "And...what do you think?"

"You look beautiful," he said. "You did that all today?"

"Right after I was done with coding invoices. I also signed up for a painting class. In fact, I got in the last space that was available."

Brian tilted his head and smiled at her in his way that made her know he was genuinely happy for her. She exhaled, thinking about how she was going to go to the art store the next day for some new supplies.

After they finished dinner, and Brooke and Devin had once again ensconced themselves into their rooms, Saylor looked at Brian. "I need to tell you something—can we leave our phones behind and go for a walk?"

"Why can't we just talk right here?" Brian narrowed his eyes.

"Don't worry," she said, "this isn't about my anxiety. I just don't want to be interrupted." She called Neptune from under the kitchen table and asked if he wanted to go for a walk.

Neptune wagged his tail and went straight to the door. "Besides," Saylor said, "Neptune looks like he wants an evening constitutional."

They strolled down the street, Saylor holding onto Neptune's leash. Alone with Brian in the spring night, Saylor wondered why they didn't do this more often. Enjoying the gentle quietude of the hour, she fell silent.

Brian nudged her as if to waken her up. "What did you want to talk about?"

She had wanted to tell him about Billy right away, but first she needed to know—needed to know if he'd noticed. "Do you see a change in me—besides just how I look? And can you see that the kids are doing better, too?"

"It seems so." Brian cleared his throat. "I'm sorry that I haven't said so yet." Then in a voice so sheepish that she had to lean in to hear him, he said, "I have to admit that hiding my head in the sand didn't help matters."

"You do?" A sense of relief washed over her.

"We're a team. I just needed a friendly kick in the pants from Nathan Greenberg to remember that." He laughed. And she smiled under the moonless sky.

A moment later, a jet passed overhead, its thundering rush making her heart beat faster—but in a good, exhilarated way that was different from panic. "I wonder where it's heading," she said, turning to face her husband. She knew she was stalling. She swallowed. It was time. "Brian, I need to tell you something, but before I share it with you, I want you to promise that you'll take it seriously."

"I promise." Brian's weary tone said it all; despite her telling him that it wasn't about her anxiety, he was still afraid she was going to weigh him down with yet another irrational fear. "What," he said through gritted teeth, "is it?"

"Remember how I had found Billy living under the pier?"

"The homeless guy?"

She heard the oh-no-not-again wariness in his voice again, but continued on. "I found out today that he may be my half-brother." She felt her words sputter out, still not sure what she believed.

Brian stopped mid step. "Who told you this?"

"My mom. But she swears that it isn't true. She said that it's a lie that Faith made up just to be vindictive."

"Who knows between those two? I think they're both a little nutty." Brian let out a low whistle. "But, why would Faith lie about something like that? What good would it do her?"

"That's what I thought too. Also, my dad did have a tendency to go after my mom's friends. My mom, of course, won't believe that my father could have possibly betrayed her." Neptune tugged on the leash and they continued on. She felt Brian's arm around her shoulder and leaned against him. "But I don't know. Even though Billy and I really don't look that much like brother and sister, there's something about the shape of his mouth..." Saylor bit her lip. "Maybe Faith and my dad did have an affair before she and her husband Cliff even started hanging out with my parents. Maybe her pregnancy coincided with what would have been the right time for Simon to be the dad, but still, Billy is really Cliff's biological son. Maybe Faith doesn't even know the truth herself."

"Does Billy look like Cliff?"

Saylor shivered. "I had always assumed that Cliff was Billy's dad, so I never really compared them. I haven't seen Cliff in so many years that I don't remember him that well—it was Faith who people always noticed, not big, quiet Cliff."

Then Brian said something she never expected to pop out of his mouth: "But what does your intuition tell you?"

"My *intuition*?"

"Yeah," Brian said as if he had always believed in the power of insight.

She knew her answer without even having to think. "It tells me that it doesn't matter," she replied. "No matter what, he still feels like my brother, still feels like a person I want to always have in my life." She nodded. "And I am going to find him again."

"And if you do?"

"Nathan Greenberg says that he can get him a space in Serenity House."

"Serenity House? Isn't that expensive?"

"They serve both private and county clients." Nathan had assured her that Serenity House not only helped adults struggling with mental illness, but also focused on the long-term goal of independent living. No matter what, she knew she'd be able to visit him most every day. "I'd like to help him transition here first. If that means he camps on our couch for a time or even in a tent in the backyard. I hope you'll understand."

"You are one determined woman, aren't you?"

Saylor squeezed his hand.

CHAPTER TWENTY-THREE

Just as Saylor was reaching for a tube of cerulean blue paint, her phone rang. It was Erika. The art store was not a place that she wanted to sully with the emotional stuff of her mother, so she waited until she had bought her supplies, was out the door, and walking with the wind against her face.

Holding her breath, she called back. "Is everything okay since we talked yesterday?"

"I'm perfectly fine," retorted Erika, sounding more like her usual brisk self. "I am just checking in about Easter. I would like to have you all come down and be with me for a change."

Saylor waited for the crosswalk light to turn green, wondering if her mother was ever planning on broaching the Billy subject again. "We've already committed ourselves to going to Brian's family. But you are more than welcome to come up here—"

"I'd appreciate it if you changed things around and visited me instead."

Saylor hurried across the street. "I want to talk to you about Billy—"

"I'm going to stop you right there," Erika said, the tone of her voice raising the hair on the back of Saylor's neck. "I will not speak any further about Billy. I only told you what Faith said so that you would be prepared if she ever saw you or Lucy and tried to poison either of you with her lies. You must not obsess about this. I know you well enough to know that it is not good for you."

"But I know myself a hundred times better than you ever will." Saylor hadn't meant to be so blunt, or sound so defensive. Her mother's exacerbated sigh came through the receiver loud and clear, yet Saylor continued on, "And going down there to try and help him is something I *want* to do." A passerby stared at her, and Saylor realized how guttural her voice had become, but didn't care.

"Stop letting your imagination run away with you, Saylor. He is *not* your brother."

Saylor marched down the sidewalk, ignoring the beating inside her chest. "That doesn't matter."

"Don't be so foolish. You wanting to help him is silly."

"And you are..." Saylor tried to swallow the sudden lump in her throat. "You are not to talk to me that way again. I don't deserve it."

"Nor do I." The phone went dead. Saylor paused in front of the bookstore, staring at her screen. Just like her mother to turn it around. She drew in a breath and continued down the sidewalk.

In the office, Saylor prepared a stack of invoices that she had to input before the day's end. She hadn't heard back from her mother, but was too tired to initiate contact. She shrugged and turned on the computer. Her mind was already set on going down south the next day to try and find Billy, so she decided that she'd carry on with work while trying to ignore the rebound stress of having to deal with her mother. But something different than the upset of anxiety made it hard to focus, something shadowy that flitted in the back of her mind she couldn't name. She shut off the computer and told herself that all she needed was a quick walk and then she'd get right back to work. Neptune followed her out and went straight for his leash hanging on a patio chair. Saylor hooked the lead to his collar. Wishing she could understand the furtive, underground-like feelings mounting inside, she increased her pace.

When they made their way down to the beach, she unleashed him so that he could run at his leisure, but the tide was high and there wasn't much sand. Saylor noticed a man sitting on a log beneath the cliff, and wanted to warn him about the rare rockslides that had killed people in years past. Yet he looked so content, gazing at the ocean, the sun shining on his bald head that she remained silent, hoping that this would not be the one moment in time that the cliff would decide to collapse—and thinking that if it did, his death would be on her. She followed Neptune, realizing that she was doing what Nathan Greenberg labeled as "catastrophizing," and chastised herself for back-stepping. But this random what-if thought was still easier to contend with than the disquieting undertow. Gingerly making her way over the slippery rocks, she had to pause each time the tide swirled around her ankles. Finally, she made it around the point to where a dry patch of beach lay between the cliffs and a sandbank held back incoming waves.

Still fighting the nightmare-like apprehension, a heated exhaustion overtook her and she kneeled in the sand. A piece of broken glass stuck up razor-sharp in front of her, and she stared at it, her heart racing. Like a prompt of something as simple as seeing a spoon on a table or some silly remark that brings back forgotten images from a dream the night before, the memory began to materialize. Saylor looked up to the sky, remembering the quick pain and the warm smear of blood under her grip. Neptune whined, and she patted his head, knowing he was sensing her upset. She reached for a piece of driftwood and threw it a few feet over for him to chew. Surprised by the abrupt twist in her belly, she tried to hold it back, but couldn't control the growing nausea. She retched into the sand. Over and over again, she vomited, not able to move, as the memory bubbled up and fully surfaced.

"You shouldn't wear that." Her father laughs, pinching her mother's stomach, exposed and vulnerable between her white shorts and red-checkered halter-top. He leans against the counter, gulping down grapefruit juice. "But on Faith that would look perfect."

"Do not compare me to her—"

He slams his glass down so hard that it shatters across the kitchen counter, but he doesn't make a move to pick up the pieces. Instead, he grabs her mother's hair and tugs so hard that her face becomes a tight, frantic-eyed mask of fear. Between clenched teeth, he says, "It's Faith who really understands me. It's Faith who believes in my art. Not you."

Saylor stands at the kitchen's threshold, terrified that she's going to be seen. She takes a step back, but her father jerks his head up and glares at her. Saylor freezes. He doesn't say anything, keeping his grasp on her mother's hair. Her mother, though, narrows her eyes and stares at her as if this is somehow her fault. Grimacing, her father finally releases her mother and gets himself another glass from the cupboard.

Saylor wants to bolt out of their sight, out the front door, out into the world, but her legs will not move. She is stuck in this house. There are no chances of a safe escape, not at her age.

Instead, her fourteen-year-old body shakes and she finds herself yelling out what she wishes her mother would say: "Why don't you just leave, then?" She faces them both, but clamps a hand over her mouth, wondering why she allowed herself to blurt out what she knows will only make things worse.

For several moments, no one moves, a terrifying silence cementing them all in their places. Her father stands so still that his body has become a block of stone, yet his eyes are filled with so much hatred, they shine. "You fat, dumb girl." He smiles at her as if he's just paid her a compliment.

Saylor doubles over. Through all his past outbursts, he has never been this cruel. With shock and shame, she looks at her mother, hoping for some kind of help. But, instead, her mother is nervously rubbing her hands together, a pleading look of panic on her face.

"You are never to disrespect your father again," her mother's voice shakes as if she's a little girl.

"But I..." Saylor cannot finish her sentence. The words that she had wanted to say vanishing from her mind.

"But you..." her father mimics her with a nasty tone, "are just a fat, stupid girl who shouldn't be allowed to say such disrespectful filth."

Her stomach lurches. She wants to run to the bathroom, but knows that she won't make it. So, she races to the kitchen sink. Holding back her nausea, her hands grip the edge of the counter. Briefly, her father touches her shoulder, but not in the way that makes her feel he's angry. Rather, his touch is a warning. Through all his cruelty, he still loves her. Still, she cannot respond and slivers of glass cut into her palms. She retches uncontrollably, oblivious now to whatever her mother and father are saying.

The memory having surged through her body, Saylor called Neptune over, and wrapped her arms around his neck. "I'm okay," she whispered into his fur, wondering why her mother could have stayed with such a sick man. Then, thinking that Erika must have been terrified of what he'd do if she had stuck up for Saylor, she realized her mother had only been trying to protect them both by making Saylor apologize. It wasn't right, but now she knew that Erika had been afraid. She could understand that.

Her body weak from all the retching, Saylor cupped her hands into the sand and covered her mess. Then she dug a hole next to it and dropped the piece of glass in, burying it so that other beachgoers would not inadvertently cut themselves. She sat back and watched the waves crash, their blue-green faces eventually flattening into lacy white foam.

Mesmerized by the constant movement of tide, a realization struck that was so simple, yet so true that she closed her eyes for a moment, telling herself never to forget. The journey from fear to courage was more than winning an inward battle; it encompassed the ability to accept change. If everything else—happiness, sorrow, even certain memories—were fleeting, then fear could be transitory as well. She took in a huge inhale and stood, peeling off her T-shirt. Without hesitation, she leaped off the sand bank into the tide, the shock of biting cold seawater making her heart pound with such force that she imagined her chest ripping open. But she liked the sensation, and with the water's chill surging against her body, she dove under an incoming wave, immersing herself within its pull.

Before heading back to the office, Saylor gathered the new art supplies and set up her easel in the backyard. She was going to wait until classes began, but what just happened on the beach brought on such an immediate desire to create that her whole body itched in anticipation.

Without even penciling in an outline, she began painting the trunk, then branches, and then new leaves of the oak tree. She brushed on layers of burnt sienna, raw umber, light green, a connected sense of calm settling inside her. Everything else in the world—and her past—became distant points beyond the canvas.

When she was done, she stepped back from her work, looked up to the sky and knew that she possessed the strength to finally confront her mother.

CHAPTER TWENTY-FOUR

Her hollow-cheeked mother answered the door. "What are you doing here?"

"I told you that I was going to find Billy."

Erika stood mute, her swollen eyes making it look as if she'd been crying nonstop. She had definitely lost too much weight, her already thin body now whispery frail. Faith telling her about Billy supposedly being Simon's son must have really gotten to her—either that or she was sick. Despite her anger, Saylor reached for her mother's hand. "Have you been ill?"

"Of course not. I never get sick." Erika pursed her lips. "You got a haircut, I see—" she gave Saylor her up and down look of scrutiny, but also with a flicker of approval. "And some new clothes too."

Saylor hadn't expected any compliments and berated herself for how much she appreciated her mother's curt acknowledgement. "I need to talk to you, Mom."

Erika stepped aside, her baggy sweater and loose skirt making her look even more vulnerable. "I already explained to you that I will not speak to you about this Billy nonsense again."

"It's not about Billy." An invisible weight pushed against Saylor's chest. "Can we go into the living room?"

They sat on opposite couches, the afternoon light making everything look like it was coated in amber.

Her mother crossed her legs, her hands, like dry twigs settling on her lap. "Well?"

"Why did you stay with him?"

"What are you talking about?"

"Why did you stay with Dad? He was awful to you, Mom. I don't understand it."

"Is this because I told you about Faith's lies?" Her mother's body shrunk into the cushions. "I knew you'd obsess about this, Saylor."

"No, it isn't." Saylor glanced down the narrow hallway toward the kitchen. "He was cruel to both of us. Why did you let him stay?"

"This isn't going to get us anywhere."

Saylor's heart clenched. Erika's denial was impenetrable. But then she said something that she hadn't planned: "Why didn't you love me enough?" Panicked, Saylor swallowed, having no idea how her mother would react.

Erika's eyes widened, but she didn't say a word. After several long moments, she finally spoke in a dry, thorny tone, as if saying the words physically pained her. "I did love you." Her fingers tightened into a bony knot. "I promise I have always loved you. I love you more than you know, but..."

"But what?" Just like she did when she had been fourteen at the scene of her parent's sick fight, Saylor shook uncontrollably.

"No matter how irate your father seemed to you, I knew it was because he was in constant pain. You only know the tip of the iceberg about how horrific his childhood was. I had to put him first—even before you."

"But I was your child," Saylor said, hearing the rage grow sharper in her own voice. Her mother's face turned white, but Saylor wouldn't stop. "You should have protected me."

"But you were such a strong-willed girl—"

"Strong-willed doesn't mean I wasn't scared, Mom." She held back tears, wishing that she felt safe enough to cry in front of her own mother. "And now that he's been gone for so long, I don't understand why you're still so hard on me." Her mother would probably never change—but, still, Erika only had a handful of years left. At this point, what good would come of any unreal expectations? It was time, though, to release the jammed-down words that had pressed against her chest for what now seemed a lifetime. "I can't let you treat me like this anymore. I'm not your enemy." Saylor tried to catch her mother's eye. "I'm your daughter."

Everything in the room stopped. Even the sound of the tide's roll beneath the house paused in Saylor's ears. She waited.

After a thick silence, Erika finally looked back at her. "Saylor..."

"What, Mom?"

"You are the only one..." Her voice struggled. "You are the only person in my entire life that I have ever felt truly safe with."

"I'm the only one you've ever felt safe with?" Utterly confused, Saylor studied her mother's quivering chin. "I don't understand."

The jagged tone of regret punctuated her mother's words. "With your strong-will came an unquestionably loyal heart. I have seen it in you since you were a very young girl." Then her mother did something that she had never done before. She tucked her head down in what looked like genuine shame and cried.

Saylor watched, not wanting to break whatever was happening.

"I was afraid..." Erika fingered a wadded-up tissue that had been tucked under the wrist of her sweater and wiped her nose.

Saylor wanted to reach out, but hesitated. "You were afraid?"

"I had always told you that my father died of cancer. The truth is that he was a drunkard, and when I was a little girl ..." Erika took in a ragged breath, her body looking as if it were shrinking in on itself. "He disappeared."

"You never saw him again?"

"I did not." Erika stopped as if uttering one word more would stop her from breathing. All at once, Saylor pictured the black and white photo that her mother kept on her bedside table. A ten-year-old Erika in a plain collared dress, flat black shoes and white ribbon in hair stared into the camera in what always looked to Saylor as angst. Now she was beginning to understand why.

Saylor wished she could go back in time, hold her mother's little-girl hand and tell her that she was okay. "Did you ever find out what happened to him?"

Erika shook her head as if admonishing herself. "My mother always made sure to tell me that it was all my fault."

"It's never the kid's fault, Mom. I hope you know that."

"I loved him so much that even though he could be harsh, my heart broke."

Saylor wasn't sure if her mother was talking about her own father or Simon—or perhaps for the memory of both. "But what about yourself? What about me?"

"We were both stronger than your father. He was a lost man, a bird without wings. I knew you'd be able to fly, but never Simon. Deep inside, I knew he'd never be free—even though I tried to convince myself that I could help."

Saylor drew in a breath, readying herself. It was now or never. "But it still doesn't make how you treat me okay."

"I loved him so much..." Tears still in her eyes, Erika paused. Her mother's gaze became unfocused and she spoke as if she were in a trance. "I know this doesn't make sense to you, but even after his death, I couldn't stop the des-peration in not being able to help him."

Saylor dared not mention that Simon's "accident" might very well had been a suicide—unconscious or not. As calmly as possible, she straightened her back. Her mother's identity had been so wrapped up in protecting Simon that she continued to languish in the past. Although it was a broken past that she hadn't been able to fix, and a childhood past steeped in abandonment, it was still the past. "But what a waste when I've been here all along, Mom."

Erika reached her trembling arms in Saylor's direction. "I *do* love you."

Stunned, Saylor sat for a moment taking in the urgent tone of her moth-er's declaration. Then she crossed over the living room carpet that held the layers of dust from her childhood and sat next to the papery-thin woman who was her mother. She smelled the scent of Erika's salty remorse and for-gave her.

Through the window, fading sunlight threw shadows on the worn carpet. Saylor placed her arm around her mother's brittle shoulders. "I love you too, Mom."

CHAPTER TWENTY-FIVE

When Saylor arrived at the parking lot, the sun was just about to set. Against the golden light of the horizon, she made out Wex, his back to her as he sat alone in his wheelchair watching the day's end.

She came to his side and grazed his shoulder with her fingertips. "It's going to be a pretty sunset, isn't it?"

He glanced up, sorrow and kindness softening his face. "How is my fellow coyote?"

She smiled. "I've been good, Wex. How've you been?"

"He's been waiting to see you."

Saylor's throat went dry. "He's here?"

"He told me you'd come back." Wex turned his gaze on the horizon. "And I believe he's ready."

"I hope so." She studied his profile, wondering how he knew.

Wex nodded. "If he goes with you, you'll take good care of him, won't you?"

Holding back tears, Saylor squeezed his shoulder. "Of course."

"Well, I guess my job is done, then." Wex looked at her and cocked his head toward the pier.

"Thank you, Wex." She let her arm fall down and for the briefest of moments they brushed hands.

Before the last sliver of sun slipped away, she turned around and walked under the pier. In the shadowy light, she looked for Billy. She was finally going to see him again. But as she weaved between the pilings, she began to wonder if Wex was wrong about Billy being ready. Maybe he was just there, but got scared when he spied her talking to Wex and bolted again. She raced all the way down to where the ocean met the sand, peering left and right. In a panic, she ran back to where Wex had been, but he was gone too.

She went back under the pier and searched again. There wasn't any trace of Billy. She sank to her knees and bowed her head. Her crazy hope had blocked the sadness of reality. A man struggling with mental illness, who'd been homeless for so many years, who was afraid to even go indoors, wasn't about to let her take his hand and go home with her.

She stood, telling herself that it was okay. He'd already survived this long and he did have Wex. Who was she to try and change his life now? But still, she searched one more time. Just one more time before she slumped away. Slowly, she walked along the shore. For what seemed like an eternity, she continued to search. Then, just ten feet away under the pier, he appeared as if he were an apparition. But it had to be her imagination. She closed her eyes and opened them again. He was still there. Her heart was so full, so thick with emotion, she couldn't speak. She stood still, not ever wanting to forget what Billy looked like in that moment. A found man sitting stoic calm as he stared at the incoming tide.

Finally, she walked up to him. Finally, she found her voice. "Billy, I'm here."

His gaze locked onto her. Even under the pier's diminishing light, his green eyes were just as bright as she had remembered.

"Let me see you," he said.

She kneeled next to him.

He turned, keeping his whole attention on her. "You unshackled yourself."

"I did, Billy."

"Sometimes my mind doesn't work like it should," he said. "But I can tell these things."

"I know you can." She reached out and held his hand in hers.

"And your family," he said, "you've been able to help them, yes?"

"I have." She hoped she was passing his test.

Billy continued to study her. "Have you ever thought about how running into the bad can sometimes be the best thing for you?"

"Why is that?"

"Think about it." He closed his eyes, his body like a boulder embedded in the sand.

Saylor took three deep breaths, waiting. But he kept silent, and she finally closed her eyes as well. Then she thought about what he said and it dawned on her: If it hadn't been for the awful man from the bookstore making her think that her irrational fears had come true, she wouldn't have felt so desperate to find Billy or had fought so hard to climb out of her fear.

Billy tapped her on the shoulder. "You see what I mean, don't you?"

"I do."

He nodded. Then he crouched on the edge of his blanket and began scooping away handfuls of sand.

Saylor waited, wondering what he was digging for with such serious intent.

Finally, he looked up, beaming as if he had discovered a hidden treasure that he'd buried a long time ago. "Here it is." He uncovered a deflated raft.

"I can't believe you have that," she said. She reached over, tracing her fingers against the faded stripes. "It looks just like the ones we rode together."

"We can patch it up, Saylor. And then we can go back into the ocean one day and ride it."

"Yes, let's do that." She stood, holding out her hand. Then the words came out without her even having to think about them: "Come home with me."

"Home?" he whispered. "Go home with you?"

"Yes." She wanted to grasp his hand right then and there, but could only stand with her arm extended, waiting.

He froze for several long moments, and Saylor worried that she was losing him again.

"Please," she said. "I want to be there for you."

"Before I do..." He paused. "I want to hear you say it."

"Hear me say it?" Did he mean that they were brother and sister? But she looked at him and somehow knew that wasn't it.

"Yes, Saylor, say it out loud." He tilted his head as if trying to hear some far-off sound. "Tell me something we both should know."

She listened to the rhythm of evening tide lapping against shore, searching for the right words. Then as simple as Dorothy's way back home, she knew what to say. "Whether or not our fears are real, we have each other." She watched trust smooth away the trepidation on his face and a hundred birds fluttered in her chest.

"Yes. We will always have fear, but now we'll have hope because we can be there for each other like we should have always been," he said. "Like brother and sister."

"Like brother and sister, Billy?" Saylor's skin tingled. She reached for him again, but his hands remained in his lap, and then he squeezed his eyes shut, seemingly digesting his own thoughts. An evening breeze blew toward them from over the Pacific, and Saylor held her breath, hoping he'd be able to believe. Billy nodded to something invisible and finally stood, grabbing the raft with one hand and grasping her palm with the other.

"I will go home with you, Seraphina."

Stunned, Saylor paused. "You know my real name?"

"I've always known it," he answered, and grasped her hand in a way that made her want to cry with relief.

They faced each other, and then walked from under the pier onto the open beach. An insistent caw came from above. Against the final glow of the horizon, silhouettes of wings flew overhead, all heading in the same direction.

END

Book Club Questions: The Grace of Crows, Second Edition

1. Empathy is a theme throughout the narrative of *The Grace of Crows*—not just empathy toward family, but also empathy toward strangers and even oneself. Discuss the significance of empathy in *The Grace of Crows* using specific examples.

2. Saylor's main motivation is clear: She desperately wants to banish her anxiety. What motivates Brian, Brooke, Devin, and Erika? How do their different motivations conflict or align with Saylor's?

3. How does the author's use of setting enhance your understanding of the characters? What do you learn from the descriptions of interior spaces and outdoor surroundings?

4.The relationship between Saylor and her mother Erika is one of the most complex in the novel. Although Erika is judgmental and combative with her daughter, Saylor is able to see the fragility behind her mother's narcissism. Discuss ways you have dealt with difficult loved ones — and have learned to see past their contentious exteriors.

5. Even though Billy only appears twice in the novel, Saylor's conviction to connect with him again is an ongoing quest throughout the story. Discuss how this affected both the plot and you as the reader.

6. In chapter two, Saylor thinks: "Everyone dies in the end, and in billions of years, the sun will explode and melt the earth." Saylor is aware that these thoughts are morbid, but they calm her

by putting her fears in perspective. When you have faced emotional turmoil, what thoughts have helped you carry on?

7. Discuss Saylor's epiphany about the "grace of crows," what it means, and how she applies it to her life. In what ways do you experience Saylor's understanding about the "grace of crows" in your own life?

8. Besides the crows, what other animal symbols can you identify and what aspects of emotional health or personal growth might they signify?

9. In the beginning of the novel, Saylor is aware that she suffers from anxiety. She knows her fears are irrational, yet she's unable to control them. Discuss how her struggles compare to your own emotional challenges.

10. Saylor's first encounter with her long-lost friend Billy sparks her journey toward self-awareness and healing. Later, a breakfast with a stranger leads her on a deeper journey toward emotional health. Discuss ways in which someone from your past — or even the kindness of a stranger — has helped you in some profound way.

11. Discuss the beginning and end of *The Grace of Crows*. Why does it start the way it does? Did it end as you had expected? What kind of future do you envision for each character?

12. How did the novel expand your awareness? Did reading it help you understand a family member or friend better? Describe any personal insights that *The Grace of Crows* may have sparked.

About the Author

Tracy Shawn lives and writes on the coast of California. Her debut novel, *The Grace of Crows* (now out as a second edition with expanded development), won several indie book awards. Her second novel, *Floating Underwater*, won a silver medal for General Fiction with the 2023 Living Now Book awards, and placed as finalist with Next Generation Indie Book Awards for General Fiction and The Wishing Shelf Book Awards for Adult Fiction. Tracy Shawn's short stories have appeared in several literary journals, and her poetry has been published in two best-selling poetry anthologies. Ms. Shawn has written numerous articles for print and online publications. She is currently working on her third novel and hopes to keep writing books that both entertain and enlighten.

Read more at https://www.tracyshawn.com/.

Printed in the USA
CPSIA information can be obtained
at www.ICGtesting.com
CBHW031415140324
5378CB00010B/611